EXTINGUISHING
Shadows

A New Adult Paranormal Fantasy

Heather Beal

Black Rose Writing | Texas

ISBN: 978-1-68513-282-8
PUBLISHED BY BLACK ROSE WRITING
www.blackrosewriting.com

Printed in the United States of America
Suggested Retail Price (SRP) $22.95

Extinguishing Shadows is printed in Calluna

*As a planet-friendly publisher, Black Rose Writing does its best to eliminate unnecessary waste to reduce paper usage and energy costs, while never compromising the reading experience. As a result, the final word count vs. page count may not meet common expectation

Mara wants me to tell everyone that this book is dedicated to not only the other authors out there hearing voices (and we know you are out there my friends); but to all the readers who can't wait to join our wild spirits on the exciting and unpredictable adventures they take us on!

Thank you for joining Mara and Terrill into this world of vampires, Viajantes, and the unexpected.

I owe a special thank you to Pamela Taylor, author of *Second Son Chronicles* and editor extraordinaire! Thank you for helping me fine-tune and smooth this story into shape.

I also want to thank Christy Cooper-Burnett, KJ Fieler, Karen K. Brees, and Pamela Taylor, all great authors in their rights, for taking the time to encourage and mentor a new author in the field.

Thank you to Black Rose Writing for taking a chance on me. I especially want to thank Regan Rothe for his kind and helpful interaction and David King for his amazing cover.

I want to thank my husband Rob for putting up with my author craziness and listening patiently to the latest thing my characters said or did that surprised me. Sorry baby, its unlikely to stop any time soon.

Finally, I want to thank my kiddos Leilei and Nickolai for being my cheerleaders. I hope this inspires you to continue to imagine and dream big.

EXTINGUISHING
Shadows

CHAPTER ONE

Mara let the fading sunlight filter across her body, its heat still warm against her cool skin. The wind kicked up the ocean spray from the rocks below, creating a fine, salty mist. She smiled as it danced against her face. The sun set and she watched the salt crystals shimmer in the shadowy twilight. She sighed. Time to go. She climbed up and over the so-called barrier preventing pedestrian access to the cliffs and slid into the driver's seat. The simple sense of peace and serenity that brief stop had given her dissolved, leaving instead the unmistakable vibration of danger coming, and coming fast.

Mara slammed the door and turned the key. She headed toward the rapidly darkening skyline as the threat closed in behind her. Damned if she would make it easy for these two, and she knew there were two of them. She kept an eye glued on the rearview as she navigated the treacherous curves, rewarded finally by the appearance of headlights. She smiled grimly. Right on cue.

Her brow furrowed. She'd hoped for a little more distance. Either these guys were really good or worse, really determined. If the latter, lots of troublesome questions needed answers - fast. She tried to sort it out as she snaked along the deserted highway. They shouldn't have expected her to isolate herself like she had by cutting through the mountains. Most mortals would have reached for the illusion of safety in public, so her choice of escape should have at least confused them. Unless . . .

Damn!

What if her actions had backfired and she'd somehow inadvertently revealed something about herself or her intentions, increasing their desire to obtain her at any cost? She groaned in frustration at her arrogance. She'd believed she could enter the city undetected. She was certain her mortal camouflage hadn't failed her, but how had they caught her trail again so quickly? She needed to lose them, and quickly.

She clutched the steering wheel. This was going to suck. She needed to disappear, but to do that she had to ditch the car. She swore to herself. She'd really been looking forward to putting it through its paces. Worse, this wasn't going to be a crash she'd walk away from unscathed.

Focus!

She shook her head and concentrated on the occupants of the car behind her. If the high-octane gas tank didn't explode on impact, she could easily ignite it spontaneously. The trick would be escaping in one piece. She only hoped she wouldn't be so badly hurt that it would compromise her ability to disguise her presence. To top it off, she'd have to project a reasonable semblance of fear or surprise to accompany the illusion. Few of her kind were able to pull off something like that successfully, but she could.

She grabbed her backpack. The next curve. That was the one. She poured more power into the image she sought to project and let it envelop her, then her car, expanding it to include the vehicle behind her and the surrounding area. She didn't attempt to contain its limits. Better too much than too little she figured. Neither one of her pursuers saw her roll out of the open driver-side door, smashing and bouncing off the pavement, nor did they see the door close behind her of its own volition as the car took flight over the cliff.

It would appear to anyone who might investigate the crash that she'd simply taken the curve too fast and lost control. By the time anyone got down to the wreckage and discovered the lack of remains, she'd be long gone. True, the fire would only temporarily keep her pursuers from discovering her escape, but if she was lucky, it just might buy her enough time to learn something about them as well.

She winced as she heard her beautiful car smash into the rocks below, flames and smoke exploding up into the now ink-black night.

Tires screeched to a stop, forcing her to move. She grimaced as she propelled bruised and sore limbs into motion, silently crossing the road and ducking out of sight of her trackers. She heard car doors wrenched open even before the car came to a complete stop. The occupants emptied the vehicle and stared down at the burning wreckage. The one who'd been driving leaned over the rail and looked curiously at the charred remnants before spitting over the edge.

"What are we going to tell them?" his companion asked. His high-pitched voice echoed across the distance separating Mara from her pursuers. Even in the gathering darkness, enough light remained to see him clearly. He was slightly built with weasel-like features. His eyes darted back and forth between the crash and the driver. "They said you could track her and bring her in. They aren't going to like this."

Mara heard the whiny accusation in the man's voice, and her eyes were involuntarily drawn to the driver's face as he turned toward her. His emotionless face transformed into a menacing smile as he walked toward the smaller man. She braced herself for the onslaught of violence she felt building.

She blanched. Oh my god, he was a Vampire! She literally had only seconds to learn why they were after her before he killed this mortal stupid enough to have confronted him. She wasn't confident her skills would let her touch the Vampire's mind without him noticing – not yet. There was way too much to lose if he discovered her probe. She lightly touched the weasel's mind instead, surprised to discover it was somehow protected.

Oh crap! She hadn't expected that. She didn't have enough time to unravel the lock without giving herself away either. Quickly, she used her powers to push around the edges of the barrier protecting his mind from her and extracted as many partial memories and details as she could. The driver's name was Claudio and the weasel was afraid of him. They'd been given a mission to find and capture her, but she couldn't learn why or for what purpose. Did they know who and what she was, or was she just a random target? Mara struggled to sort out the confusing jumble of fragments and images.

Before she could discover anything more, Claudio spoke. "There was nothing we could do. I'm sure they will understand."

His words were spoken calmly and his voice conveyed sincerity and trust as he closed the distance to his companion. Mara's eyes widened at the horrible incongruence between his words and what she'd picked up about his intentions. She heard the immortal persuasion in his voice. It was an extremely effective tool against mortals and even occasionally against the unwary immortal.

The small man hesitated, clearly confused, as he looked down at the crash burning brightly below him. It appeared that whatever protected him from her mind penetration also limited the seductive influence of Claudio's voice. Limited it, but didn't completely eliminate it.

Claudio attacked before the mortal realized the danger, smashing a fist into his victim's stomach, doubling him over, and leaving him gasping for air. He yanked him upright by the collar and brought him within inches of his face. Mara could see the saliva gleaming from lengthened fangs in Claudio's mouth as it dripped onto the man's face.

"Stupid mortal" Claudio hissed as he lifted the younger man off the ground using only one hand to hold him in place while he shook him. "You have no idea what is, or is not, important." He sneered, his disgust transparent at the weasel's feeble attempts to protect himself. "I don't understand why we bother with your kind at all."

Mara froze as he sank his teeth into his terrified victim's neck. Within seconds the man's struggles slowed then stopped completely. After he drank his fill, Claudio callously dropped the lifeless body over the cliff and wiped the remaining blood from his mouth. Mara saw him lick his fingers, and she fought down the bile that rose in her throat.

The complete disregard for life the Vampire species seemed to have was something she'd never understood. Life was precious to her kind. Perhaps it was because they didn't prey on mortals, or maybe it was simply the way they lived their lives.

She was a Viajante – a traveler – an ancient immortal species that lived hidden among the humans, or more accurately, on the fringes of human society. Throughout history they had occasionally been identified by mortals as nomads, gypsies, or tribes, their true nature hidden, suspected of nothing more than a curious desire to limit contact with outsiders.

Their one natural enemy was the Vampire, another ancient immortal species existing among mortals like themselves. As far as Mara was concerned, immortality was where the similarity ended. She could only guess what strain of stupidity – or insanity – had inspired this particular group of mortals to align themselves with Vampires voluntarily.

She brushed her hair back from her face with shaky fingers and shook her head slightly, saddened by the irrational desire for power and wealth among mortals that typically led to such a senseless loss of life. She strengthened her shields as Claudio scanned the area for witnesses and, more significantly, any trace of her. He didn't seem as convinced about her demise as his companion had been.

He stretched, flexing his muscles, and grinned into the darkness where she lay hidden. He couldn't find her now, but she had no doubt he would keep trying. The game wasn't over yet. He sauntered back to his car and left, not wanting to be discovered by the sirens becoming discernable in the distance.

Mara didn't realize she'd been holding her breath until that moment. She gulped air into her lungs. That had been too close. She stepped deeper into the shadows and pulled her hoodie and favorite ball cap out of her backpack and put them on before slinging the pack over both shoulders and taking off east at a light jog.

She crossed a field leading toward deeper woodlands. She moved as if in full sunlight, easily avoiding obstacles at a run that would have made walking difficult for mortals. The darkness was now her ally, hiding her presence and preserving her anonymity.

To keep her mind off her injuries, she replayed the night's events. What had just happened? Granted, her experience with Vampires was still limited, but why hadn't she detected Claudio's presence immediately? And why had that mortal had a mind block? Was it possible he didn't know he was dealing with Vampires? No, the presence of a mind block made that unlikely. So it must be that they didn't trust the Vampires. No shocker there. But the more troubling question was whether or not the block was deliberately directed at her species as well. As for why she hadn't detected Claudio, she must have been careless. She wouldn't let that happen again.

She estimated she'd only come about ten miles or so. The next bus depot was still about forty miles away. She picked up the pace. It was going to be a long night.

Mara awoke to sunlight peeking into the darker recesses of the bus, streaming through half-closed curtains. She heard the driver call out their arrival in San Luis Obispo. So far so good. She scanned her fellow passengers once more, easily erasing the vague memories they had of her before switching buses again, this time bound for San Francisco.

Once she had settled into her seat, she pulled her laptop out of her backpack. She was still amazed it had survived the roll out of the car. She imagined some ad exec using crash resistance ratings to boost sales. Probably not much market for that in the mortal world. She laughed silently to herself and fired it up. By the time she arrived, her new identity was firmly in place. She cleaned up at the bus depot before hailing a cab for the airport where, with a few subtle 'pushes' she slipped through security onto a commuter flight to LA and her planned hunting ground.

A few hours later she pulled into the secluded estate nestled in a still expansive forest area. The property provided both privacy and a reprieve from the sensory overload such a large city would cause her. She punched in the alarm code and waited impatiently as the enormous gate groaned and lurched open. She'd have to do something about that. After verifying it closed securely behind her, she continued up the drive.

The real estate agent had gushed about the view of the San Gabriel Mountains over the phone. She grinned wryly in remembrance. There wasn't much the woman hadn't gushed about. She must have been trying to sell the place for a long time. At the price she had been asking, Mara wasn't surprised she'd had few takers. Looking at the view though, she conceded that the agent may have been on to something.

That sense of unease she'd gotten as she had stepped off the plane hadn't dissipated. No matter how much she tried to forget it, she kept returning to the moment of her arrival. It was almost as if something recognized her. No one – mortal or immortal – had ever seen through her disguise before, yet she had the distinct impression that this time something or someone had. And now, it hunted her. Not her kind, but her specifically.

Her close call outside the city must be making her paranoid. She was just tired. She stared out the window and tried to relax. The deepening red horizon stained the afternoon sky and highlighted the jagged mountain peaks silhouetted in black. It really was beautiful. She was still trying to convince herself there was nothing to worry about when she finally succumbed to sleep.

* * *

He'd sensed her presence the instant she entered the city limits. She was young, but she'd hidden well, he grudgingly admitted. Her presence remained undetected by his kind, save himself. A remarkable feat, all things considered. He wondered how she was able to conceal her presence so successfully. He smiled in anticipation. He looked forward to finding out. Looked forward to finding out that and a lot more.

Did she yet realize how much of her journey was of her own volition and how much because he'd summoned her? He reflected on how that scene might play out once she realized exactly what he'd done and who he really was. His eyes narrowed. That battle of wills he also looked forward to.

"She's here at last." The soft voice to his left startled him. He grinned. At least he came by his stealth honestly. "The one who called you back. Your soul. You've been waiting for her a long time."

"She'll fight me. She won't want to accept the truth." He stopped, unwilling to share everything he'd learned about her and the reasons why she'd fight him. He needed a plan she couldn't escape from – one that gave her no choice but to accept what he already knew to be inevitable. That she was his.

The woman with him frowned. He could tell by her expression that she knew he wasn't telling her everything. Her visions might reveal what he wished to remain hidden. She stepped forward, touching his arm so that he turned to face her. "She hides things from herself as well."

He acknowledged the statement with a nod and looked up at the night sky, savoring the evening sounds. "You have no doubt though, she is the one I've been seeking?"

"Yes," his companion said. "You have doubts?"

"No, all will come to pass as planned." He spoke nonchalantly, but the plans he'd put in place to guide her course to him were anything but.

CHAPTER TWO

Mara took one last glance at herself in the mirror, her green eyes luminous against her pale skin. The extra reds she allowed to burst through her artificially darkened black hair presented a dramatic, yet striking Goth picture. Good, she fit the part, one more 'mortal' styling herself as a Vampire wannabe. She retained the ability to blend into the darkness at will but still wanted to be able to attract attention. She'd learned that ability ranked right up there as one of her best weapons to get what she wanted quickly from mortals, short of tapping into her powers and risking detection.

Her eyes burned with sizzling energy as she perfected her mortal façade, temporarily erasing her Viajante characteristics, not just on the sensory level but sustaining the illusion down to a cellular one. None of her kind had ever attempted the type of long-term disguise she'd repeatedly been using and never to the degree to which she exposed herself. The elders would have been furious if they knew this was what she practiced while in Sanctuary.

Now that she was eighteen, they could no longer control her actions or prevent her from leaving – something she'd been trying to do for years. She'd seen the Council of Elders let others leave after they'd turned sixteen or if they'd completed their training early. But even though her training was completed long ago, every time she'd brought it up it had been summarily shot down. Even her aunt, Yasmine, had fought in her defense. If Yasmine hadn't accused them of sentencing her to an eternity of pain by preventing her from finding her soul – her other half – which obviously wasn't in Sanctuary, she'd probably still be there. She'd never made much time for boys before, not that she had any plans to change that now, but if it bought her the freedom she desired, she'd say whatever they wanted to hear.

Mara knew her aunt didn't believe she'd left to find her soul, but Yasmine knew it was Mara's destiny to go and their family had never been the type to fight destiny. She'd warned Mara to avoid contact until after she found what she was looking for. Yasmine thought the elders might come after her if they learned what she was up to and didn't want to be used against her niece. If she didn't know Mara's plans or location, she'd explained, she couldn't give anything away.

Mara understood her aunt's logic, but it really hurt to cut off contact. It still did.

Once outside Sanctuary borders, she'd felt drawn west, and once in California, drawn to LA. She didn't know why yet but was certain she soon would.

She'd accomplished a lot since her arrival a month ago. She wanted justice for the death of her family and she felt feisty enough to want a piece of whoever was responsible for chasing her all over the coast and delaying her entry into the city. Especially if that delay had removed whatever had drawn her here. Despite the odds, she decided to stick around and see if anything evolved.

Attacks against Viajante or Vampire were actually quite rare, despite the high tensions between the two. The attack on her family had been different. Mara knew there had been a specific significance about it that the elders mysteriously refused to acknowledge. She knew that with as much certainty as she knew she was different from any of her kind.

As with all Viajante, she had mind-bending abilities – the telepathic ability to pick up on and control the thoughts of others.

Since childhood, her finely tuned senses had allowed her to control situations and divine things invisible to most elders and even some Shamans. Not only could she pick up, store, filter, and control the thoughts of another, but she could simultaneously control numerous mortals and Vampires, all while exercising other unrelated powers like those of disguise or telekinesis.

She'd also developed and practiced others powers like broadcasting and controlling the images others saw in the external environment. It was that very ability that had saved her life so long ago and was something she still counted on today. She shook off the images of that day, grabbed her things, and headed out.

She entered the club, confidently breezing through the line designed to limit undesirables. She lightly pushed into the mind of the bouncer, convincing him to drop the red rope and rush to open the door as she glided into the acknowledged Vampire social stronghold and feeding ground.

Mara relished the challenge contact with her enemy provided. She eagerly sought out their areas of congregation, using the opportunity to study them as if one might a bug under a microscope. She tried to understand their behavior, sifting through the rumors and myths taught to her as a child for the real truth and more importantly, the answers to the questions that haunted her. Why had her family been murdered, and why or how had she become considered a threat? She was discovering there was a lot she hadn't been taught.

The comforting noise of her favorite techno bands pulsed in the background. Mara unconsciously dialed down the volume in her head and took her normal seat in a back corner of the dance floor. Since she'd found this club a week ago, she'd determined that location to be the safest and most advantageous for her purposes. She liked it because of the vantage it gave her of the rest of the club, including the upper VIP levels, but more importantly for its proximity to an exit not readily apparent to other club members.

The need for one was a lesson she'd learned from her first Vampire encounter in the city's bar scene.

She'd been in mortal disguise, back in a darkened corner of the bar much like this one, when trouble approached in the form of a gaunt Vampire male intent on using his powers to persuade her to leave with him. Not sure how to respond without giving herself away, she'd panicked. Her terror had increased as they were joined by another Vampire couple.

The girl, who later identified herself as Morgan, seated herself next to Mara. She'd smiled when Mara unconsciously shifted her body to put more space between them. "Pierre, are you bothering this girl?" she'd asked.

The Vampire who had propositioned her glared at the woman and her companion. He'd looked pissed. "I was not bothering her. We were about to leave," he'd said. "You're interrupting a private conversation." He'd turned his angry black eyes back to Mara and tried again to force her compliance.

It didn't work, but before she could respond the male with Morgan had cut in. "Not looking so good for you, old man. She doesn't look too interested. Best try your luck elsewhere, eh?"

Mara had watched in fascination as the outnumbered Vampire scowled and clenched his jaw before stalking off. The question she found herself asking was whether or not her rescuers also considered her a late-night snack. She'd turned back to them and affected a grateful poise, curious and nervous about how the encounter would end.

The male Vampire identified himself as Caleb. What had followed was a surprisingly delightful and interesting conversation during which Mara had found herself relaxing – so much so she'd given them her name. Over the last few weeks, she'd run into them from time to time in various bars and clubs.

While part of her questioned the frequency of their run-ins, she couldn't detect anything premeditated about their meetings and assessed the danger as minimal. She was, after all, hanging out in known Vampire haunts, right?

"Mara, you came!" A delighted voice broke into her reverie, announcing Morgan's presence to both Mara and several of the club patrons closest to her.

"Finally! We were wondering if you'd ever get here," Caleb said. He sounded mildly irritated, but the twinkle in his eye ruined the illusion. "Now she can stop hounding me about what time you said you were going to show up. Good to see you, Mara."

Mara smiled in response to their light banter. Rarely did she let herself feel true emotion. She hadn't been close to anyone except her aunt back in Sanctuary. She thoroughly enjoyed this rare opportunity to just act normal, as well as the too-short respite from her vigilance.

She stole a look at her Vampire companions. Morgan was a statuesque redhead who could have easily graced the cover of any fashion magazine while Caleb, her athletic and self-assured companion, had an aura of European money about him. The laid-back appearance he projected hid a well-contained power she suspected most couldn't even pick up on. She found it intriguing that he sought to portray such a non-threatening persona when he was so clearly capable of wielding serious power.

"Morgan, I told you I'd try to make it before twelve. Caleb, didn't I tell her that? It's only a few minutes after, really."

It normally went against all her self-preservation instincts, but Mara had allowed this relationship to blossom. As irrational as it sounded, there was something about them – Morgan in particular – that made her want to trust them . . . within limits of course. Besides, there were other benefits to the relationship. Unbeknownst to them, Morgan and Caleb served as lightning rods for detecting potential danger, allowing Mara to stay a crucial few steps ahead of any other would-be Vampire threats.

Caleb chuckled. "You did tell her that. She just couldn't believe you meant it this time."

Morgan slugged him and pouted. "Caleb, go make yourself useful. Get Mara a drink." She plopped down next to Mara. "Your usual? Sparkling water, unopened?"

"Please."

Mara scanned the bar and its occupants again, searching for the source of the discomfort she felt slowly creeping across her skin. Something was about to happen. She strengthened her mortal projection and checked for anything that might give her away. She didn't detect anything.

Caleb returned a few minutes later with her drink, and he and Morgan made a few half-hearted attempts at conversation before drifting off when they saw Mara's heart wasn't in it.

Mara mentally calculated the location of the Vampires throughout the club, noting that there seemed to be a larger-than-normal population out that night. The name Victor Terrington kept coming up. There were those goosebumps again. Something about that name resonated. He was hosting some sort of charity ball soon. Maybe this was the break she'd been looking for. Mara vowed to learn everything she could about him once she got home. This holiday event might give her the excuse she needed to learn more and to see if there was anything to the unnatural reaction his name caused her.

* * *

It might have been the effort to focus on so many conversations that caused her to miss his presence during her previous scans. But then she saw him. It was his eyes that caught her. Caught her and held her hostage. They were smoky gray. Even through the murky darkness of the bar, she could see that. He was tall, with dirty-blond hair not quite reaching his shoulders but almost haphazardly tucked behind his ears. Hot in any language and by any species standard.

He leaned back casually against the bar, but still maintained a presence that screamed power. The contradiction only enhanced his very bad-boy look. She must be crazy. No way had he been staring at her. She must have imagined it.

She looked away, unwilling to draw undue attention to herself. She fought to get her heartbeat under control. If she saw him again, there was no chance she'd be able to pretend he hadn't caught her attention – not after that searing eye contact.

Against her will, she felt the need to look up and was once again caught by his stare. No, stare wasn't the right word for it. The intensity of that look could melt ice, bring it to a boiling point and then evaporate it in a second flat.

It was suddenly obvious to her that he hadn't looked away. Not once. She wasn't even sure if he'd blinked since she'd first noticed him. She inhaled deeply, trying to calm nerves already jingling in alarm, and double-checked her shields again.

All right, enough of this. Time to take the ball out of his court. She wasn't about to let him intimidate her. She wasn't the uncertain teen she used to be. She returned his stare with one of her own, her eyes flashing a defiant and dangerous green. So there!

He looked slightly surprised like he hadn't expected her to dare give back as good as she got. An amused smile lit his face and he raised his glass in a mock salute before disappearing into the crowd.

Laughed? She had the distinct impression that he'd actually laughed at her. She wasn't sure what pissed her off more – his attitude or her stupidity for spending anything more than one millisecond thinking about him. This guy was a serious threat to her sanity, and here she sat like some stupid schoolgirl mooning over his reaction to her challenge instead of worrying about the significance of his attention in the first place. Stupid Mara, she castigated herself, really stupid.

"Mara, you look like you saw a ghost." She heard Morgan's familiar and comforting voice and immediately relaxed her features. She didn't want them worrying.

"Of course not," she said, waving off the concern with a flick of her wrist. "I just noticed some guy staring at me and it caught me off guard. A little too intense, if you know what I mean." She laughed nervously.

"Really, Mara, as gorgeous as you are?" Morgan said. "That hardly seems cause for surprise."

"Where is he?" Caleb asked, scanning the crowd. "What did he look like?"

Mara described him and caught the guarded look Caleb and Morgan exchanged. "What aren't you telling me?"

"Nothing," Morgan said, patting her arm in reassurance. "Don't let my stranger fantasies get you paranoid." She laughed and raised an eyebrow. "Bad boy, huh? He sounds hot. Caleb, you run away and let us girls talk." Morgan placed her elbows on the table and rested her head on her hands, mockingly pantomiming eagerly waiting for details. Mara couldn't help but laugh.

"I'm not sure I got that good a look," Mara said, smiling at Morgan. "It's no big deal, really. Definitely not my type." She couldn't stand the knowing look Morgan gave her so she threw the first thing that came to mind in a desperate attempt to change the subject. "Want to dance?"

Almost as soon as the words left her mouth, she found herself dragged onto the dance floor. Mara tried to let the blaring music erase her concerns.

When she finally returned to her earlier position in the corner, nearly two hours had passed and the crowd had thickened even more. She was finally beginning to feel confident that she'd avoided whatever danger the tall, intense stranger had presented.

Just keep telling yourself that. She heard the taunting voice echo softly in her head.

She stiffened. *Who are you? How can you talk with me like this?* She bit her lip to prevent a more colorful version of the question from slipping out, annoyed at herself for responding at all.

He didn't answer.

Mara felt a presence building in the corner nearest her. A presence designed to demand her attention as well as cut off her exit. The stranger from earlier that night stepped out of the shadows and flashed a Cheshire grin. He unconsciously projected an image of casual elegance overlaid with a power she found so impressive that she truly was intimidated. Not that she would let him know that!

He bowed slightly, a crooked and self-assured smile on his face. *You didn't really mean it when you said I wasn't at all your type, now did you?*

Yes. She sniffed haughtily.

Liar. He grinned in obvious satisfaction. *I can read your thoughts. You were looking for me.*

Mara struggled to retain her composure and hide her growing fear. She could feel him pushing into her mind, studying her.

It must be hard to maintain that incredibly aloof poise with your every instinct urging you to turn and run. And yet you don't. Interesting, very interesting . . .

"I don't know what you mean," she said aloud, needing to change the nature of their conversation back to a less intimate form. "I wasn't looking for you. Or anyone else for that matter."

She forced herself not to scan the bar for Morgan and Caleb, knowing he could easily be a threat to them as well as her. She had no desire to involve them in any danger, especially not any of her own making.

"You weren't looking for me? Really? How very odd. And I had the distinct impression you were looking for someone exactly like me." He flashed a breathtaking smile at her as he wickedly projected the image of a very powerful Vampire. "I was so sure that I was exactly what you were looking for . . ." he leaned in as if to whisper in her ear, then continued through the private path between their minds, *Viajante.*

She gasped, temporarily losing all pretense of cool and collected. How the hell could he possibly know that? Her disguise was flawless! She hadn't detected any doubt or question in his voice. He'd made a statement. He was certain.

She pulled herself back from her chaotic thoughts. He'd been watching her, and from his expression, he'd seen too many of them played out on her face. Yasmine was forever chastising her to better hide her facial expressions.

I've never met a Viajante like you before. I find myself extremely curious . . .

He was good, Mara admitted. Either he really had figured her out, or else he was one hell of a good guesser. "You think you have me all figured out, do you?" she asked, keeping her voice light as she gathered her powers silently, preparing her next move.

"You misunderstand." He moved still closer, his hand reaching up to brush away a stray hair from her face. He looked momentarily surprised to find his hand there before lowering it to skim her neck and ultimately resting it on the antique onyx amulet hanging there. He lifted it for a second in the dim light to examine it before dropping it. He leveled his gaze back to her eyes. "I don't know everything about you yet, Mara," he said, "but I plan to."

In an instant, she was at the back door. She paused long enough to snatch a last glimpse of him before she fled. Even through the gloom, she read the shock on his face. He narrowed his eyes and glared.

Mara focused her energy, drawing a path only visible to the stranger who'd challenged her. Vampire, the projection shouted, then she disappeared.

CHAPTER THREE

How in the hell had she projected that image? Viajante were not Vampire and absolutely could not emulate them, period. She had just projected an image of a Vampire as real as he was. He leaned against the wall of the club, touching his chin with his hand, and allowed his thoughts to wander, trying to digest the strange riddle she presented. He found himself a little shocked, but honestly, much more thrilled than upset. Finally, a worthy challenge. He smiled. She thought she'd escaped him. Not even close.

"So what's the next move, bro? You want us to follow her?" Caleb tapped him on the shoulder. "Hey, Terrill?"

Terrill turned to Caleb and shook his head. "No. Just keep an eye on her if she shows up again. I think I may have spooked her."

"How'd she get out of here so fast? There's something different about this girl. I've never known you to take such an interest in any mortal before. What gives?"

"If I told you now, she'd pick it up somehow."

Caleb frowned. "How powerful could she be? Something about this little deception seems a bit like overkill."

"She isn't exactly your ordinary mortal. Let's leave it at that. Until I can figure out exactly what she's up to, I need your help."

Caleb grasped Terrill's arm in the age-old symbol of solidarity. "We're here for you, bro, whatever you need. You know can count on us." He released his grasp and shrugged, "I've got to admit though, Morgan and I are starting to like her. This cloak-and-dagger drill isn't your normal MO. Seems like a lot of effort. I hope she's worth it."

Terrill ran his fingers through his unruly hair and impatiently pushed it out of his eyes. "Let me know if anything develops while I'm gone."

He exited the same way Mara had. He inhaled the night air deep into his lungs, finding the faint psychic power trail she'd unconsciously left behind. She may be many things he had yet to discover, but he was certain she was worth the chase. That and a lot more too.

Terrill continued to follow her trail, again impressed with her ability to disguise and mislead. Were it not for prior surveillance and his formidable tracking skills, she might have been successful in losing him a couple of times. Too bad she'd have to be disappointed. He emerged from the woods and saw her window in front of him. Nope, losing track of her wasn't likely.

He settled in to wait. When he finally approached her, she wouldn't be expecting him. He wanted her off balance – needed it even – for his plan to succeed.

* * *

Mara arrived home jumpy and nervous. She'd done her best to hide her flight and dissuade any attempts to follow. In all her recent experiences with Vampires, she had *never* come across anyone like this one. She couldn't afford any mistakes – not now. She doubled her safeguards, drawing a protective curtain around her home, and slowly, as the hours passed, began to unwind.

She washed the artificial black coloring out of her hair and let the hot water soothe away the stress of her evening. It had been especially difficult that night. The thoughts of that many mortals and immortals alone would have left her drained, but her encounter with the stranger had amplified her level of effort and consequently drained her energy level. It would take time to restore her balance. Worse, she'd have to resort to some drastic measures if she wanted her strength back quickly, and she did.

She stared at her reflection as she towel-dried her hair. God, she'd been stupid. Yasmine was always warning her about the dangers of giving in to that streak of temper of hers. What on earth had made her challenge him? That he could get that close to her was a clear sign she was way over her head. And then what had she done to top that? She'd challenged him – confronted him head-on. Definitely stupid. It was indisputable. She was out of her mind.

Mara slipped on a comfortable pair of jeans and an old surf sweatshirt. She didn't bother covering her bare feet as she walked into the kitchen to make coffee. Even though her body begged for sleep – the thing she needed most to heal the damage of the evening – she still had work to do before dawn and couldn't afford to give in yet. She wrapped her hands around the mug. The fresh aroma tickled her nose as she enjoyed that first sip. She turned back to the table and almost dropped the mug on the floor.

"Surprised?" Terrill's smile was casual as he stretched out in one of her kitchen chairs looking very pleased with himself.

"How did you get in here?" Mara asked. She kept her voice calm as she scanned the area for additional threats and possible escape options.

"Oh, you mean your safeguards? I think you'll find them all still intact. I prefer not to unravel something you took such care to do. Out of respect, of course." He frowned as if considering something. "Are they usually so ineffective?"

"They've served quite well until now." Mara took a sip of her coffee, trying to maintain a safe distance between them while hiding her terror that he'd just breached her safeguards so effortlessly. Just how powerful was he?

"Have a seat, Mara. I think our conversation may take some time and you'll be uncomfortable standing so long."

"No, thank you. I prefer to stand."

He laughed. "Now you're just being contrary." Before she could blink, he was in front of her, pressing her back against the counter. "I'm afraid I'll have to insist." He smiled a sexy smile as he removed the cup from her hand and placed it out of her reach on the countertop behind her.

"Hmm . . ." he raised his eyebrow suggestively, "now that you mention it, I believe I do see the benefits of standing." He covered the slight distance remaining between them, sending her heart into overdrive. He brushed his lips against her sensitive ear as she stood paralyzed. "Won't you please join me at the table?" he whispered.

Terrified by her body's reaction to him and sensing the subtle push in his voice, she decided some semblance of distance was her safest option. She nodded and reluctantly allowed him to lead her to the table. After she sat, he placed her coffee on the table in front of her. She'd already forgotten about it. He took the seat next to hers and turned the chairs so they faced each other, almost touching.

What do you want? she asked.

Had he wanted her dead, she'd be so already. Instead, he seemed to be toying with her. He was powerful beyond anything she'd ever dealt with. It scared the hell out of her. He didn't seem to be using even a fraction of his considerable powers against her, even after proving just how vulnerable she was.

I'm not toying with you. His answer told Mara that he could easily read her mind. Great. Now, what was he after? *You present a mystery, and I need to know if you present a threat.* He shifted his weight and leaned back in his chair. *Surely you can appreciate that?*

Nothing was ever that simple. *You're the one in MY home, so tell me again, how exactly do I qualify as the threat? Who appointed you the almighty assessor of threats anyway?*

His lips twitched in the semblance of a smile. "You know exactly what I'm talking about, Mara. It's why you're here. Let's not play games."

He stretched his arms in front of himself and rolled his shoulders back before continuing. "I have no objection to remaining civilized. Perhaps we could start with introductions, yes?"

She glared at him. He acted as if he hadn't noticed.

"I'm Terrill Kristiansen," he said, "and you are Amara Martinovic. A Viajante who goes by the name Mara, pretends to be a mortal, and foolishly tries to collect information about Vampires in the middle of their claimed territory." He looked directly into her eyes. "Did I miss anything?" He sighed at her silence. "Why are you really here?"

Although he said the words in a nonthreatening way, Mara didn't doubt he would do whatever it took to get the answers he wanted. Sorry, but that wasn't something she'd allow, no matter how powerful he might be.

Mara took a sip of her coffee and set it down with a sigh of capitulation. She knew she'd only have one chance. She made it as far as the door to the next room before he caught her. He pinned her against the wall with his body and held her hands in a vice-like grip at her sides, blocking any attempt to escape. *Going somewhere?*

Mara felt the long length of his body, muscular and solid, pressed against her. He pushed her hands behind her back, forcing her forward against his chest, and she saw male satisfaction shining in his eyes as he leaned in toward her neck.

Mindless terror threatened to overtake her, and she fought childhood memories of the attack struggling to surface. Violence and fear. The horrible pain of flesh ripping. Fangs piercing. She blocked out the slurping sound pounding between her ears and tried to forget the pain that had burned through her veins as she struggled to get away from him. No, not again! She wouldn't let it happen, not ever again!

Mara, stop, look at me!

She heard the concern in his voice and saw the shock in his eyes.

Even with his access to her mind, he couldn't tell if her experience was real or just her fears of what might happen. He wasn't going to bite her. She struggled to get her breathing back under control. He looked at her curiously.

He switched his grip to hold both her hands with one of his own as he brought his free arm around to cup her face, lifting her chin so that she met his gaze. The silver in his eyes turned liquid. "What is it about you?" he asked as he drew her face closer to his.

She felt the jolt as their lips made contact, her shock turning to a delicious system overload as he deepened the kiss.

This was nothing like the chaste kiss she'd experienced when one of her schoolmates had asked her to participate in what he'd called a practice session at one of the few parties she'd attended. He'd claimed he wanted experience for when he found his soul. She'd been curious so she'd gone along and, thanks to his bragging, had earned quite a reputation. That was the last time she'd ever gotten that close to someone of the opposite sex. If only she had known it could be like this, she might not have been so hasty to ban all contact with them.

When Terrill finally pulled away, she was surprised to find both his hands wrapped in her hair. She saw his gaze move to her hair. He shifted the strands in his hands. *So, it changes color with the, ah, proper motivation. Fascinating.*

Mara blushed, still reeling from the sensations their contact had sparked. Her green eyes were dark with desire, and she made herself look away, focusing instead on her hands. Embarrassed, she discovered them on his chest and quickly pushed them away. He was a Vampire. Was she suicidal?

He took an indulgent step back. "I have business that can't wait, so I must go. I am willing to delay our conversation for that small duration only. You will be here when I return. No running."

Was that a sample of the punishment for running?

Promise me you'll be here.

She didn't want to promise him anything. "Yes." Surprised to hear the word pass her lips, she looked at him suspiciously. Had he somehow forced her to say it?

He smiled an enigmatic smile, then slowly dropped his arms and stepped back. He indicated with his arm that she should return to the table.

"No." She stopped, refusing to move just because he had given her permission to. "What do you want from me? Do you want me to promise to leave the city, that I won't threaten you? What?"

"No. You won't leave the city. Not without my permission," he said. "I want answers about why you're here and what you're trying to find."

"I can't tell you."

"And I can't ignore your presence here. Your actions put yourself and my people at risk." He took a step closer. "Tell the truth. Who is Victor Terrington to you, and why are you willing to risk your life to get to him?"

Mara froze, backing away from Terrill before she could help herself. She hadn't realized just how much he had been able to see about her intentions – perhaps even more than she'd seen herself.

He placed an arm on either side of her, once again hedging her between the wall and his muscular frame. "Shall we strike a bargain then?"

"You would trust me at my word?"

"Should I not?"

"I wouldn't."

His eyes narrowed. "Stay away from Victor. He's dangerous. Out of your league." Terrill stared at her a few seconds longer. "I'll be back in a few days. Can you manage to stay out of trouble that long? Or maybe I should take you with me?" He laughed and Mara realized she had once again clearly failed to hide her expression. "I'm sorry you find that prospect so unappealing. Perhaps there is something I can do to change your mind?"

Mara stiffened, glaring at him and wishing she had enough strength left to destroy or at least diminish his self-confidence and over-inflated ego. Damn him! She'd swear he was laughing at her again. The sooner he left the better.

Try not to miss me too much. He winked.

Mara found herself swinging at empty air where just seconds before he'd been standing. Somehow, he'd managed to disappear just as mysteriously as he'd arrived. Her safeguards hadn't even registered a flicker of resistance. She plopped down at the kitchen table and took a long drag of coffee before spitting out the cold liquid. After cleaning up the mess she'd made, she dumped out what was left in the cup and poured another.

With a wicked gleam in her eye, she headed straight for her computer. The very first thing she planned to do was look up Victor Terrington and the annual holiday charity event she'd heard about. The hell with any promises she'd made. She had been waiting too long for answers. No way was she stopping now. Besides, Terrill said it himself. She had two days. Plenty of time.

Mara sat down at the computer, digging into everything she could find. She used one of the many false identities she'd created and paid some online bloodhounds to search for anything related to Victor Terrington, any variation of that name, or any location referenced. She spread the requests across various research agencies to form a plausible genealogical cover search.

It would take at least a few hours for the agencies to respond, so she decided to check her anti-tracking software. She used her powers to amplify it, expanding the number of ghost hops it routed through, even as she set up random IP address rotators at the various stops, expertly tapping into impenetrable firewalls to create false trails. No one would be able to trace the results back to her.

She stood and stretched. As much as she disliked the idea, she needed blood to get back to full strength before confronting Victor. She had less than thirty-six hours. Nothing, and more importantly, no one would dissuade her from her planned course of action.

Mara touched her fingers to her lips, tracing the path Terrill's mouth had taken. She couldn't get the taste and smell of him out of her head. It was like she could still feel the heat that the contact of their mouths had generated. She didn't want to think about what would have happened if he hadn't broken off contact when he did.

As to her promise to comply with his edict, he couldn't honestly expect her to follow that, could he? She closed her eyes, trying to clear her mind. Despite herself, her thoughts kept wandering back to Terrill and she wondered how a second encounter might play out. She shuddered. It would be in her best interest to avoid one altogether.

* * *

Mara leaned back in the chair and let the life-giving blood flow into her veins. An unusual side effect from her near-death experience as a child – that was what Yasmine had called her occasional need for blood transfusions. They both knew it wasn't anemia, but they'd conspired to hide the truth from everyone else. It wasn't something they could afford to let others know about – not if she wanted to continue to live that is.

Mara sighed. Half Vampire. One foot was partially in their world, but the rest of her body and soul were firmly in the Viajante realm. Even having been raised Viajante, she often felt like a stranger among her kind, forever fearful they would discover her secret. No one had ever heard of such a half-breed. No one thought it was possible.

Vampire blood killed Viajante, just as it did mortals not selected for conversion, and she hadn't been. This was the one law both species had agreed on. Live and let live. It was forbidden for Vampires to convert or kill Viajante just as it was forbidden for a

Viajante to kill a Vampire. Unfortunately for her, that law had done little to deter her family's attackers or prevent her current condition.

She doubted the elders would care who had done the deed, they would instead focus on resolving the problem, i.e. her. And should Vampires find out, she'd lose the only advantage she had there as well. She thanked God that this secret, if no others, at least still seemed safe. Even Terrill, with his exceptional powers, didn't appear to have figured it out yet. She didn't kid herself. If he got the opportunity, he could, and eventually, he would.

Her transfusion finished, she hid all the evidence and set to analyzing the results her searches had produced. She sifted through the voluminous data, processing in minutes what would take mortals days or even weeks to cull through.

The hairs on her neck stood up. There it was. A Victor Terrington had been listed as a prominent member of society in the same region of Spain where her family had been attacked and killed. That couldn't be a coincidence. Not long after their deaths, he'd disappeared for a while, resurfacing to travel through Europe before eventually ending up in Los Angeles.

She thought about the implications of what she had just discovered. Victor had somehow been involved. He'd left for somewhere in Europe immediately after the attack. Her family's killers must have believed her dead else they would have come after her, right?

She was ready to put the next phase of her plan into action. Contact was always a dangerous option, but in this case, the only one. She needed to see him up close. Proximity was the only way to pick up the missing information and learn his weaknesses. The charity event she had heard about was a holiday ball for Los Angeles's elite. But being the generous patron of the arts that he was, Victor always held a number of tickets in reserve for promising students at the local art and music schools to encourage the intermingling of the two worlds.

She checked the calendar. It was scheduled for the night after next at his private estate. Thanks to her association with a socially in-tune Morgan, she knew exactly who to call on to finagle one of those student invitations. It would be cutting it close. She hoped desperately that Terrill's business would keep him away at least that long.

CHAPTER FOUR

Terrill lifted his head as he identified her scent and his senses drank in her unique fragrance. He would have known it anywhere. She stood at the top of the staircase and his gut clenched at the vision she presented. Damned if she didn't look like some sort of pagan sacrifice. Too caught up in the sensations her presence inspired, he momentarily forgot it was exactly that presence he'd forbidden.

Dressed in a vintage, off-white, sequined dress that accented her graceful neck and shoulders, she looked almost regal. The intriguing antique black onyx amulet he had noted her wearing at their last encounter perfected the image. Her radiant red hair was elegantly piled in layers upon her head. Tendrils escaped at random spots, rebelliously attempting to cascade down her back as they caught in the light, sparkling and shimmering with a multitude of colors.

His spine stiffened and he barely prevented a low growl from erupting as he became aware of the attention her entrance had generated. He wasn't the only one of his kind to notice her allure. Conversation in the gallery had dimmed as Vampires and mortals alike turned to observe her descent down the staircase. He didn't like that her appearance alone could cause such a physical response among the males of his kind, something he discovered himself ironically susceptible to as well. His eyes narrowed as he followed her progress. He stood silently and bided his time. She had no idea how dangerous a game she played.

To the casual observer, Mara appeared immune to the effect she had on others. But Terrill's scrutiny was anything but casual. It revealed an almost imperceptible resetting of her shoulders, sort of like she'd steeled herself for something to come. As she scanned the gallery opening before her, he willed her to notice him. They locked eyes. To his intense satisfaction, she responded with a slightly shocked expression on her face at recognizing him. Then there was the slightest tremble of her hand as she reached for the banister. So, his presence had affected her.

The corners of his mouth lifted slightly, and he was rewarded with a brief flash of anger from a certain deep-green gaze, indicating not only her general irritation with his presence but greater displeasure at her own reaction. What she should have been worrying about was the promise she'd broken. A mistake she'd not soon make again.

His posture and the intense emotions churning inside him succeeded in drawing his mother's attention. He didn't spare a glance at the petite, raven-haired beauty beside him. She tilted her head in inquiry. She raised her eyebrow in speculation and followed the direction of his gaze back to Mara, where her own gaze rested in deep consideration before returning to Terrill. *So, this is her?* she asked. *I've never seen you so distracted. A mortal, no less. That I didn't see in my visions.* Terrill tried to find the words but merely shrugged his shoulders, unable to explain. *She is not quite mortal though, is she? I wonder . . .*

Terrill momentarily broke his gaze away from Mara and addressed his mother. *I know what I'm doing.*

He refocused his attention on Mara, trying to see if he could pick up on what his mother alluded to. Gabriella had extraordinary skills. He should know – he'd inherited many from her. He sighed in relief. His examination revealed little of Mara's secrets. His relief was rapidly swallowed by anger and fear. Fear that she risked her life for no reason he could ascertain, followed closely by anger over his inability to understand what the bloody hell she expected to gain from this dangerous charade. Despite his anger, he couldn't prevent the unwelcome need to protect her from herself and others from rising within him.

Terrill silently acknowledged his father's arrival. Unlike Gabriella, Lauris had an older, more distinguished air about him. His physical stature guaranteed his powers were never underestimated like Gabriella's often were. Lauris squeezed Gabriella's hand and turned knowing eyes to his son's face and the expression written across it.

Terrill nodded slightly. *I'll explain later.*

Of course, I'll need to figure it out myself first. He headed to the base of the stairs, thankful no Vampire he'd ever met had anything close to his family's extraordinary perceptive abilities. Mara remained safe in her guise as a mortal, if you could call a mortal in a room full of Vampires safe to start with.

* * *

On fire. There was no other way to describe his eyes. His look burned straight through her. Staking some sort of a primitive claim on her, daring her to object. Either that or he was even more pissed off than she'd realized. She could tell he wasn't the type to tolerate deceit, and worse for her, she could tell he was used to getting his way. It had been dangerous to defy him, and she'd probably end up regretting it, but she hadn't had a choice, had she?

As she descended the last stair, he proffered his arm. *Your choice – a scene, or you allow me to help strengthen your cover.* She hesitated but a second before taking his arm. "You want to die, do you? It's a death wish you have?" He sighed. "They have counselors for that you know."

Yup, he was pissed. She deliberately misinterpreted his words. *So the price for disobedience is death?* She wasn't sure how much of the anger was directed at her for disobeying and how much at the situation he considered dangerous. She suspected the latter and hoped her powers of perception hadn't failed her.

"I warned you there would be consequences."

"But not now," she said with more confidence than she felt. Mara knew she'd assessed his intentions correctly. He was concerned, but why? She'd taken every precaution; the risk was minimal. What had she missed?

"Not now, Mara," he agreed, "but later. There will be a reckoning." Her head rose at the promise resonating in his voice.

He chose the more secure path for the next bombshell. *My mother knows you're not mortal.* Mara tensed. *Good,* he said, *you're starting to get the picture.* The hand on her arm tightened. *What the hell were you thinking entering the lion's den pretending to be something you're not? Did you think we're all so stupid you'd get away with it? Or has that damnable arrogance in your abilities given you such misplaced confidence that you don't realize the position you're in?*

And what position is it exactly that I find myself in? Based on the tone of his voice, she was pretty sure she wouldn't like the answer.

He smiled, his eyes darkening to shimmering pools of mercury as he met and held her wary gaze. *Why, dependent on me for your survival tonight, of course.* His words coursed through her blood, causing her heart to thump loudly as she imagined the payment he would demand for such dependence.

The approach of a distinguished and powerful-looking man interrupted their private conversation. Chocolate-brown eyes stared purposefully at her from a square-jawed face framed by lustrous brown wavy hair. She recognized him from the press clippings. Victor.

He was a handsome man, but she found that she wasn't even remotely attracted. Instead, she found herself fighting to control the feeling of revulsion threatening to overwhelm her as he got closer. She'd only felt that strong a sensation once before . . .

As she measured him up, she was certain he did the same. And it appeared he was surprised to see her with Terrill. She noticed an undercurrent of tension between them.

I hope you know what you're doing, Terrill said as Victor approached. "Mara, allow me to introduce you to Victor Terrington, tonight's benefactor and festivity patron."

He smoothly introduced Mara as a student and fan of the arts. The tense set of his shoulders betrayed his concern Victor would pick up on her deception.

Not likely she thought to herself. Her disguise was impenetrable.

It's not just Victor you have to worry about – it's his minions as well.

Okay, Mara told herself, here we go. Game time. Mara offered her hand to Victor and regulated the temperature, texture, and scent of her skin to fortify her mortal appearance. The skill came as easy to her as exhaling. If it's mortal they want, it's mortal they get.

The shock of contact left her breathless. She'd always been especially sensitive to perceiving violence or the desire for it. Based on her reaction to Victor, neither were strangers to him. She prayed he hadn't noticed her reaction.

"Mr. Terrington," she said, simulating the proper amount of awe and respect a man in his position expected. She'd sensed his need to be acknowledged for his position and power and found playing up to it the most convenient way to lower his suspicions.

She reconfigured her brain patterns allowing him to believe he'd gained access to her thoughts while simultaneously controlling the images, thoughts, and emotions within, projecting a nonthreatening yet intriguing persona. She would feel it at the end of the night, but it wasn't anything she couldn't handle.

"Mara," Victor looked speculatively between her and Terrill. "Welcome. I didn't know you knew our Terrill."

The sound of his voice triggered a bout of nausea that threatened to knock her to her knees. She had no choice but to smile through it. She no longer had doubts. This was the voice of the bogeyman that had destroyed her life.

Mara smiled widely. "Terrill and I met sometime back. He was kind enough to arrange for a car to pick me up."

Victor laughed hollowly. "Of course he was. Terrill's such a gentleman. We hadn't the slightest idea he'd hidden you away, although seeing you now . . . well, I can understand why."

Terrill's smile looked pained.

Victor kept his gaze on her and continued trivial chatter as he probed her mind for more answers. "Something about her seems familiar," he mused.

Mara felt Terrill's increased agitation through their mind link and casually placed her hand on his arm, helping him focus as Victor's questions to her about her artistic interests and studies continued.

He doesn't know if you are who you say you are, said Terrill.

What's he looking for? she asked.

I don't know, but I don't like the extra attention he's giving you. Being here with me may very well have placed you in even greater danger.

"I think it only fair to warn you, Victor, while I'm deeply interested in music, I don't think I possess such great skills myself," she said. "If you can tolerate my amateur attempts, I'd be delighted to join you for a song or two. I assume you'll accompany me?" She nodded at the piano. Victor gestured toward it and moved that way. He appeared certain she would follow.

Terrill brushed a curl back behind her ear. *You can sing, right?*

I can handle this. She flashed him a nervous grin as they approached the other guests. She was just relieved their proximity to others diluted the noxious influence Victor held over her.

The echoes of "Silent Night" ended with a polite clapping of hands and the guests around the piano parted as Victor took a seat on the bench. "What shall it be, Mara,?," he asked. "Something traditional?"

"I've always enjoyed 'The Wexford Carol,'" she said, joining him at the piano. Terrill stayed close. She turned to face Victor as the curious crowd around the piano grew. She guessed it wasn't often that Victor took such an active role in the festivities or, given the number of Vampires that joined them, the entertainment of mortals.

He nodded and soon the voices and sounds of the room receded. She lost herself in the richness of the lyrics. Her voice rang out true and wafted across the room like a haunting breeze. As she sang, the song wove its way around the room, drawing in both mortal and immortal. It was almost hypnotic. One look at Victor's face dashed any hopes Terrill had that its effect had gone unnoticed.

As the last notes of the music faded away, there was a moment of silence abruptly broken by a huge swell of applause, shocking and embarrassing her with its intensity. Victor rose from the bench and clapped lightly. "If that's your definition of interest and not talent," he said, winking at the merrymakers gathered around them before returning his focus to her, "I wonder what you would consider true talent." He bowed slightly. "Well done."

Victor looked speculatively at Mara while quietly addressing Terrill. "I now understand your interest. Your songbird has a special talent."

Terrill's face remained emotionless as he took hold of Mara's hand and pulled her close. "She has many talents. I have not yet set to cataloging them."

Victor smiled coldly.

"If you would excuse us, I promised Mara a drink," Terrill looked suggestively at her, "and, Mara, the chance to properly catch up that you promised me, is long overdue." Even though his words were meant for Victor's benefit, she couldn't prevent the involuntary shiver from running through her. She seriously needed to get her reaction to Terrill under control.

"But of course," Victor said, "Mara, it's been a pleasure. Terrill's a lucky man." He looked intensely at her and raised her hand to his lips. "Until we meet again."

Mara murmured an appropriately polite response and wondered about the private conversation she knew he'd had with Terrill. She'd had too much trouble overcoming her reaction to him to eavesdrop on their conversation. She'd have to convince Terrill to divulge some of the details.

Terrill took her arm and steered her toward a secluded alcove with various artwork displayed. She pretended to sip on the wine Terrill provided her from one of the servers.

"You sang well, Mara. Was there something significant about that song?"

"It was a favorite of my mother."

"Ah, that explains it."

Mara looked at him curiously. What exactly did it explain?

"It meant a lot to you." She felt his grey eyes burning a hole through her. "When you sang, the music itself took on a life of its own. You showed that life to others in your song. That's a gift, Mara, a powerful one. With practice, you could turn it into an extremely effective weapon."

"You'd have me add another weapon to my arsenal? I would have thought you unhappy to see another power I had. Or are you so arrogant you don't fear any of them?"

He laughed. "There's a lot you don't know about yourself or your powers." His eyes snared hers again, his expression now serious. "And it's that lack of knowledge that could get you killed. Especially with your fondness for taking suicidal risks. The only further risk I will allow you tonight is back here." He gestured ahead of them.

She looked at him in confusion.

"Victor's taste in art." Was he kidding? He smiled. "It may not be much to view, but it gets you out of Victor's eye for a while." Why not? It made about as much sense as anything she could think of. She didn't resist as he led her deeper into the alcove.

CHAPTER FIVE

V ictor designed this area to showcase his artistic appreciation," he said as he kept pace with her, "but it more accurately showcases his need to display his own importance. Most of these are familial portraits, supposedly of ancestors or ancestral holdings."

Heat radiated from the contact his hand made against her back, and judging by his reaction, he felt it too. She stepped out of his reach and walked toward a painting in the farthest recess of the alcove. Shock robbed her of speech as she stared at it. She didn't realize she'd dropped her glass until she saw Terrill holding it. His supernatural speed allowed him to catch it before a drop spilled. His eyes burned into hers.

What is it? he asked.

Who's the girl? she asked, unable to tear her eyes away.

Angelica. Victor's ward. He adopted her as a baby. Unusual for our kind, sure, but then Victor's always been unpredictable. Why?

Where is she now?

Vacationing with friends, I think. Victor has her attending some special boarding school. We don't see her much.

He moved closer and tilted her chin so he could look directly into her eyes. *Tell me, Mara,* he said. *You NEED to tell me.*

Mara felt the hypnotic compulsion in his voice and swallowed convulsively. She took a deep breath. She wasn't sure she could trust him but she wanted to. *It's impossible, but I'd swear I was looking at a picture of my mother.*

Whatever he'd expected her to say, that wasn't it. *She's a Vampire, raised such from birth. I've seen her as a child and watched her grow.*

Mara's thoughts raced as fast as her heartbeat. He had no idea the scope of what he'd just revealed. Could it be? Was it even possible? Now she really couldn't breathe.

How old is she? she asked once she got her breath back. Her voice faded to a mere whisper in his mind.

Terrill stared at her and prepared to answer. Before the words left his mouth, he heard the answer from hers. "Sixteen." Mara didn't recognize the husky sound as it passed her lips.

"Mara, look at me," he said. *Your disguise is slipping.*

He swiftly backed her into the darkened corner and ruthlessly took control of her mouth. At first, she was too shocked to think. Then what he was doing registered and she wasn't able to think at all. She was drowning.

She shifted restlessly in his arms, finally fighting through her fragmented emotions and strengthening her disguise. Terrill reluctantly allowed her to pull free of his embrace.

Damn it, Terrill! We need to talk about your distraction techniques. She placed her hands on burning cheeks and self-consciously checked her hair, hoping her lips were not as swollen as they felt. She knew he'd been trying to distract her, help her, but she was embarrassed that he'd been able to affect her so thoroughly. *They're not half as effective as you think they are.* The untruth of her words burned crimson rings on her face, but she was determined to make a point so she let it stand.

Terrill's smile got wider. *I beg to disagree.*

The smug male arrogance in his tone grated on her nerves.

If it were not my right to do so, you would not react thus. You prove my claim with your very reaction. Not effective? He ran his hand through his hair in aggravation. *Baby, if it were any more effective, we'd have both burst into flame.*

You would not react thus? Your claim? She sniffed as she tugged the curls back into place. *Spoiled lord of the manor, your age is showing.*

And you find it wise to argue with one so much senior to you? Laughter showed briefly in his eyes before he sighed and shook his head. *I must have the patience of a glacier. You truly don't have any idea how dangerous this game you play is, do you?*

She avoided looking at the portrait again. Of course, she was aware but wasn't about to let that stop her.

Are you able to face the crowds and continue your charade a while longer? It might raise questions if we were to leave so quickly after being back here.

Mara nodded, unsurprised to find herself again hoping the night would end quickly. As usual, she'd gotten more than she'd bargained for. Terrill still confused her – both his motivations and her reaction to him.

She forced a smile onto her face, and they rejoined the crowd. Only she and Terrill knew how much that impression cost her.

Mara made small talk and forced herself to accept the numerous congratulations and well wishes of those who had heard her sing. The headache building in the back of her mind threatened to spill over. The mortal image she projected got more and more difficult to maintain.

Her hand trembled slightly as she set her glass down on the server's tray. She raised her eyes to meet Terrill's.

Mara, I can't tolerate watching you like this. Take the choice I offer. Leave now in control of your destiny or I will take the choice away from you. Either way, I forbid you staying here and needlessly torturing yourself.

Mara could no longer deny the red haze building in her mind. She placed her hand on Terrill's forearm. *Let's go.*

He nodded curtly and all but dragged her toward the exit. He signaled to Caleb and Morgan, standing silently across the room. Morgan met them at the door with Mara's wrap. She placed it around her friend's shoulders. "Is she all right?"

"She's fine."

Caleb got out of Terrill's car and came around to open the passenger door for Mara. Once she was tucked in the vehicle, Caleb turned to Terrill. "Victor's eyes never left you two. What's going on?"

"Later," Terrill said, brushing off Caleb's concerns and getting into the driver's seat.

Mara let the soundproof interior of the sports coupe dull her over-sensitive senses as she sat back in the plush leather seat. The car, like its owner, exuded raw power. It suited him. "I've never actually seen one of these. I didn't think they were out yet."

He looked surprised.

"What? Girls can't know anything about cars?" She rolled her eyes. "Vampires aren't the only ones who like speed you know."

He pushed down on the accelerator.

Fine, two can play that game. She willed herself to block out the distractions around her and focus on mending the pain pounding at her in waves. She didn't have the strength to fully heal herself, but she might be able to at least lessen it. It would put her at a disadvantage momentarily, but she needed relief and her wits if Terrill had any intention of sticking around.

Terrill heard her occasional stuttering heartbeat and shaky breath and jerked his head toward hers. "What's going on?"

Although it hurt, she shook her head. "I'm fine." She focused on her heartbeat, trying to even it out, finally re-synching the rhythm to a healthier one.

Terrill continued to shoot concerned glances at her.

"Where are you taking me?" she asked. She was still dangerously close to overload. She needed to replenish herself but feared she'd pushed him too far for a respite.

"Somewhere we won't be overheard or interrupted."

She pulled distractedly at a loose thread on her dress.

"Terrill, can we do this some other time . . . if . . . if I promise not to run?"

He pulled his foot back off the accelerator, slowing the car to a more reasonable rate of insanely fast, and looked hard at her. "Your skin's as pale as paper – damn near translucent. I don't know you well enough to know how much you can or can't take. We **will** continue this conversation tomorrow night. Don't even think of running. Mara, I mean it."

She sank into her seat with relief.

He growled in frustration and whipped the car around. As they got closer to her home, an unexpected apprehension caused her to sit up straight and scan the horizon.

"You feel it too?" he asked.

She nodded. "Vampire."

The gate protecting the estate lay mangled and useless, permitting unimpeded access to the estate.

"She's already gone," he said.

The car roared into the drive. He turned to Mara, but she was already out the door, streaking toward the house. He raced after her and barely managed to beat her through the door. He positioned his body as a protective barrier against any lingering threats. The place was trashed.

Shock caused Mara to move slowly, trance-like. She tried to remember if she'd left anything incriminating behind that her intruder could have taken – anything that might give her away. No, she'd destroyed her internet research notes and all history of her downloads beyond any hope of retrieval. She wasn't surprised to see her laptop gone, but there wasn't anything incriminating on it so she didn't care. That wasn't what she was worried about.

As she stepped into her bedroom, her heart sank at the scent of blood that assailed her. They'd found her stash. She could only pray they didn't understand its significance. She doubted Terrill would make that same mistake.

Mara stood frozen as he walked into the room, staring at the scene with disbelief. His eyes were drawn toward the hidden refrigeration unit now exposed and the blood slashed open and draining on the floor.

She watched him process the evidence. Human blood, not Viajante. Transfusion equipment. Her weakness after expending powers. It was all there.

The last thing she remembered before everything went dark was the look of condemnation and fury that flashed across his face. She had the vague feeling she had just been tried, found guilty, and sentenced to death . . . and Terrill stood by to carry it out.

He caught her in his arms as she fell. He placed her gently in the car and headed for his home in the San Gabriel Mountains and answers.

CHAPTER SIX

S he opened her eyes cautiously and slowly took in the unfamiliar surroundings. She was still alive. Not too surprising, she conceded grimly. Terrill would demand answers before taking action.

She sat up gingerly, her aching muscles protesting the effort. Psychic overload wiped out her nervous system and always impacted her body a little differently each time. She was weak from lack of blood, but the tension humming through her veins was strong enough to send her jumping at the slightest sound.

She lay on a plush, yet functional coffee-brown sofa in some sort of a wood cabin. She could see two windows covered with heavy drapes drawn tightly shut. A fire crackled and popped innocently in the impressive hearth in front of her. She noted the masculine décor, bare beams, and sparse furniture. A few rugs and pelts scattered across the floor gave the barren surroundings more warmth and depth than the aura of semi-habitability she might have expected if she had given it any thought. But her initial conclusion remained inevitable. This was Terrill's domain. Here, he was in complete control.

Hard upon that recognition, her eyes were drawn to the shadows separating the room she lay in from a passageway into the next. Terrill slowly came into focus. He leaned against the wall, his arms folded in front of him as he quietly studied her. The feral look in his eyes left little question about his intentions.

She swallowed and nervously licked her lips, wishing desperately for something to quench the desert taking residence in her throat. Not much chance that would change any time soon.

He glided toward her, catlike, never once taking his eyes off her face. He lifted her legs momentarily to slide under them as he sat down next to her. His hands remained right above her knees. The heat of that contact burned through her clothes, a not-so-subtle reminder he now called all the shots.

"I trust I now have your complete attention?"

An involuntary chill ran down her spine at the steel behind his words. She didn't like the smile of satisfaction that flashed in his eyes.

He waved his hand at the fire. Mara watched the blaze jump and bend to his will, eliminating the draft that attempted to break through the warmth he had created.

She tilted her jaw stubbornly and returned his stare. He cocked an eyebrow. "What?"

"What's between you and Victor? Why the interest in Angelica?"

Of course, she'd known he'd ask that, but she'd irrationally clung to the hope he wouldn't. No matter how much time passed, memories of that night still packed the equivalent of a one-two punch. Just thinking about it could start nightmares. And once those started . . .

She inhaled deeply and forced herself to push it out of her mind. "My parents were both Viajante, but never found the safety of Sanctuary. They are what we refer to as the Lost Ones. –Los Perdidos." She saw the question in his eyes. "It happens sometimes that mortals are born with the ability to become Viajante, and once of age, they convert before knowing or understanding what they are. Others may have been separated from their Viajante family and raised as mortals. They become what we call lost ones."

"Are all Viajante born mortal?"

She smiled slightly, "No," she said, "just as Vampires are born, the product of a union of like species, we are too, but sometimes mortals become Viajante."

"You convert them?" he asked.

She shook her head. "Many mortals, probably more than you realize, are born with the genetic coding to become Viajante."

"Why don't they turn if they have the gene?"

Mara shrugged her shoulders. "It's not that simple. No one really knows for sure why some convert and others don't. Maybe it's some sort of genetic lottery. The elders think it may be a type of survival mechanism – some type of population control."

She ran her fingers through her hair, pushing an errant strand out of her eyes. "For example, if the Vampire population starts to expand too quickly in a given area, more mortals with the genetic coding to become Viajante convert when they turn eighteen. Of course, this creates problems for us to find them and bring them back to safety so they can develop their powers and learn our ways. Our Seekers have special tracking powers and generally, there are few mistakes."

"So only Seekers can find your people?"

She shook her head. "Like Vampires, Viajantes can instinctively spot their own. Only a few, however, can find and track the ones not yet fully Viajante – the ones about to turn. Sometimes those selected begin to manifest powers earlier so there's a trail, but not always. That's why our Seekers are so important."

"Seekers." He let the word roll off his tongue. "They sound a lot like our Warriors, except the goal of your Seekers is more of passive collection or protection, and our Warriors serve a more active defense." He scratched his chin. "Perhaps the power itself is similar. Our Warriors are also formidable hunters, seeking and finding what most cannot."

Mara didn't need to ask what they hunted. If her experiences were any indication, she already had a pretty good idea.

She moved to free her legs from his grasp and was surprised he let her. She stood in front of the fire, watching the flames shrink and expand as they engulfed the wood.

He lay back and watched her pace restlessly. "Does a comparison of our species distress you?"

She cocked her head to the side as if considering it for the first time and turned back to him, a look of honest confusion on her face. "I don't know. I guess I was always taught that our species were such polar opposites that it never occurred to me there were similarities besides immortality. Maybe our species have both evolved and developed powers to counter the other, in order to maintain this balance our elders talk of."

She sat back down distractedly. "I guess it shouldn't be so surprising. But it does little to explain the animosity between our species."

He nodded in agreement. "I've often wondered about that as well. We're brought up to distrust your kind, but few fear them." This time it was he who reached over to push her hair back behind her ear. "Tell me what happened to your family."

Mara sensed his need for her to confide in him but also felt his determination to get the answers he wanted. He'd have no qualms pulling it from her, whether she wanted him to or not. She really had no choice.

"I was only six and Celeste was two. We moved around a lot. Now, when I look back, I realize my parents had probably been running from something since before I was born. I think sometimes it was from my own people, but that doesn't make sense. They avoided contact with all immortals, judging mortals safest and easiest to control if any contact was required."

Memories flooded her mind of orange-cropped rocks rising rebelliously from the green-and-sagebrush canvas of the Spanish hillside where she lived with her family. The earthy smells and quiet serenity surrounded her. She hadn't realized how much she missed it.

Her eyes misted as she remembered playing hide-and-seek with her father in the scores of caverns and tunnels zigzagging across its vast expanse. The thoughts remained so real to her that she almost forgot where she was.

"Mara."

The wonder in his voice made her realize she'd unknowingly broadcast her memories to him. Maybe it would be easier if she just showed him.

She took him back to Spain and the beautiful place she grew up. The vision deepened to include pictures of her parents' faces. Her mother was beautiful and delicate, her father strong yet compassionate. He saw a bright, happy child playing with her little sister and the love and devotion their parents had for them and for each other.

They had been in a small house, and Mara's mother, Nicolette, had just laid Celeste in the crib next to her bed. Mara played by the fire and her father read. Terrill saw a darkness shadow her family, turning that cheery home scene into a deadly premonition of impending disaster.

She struggled against the fear that reliving the memories caused her. It wasn't really happening she kept telling herself. It wasn't really happening.

He captured her hand in his, subconsciously lending her the strength to get through it.

Through her memories, he saw her father look lovingly at his soul. Even at a young age, Mara had realized her father knew something was about to happen. Mara's mother had smiled serenely, tears threatening as she looked lovingly at her husband and children

There had been two of them. Two Vampires. Her father had tried to take on both of them as his wife struggled to get the children to safety. He managed to kill one. Paralyzed and dying from lack of blood, he'd slumped to his knees and watched in horror as the second Vampire attacked Nicolette – his soul – and then Mara. He'd poured his remaining strength into his soul, who had gathered it with her own to plunge her hand into the Vampire's chest and pull out the still-beating heart and fling it contemptuously into the fire.

Terrill looked shocked. "I've never heard of Viajante as strong as your parents were. Even ambushed, that they were able to kill their attackers. It's . . . well . . . unheard of."

The strain painted on Mara's pale face indicated her story wasn't yet over. As far as she was concerned, the worst was still yet to come.

Her vision returned him to the cabin. Her mother had called to her and forced her to rise above the pain screaming through her tiny body as the Vampire poison spread, seeking and destroying healthy cells. The sound of Mara's crying mixed with the terrified cries of the yet untouched Celeste seemed to push Mara's mother, Nicolette, over the edge.

Nicolette had tried to soothe her children. She must have been in incredible pain from the bites she'd received, but she had forced Mara to go inside herself, helping her change her cellular structure to one the Vampire poison could co-exist with. Not only had what Nicolette forced her to do healed her, but it had also done the impossible task of somehow semi-converting her.

Terrill swore and jumped up from the couch.

"It gets worse," Mara whispered.

He returned back to her side, sitting at her feet with his hands holding hers. "Show me."

Mara returned him to the cabin where Nicolette whispered to her daughter that they were going to play a new kind of hide-and-seek. Now that the hurt was gone, Mara was to hide and make Mommy see the sleeping man next to her as Mara while she made Celeste invisible. Mara had shaken her head. She didn't want to play. Mara felt Terrill cringe as she remembered the slap her mother gave her from across the room and how she'd cried. Nicolette had never been cross with her before.

Nicolette hugged her daughter and kissed the top of her head. "Be a good little girl and the prophecy will take care of you." She'd wiped her eyes and directed her to hide behind the sofa closest to the window and do what she told her. Still shocked from the blow, Mara had obeyed and projected herself as the dead Vampire lying near her mother. The illusion was perfect. Then she hid behind the couch.

No sooner had she accomplished this, than a dark presence arrived. Mara peeked around the corner and saw her mother make Celeste disappear in the crib after pushing her to sleep. Mara shared the feeling of danger and violence that had overcome her as she scurried back behind the furniture and focused on the image her mother wanted her to make.

It was another Vampire. Mara only saw glimpses of his clothing as he surveyed the scene. He must have noticed Nicolette was still alive because he dragged her up against him and bit her neck. The venom from the first bite had already started to weaken her, and his second bite did more. It wasn't long before she could no longer hide Celeste.

Mara knew the moment he discovered Celeste from the thump her mother's body had made when he released her and she hit the floor. She heard him walk over to the crib and lift the sleeping infant from her bed. "How nice," he said. "You saved me a snack."

Terrill let loose a long and well-practiced list of profanities under his breath.

The last thing they saw before the scene faded was the Vampire leaving with the baby. Mara's face was wet with tears. "Until tonight, I thought he'd killed her like he'd had my parents killed."

"What happened next?" Terrill asked as he brushed away her tears.

"He torched the place. Like Vampires, fire is the only thing that truly destroys us. I stayed hidden for a while but eventually crept out to try and help my parents. But . . . they . . . I . . . there was nothing I could do," she reluctantly admitted. "The fire kept coming closer and closer and I finally got out through the back window. That's when Yasmine showed up. She was the Seeker sent to find me. She found me hiding in the dark. It was only later I learned she was my aunt."

She stood and made her way to the fire, feeling a bit shaky on her feet. Terrill stood and reached out to steady her. "I never saw the Vampire's face that night," she said, "but the sense of violence I can feel now stems from sensing his aura that night. That's what I put together tonight. And then with the picture, there's no longer any question."

She paced back and forth. "How else could she be alive? His ward?" She spat out the last word as if it was as venomous to her as the Vampire bite that had changed her life. Her energy spent, she slumped back down onto the sofa, no longer caring what Terrill would do now that he had the truth.

He sat back on the sofa next to her, drew her exhausted body toward his, and gently stroked her hair.

"Could he have turned her?" she asked. "I didn't think you could convert Viajante."

Terrill started to shake his head and then stopped. "It may be possible, but it's something we don't do. It's forbidden to turn one who is not a soul."

"And Victor would never do anything forbidden?"

He shrugged. "Victor would do whatever served Victor best. If he did this, he must have been confident no one would ever find out. Or perhaps it would be of such value to him, he would be willing to take the risk."

He took her face in his hands, meeting her eyes. "Are you sure he suspected nothing? You were only six. Could you have pulled off a deception so complete as to fool such an experienced Vampire? Can all your people do this?"

She shook her head. "Some have skills at hiding or camouflaging their appearance, but Yasmine had never heard of anyone being able to do what we did that night."

He appeared to consider that and then shared the earlier conversation he'd had with Victor.

She returned his penetrating stare. "I've never had cause to think anyone knew about the deception that night."

"It may be only a matter of time before he puts it all together. And this prophecy?"

She shook her head. "Yasmine rarely spoke of it. Speaking of it forces her to remember how she wasn't able to save her sister."

He looked directly into her eyes. "Are you Vampire or Viajante? I've never heard of anyone doing what you and your mother did. Not and living to tell of it anyway."

"Is that a trick question?"

He raised her face so her eyes met his. "No, but one I want an answer to."

CHAPTER SEVEN

A little of both," she admitted, relieved to finally be able to tell someone. Even so, she still wasn't quite able to meet his eyes. "I was raised in their traditions and have the powers of my people. But I also have powers my people do not. Although Yasmine made sure those were not known by my people. There were already too many questions about that night and how I had escaped." She didn't mention the distasteful need to supplement her diet with blood.

One look in his eyes confirmed he'd noticed the omission.

"I think I know the day you speak of."

She glared at him in accusation and disbelief. He was part of this? He'd known it would happen and did nothing? She tried frantically to get some distance from him as tears of betrayal threatened to fall.

He held her in place. "Stop it!" His eyes blazed with anger and frustration. He shook her shoulders. "I wasn't there. Search your memories." He took a deep breath. "I know the day you speak of because I felt some of what you were going through. It's how I learned of your existence."

She tried to focus. The conflicting emotions radiating off him finally made their way into her subconscious. She could never have gotten in close proximity with anyone, mortal or not, who could have committed or ordered such a crime. It would have affected her physically, and she would have spotted it immediately. Logically, she knew that. But he scared her. Violence clung to him. Not the sort she'd spoken of earlier, not exactly. She couldn't quite shake the sense of unease his declaration provoked.

"Were you in Ireland before your family went to Spain?"

She looked at him in surprise and nodded.

"I was drawn there before this happened to your family. I resisted the call at the time, unwilling to allow something I didn't understand to direct my actions. Now I do."

"I don't."

"It's my turn to show you." He opened up his mind to her and gave her access to his memories of that day. She hesitated, questions flickering in her eyes. "Mara, let me show you, please."

She closed her eyes and saw his memories unfold. Instantly she could feel the horror and helplessness he'd felt that day.

"I didn't understand," he repeated as she scanned his memories. "I only knew I was being gripped by some unnameable dread – a need to attack or run. Some sort of abhorrent act was being carried out – something I was supposed to stop, but couldn't. I knew there was an enemy out there – someone causing pain – but didn't know how to find him, how to stop him before it was too late. Mara, I know about this day because you know about it. I felt what you felt."

"Do you mean – are you saying that you were sharing my pain as I experienced it? How, how is that even possible?"

"Mara, does your kind believe in finding one's soul?"

Mara's eyes widened. She shook her head vehemently. "Not between the species," she said. "Never between species."

"How else do you explain this connection?" He moved closer, touching his fingers to her lips, eliciting a sharply indrawn breath. "And this chemistry?" He moved even closer, invading her space. "Can you explain it?" he asked as he pressed his lips to hers, the heat between them flaring as the kiss deepened.

Mara tried to focus on what he'd said. It was damn near impossible. She pulled away and dragged in ragged breaths as she fought to slow her frantically beating heart. "It's impossible."

The Viajante call to find one's soul was instinctive. It was strongest after they came of age unless the two were lucky enough to have already found each other in Sanctuary. Sometimes, one's soul turned out to be a Lost One, but even then, the one searching always knew the other existed. When they left Sanctuary, they found each other. It was rare, but not unheard of, that it might take centuries of searching, if one was born long before the other or killed before the pair was joined.

"Why not?" he asked.

She shared her thoughts with him. "Mixing the species is forbidden."

His thumb rubbed small circles on her hand, distracting her and numbing the impact of her words. She gave him a look of accusation to which he responded with a wicked grin, but to her relief, stopped moving his thumb. He refused, however, to release her hand.

Mara felt her heart speed up again as he leaned closer, brushing her ear with his lips before teasing and tugging at her earlobe with his teeth. "When my people find their soul, Mara, nothing stops them from possessing it."

Mara shivered at his words as he reached up and pushed her hair away from his mouth. "If one's soul is mortal, it's simple. They are converted. The blood exchange makes the bonding complete."

"And if the soul resists?"

He held her gaze, his eyes a smoldering grey. "She cannot. Her life without him would be incomplete, plagued by nightmare and loss, forever searching, never finding the joy and release such a union would bring."

Mara couldn't speak. He seized her lips for a hard kiss before releasing her. She could feel the contact burning her mouth after his lips left.

"Would you deny yourself happiness? Deny your soul that fulfillment? Sentence him to eternity without joy, without hope?" He looked intently at her. "Would you, Mara? Could you do that?"

He didn't allow her to answer, simply took possession of her mouth again. She didn't want to believe what he said, but her body had no such doubts. She pushed into his mind, finding a dark, deep desire and a burning need to possess her. She pulled out, frightened by the intensity and, though she would never willingly admit it, a little excited.

"Has this ever happened before?" she asked.

He shrugged. "I don't know, and honestly, I don't care. Precedent matters little to me. The more important question, at least as far as I see it, is what we're going to do about it."

She glared at him. "It's forbidden."

"You think rules matter to me? Your presence here in LA leads me to question their importance to you."

She opened her mouth to respond, then closed it.

He chuckled before turning serious. "Our relationship aside, I was actually thinking about a more practical issue. I find I can't seem to help my protective nature as far as you're concerned. I won't allow you to keep putting yourself in danger. We need to do something about this need of yours. Why do you keep yourself so weak? It's natural for souls to share blood. Do your people not do the same to help restore strength and power?"

"Not like that, no. There is a bonding ritual where blood is exchanged by tying slit wrists together. A ceremony. A joining of two halves."

"Nothing more? No other times?"

She thought of the annual renewal of vows and the preparations and rituals the Seekers undertook before they left Sanctuary. She looked at Terrill in surprise. "I never thought about it that way. But it's hardly the same thing."

"Is it not? And you, Mara? What of your needs?"

She stiffened. "I need a transfusion now and again, it's no big deal. I could even hunt if I wanted to." She bristled at the insinuation suggested by his raised brow. "Animals, not people," she growled. "I'm not a Vampire!"

He grinned, showing a brilliant set of white teeth. "Who exactly are you trying to convince of that, me or you?" He crowded her again. "These transfusions, how often do you have them?"

Her eyes narrowed. "Every few weeks or so. Sometimes more if I use my powers a lot." She didn't like the calculating look he gave her. "Why?"

"So," he drawled, "you can hunt, which means you can drink."

"You won't allow me a transfusion."

"No." He didn't move. Mara watched his smoke-grey eyes turn obsidian as they stared unblinkingly at her. "I'll give you a choice. Take strength from me willingly, or I will compel you. Our lives are tied together, Mara, whether you want to accept it or not."

"You're not my soul!" Even as she denied their connection, she drew closer. She realized he was using his power to enhance her thirst, but she wasn't strong enough to stop him.

"Yes, I am your soul. I am what completes you. As such, I will protect you, even from yourself if I must, until you come to accept that truth."

His scent called to her, enticing her closer to the pulse beating at his neck as he held himself immobile. Her breath lingered on his throat and she felt anticipation build inside her like some forbidden thing clawing for release. Her teeth scraped across his skin, and she felt a corresponding jolt race through his body. She sighed in satisfaction at the groan forced past his lips as her teeth sank deep and she drew his powerful blood into her body.

Mara felt the strength of his blood sweep through her. The intimacy of taking his blood, feeling so connected, made it impossible for her to continue to deny the attraction growing between them. Terrill had somehow been able to temporarily erase the fears that the memories such an act should have brought up in her.

She closed the opening her teeth had made with a sweep of her tongue and opened the distance between them, blinking in surprise. Oh my god, what had she done?

Terrill moved quickly. He held her face with both hands and feasted on her mouth. Even knowing his kiss was designed to prevent her from thinking too much, she couldn't help succumbing to the dangerous distraction he provided. He lowered them both to the fur in front of the fire.

He held her captive with his eyes. "Mara, you have to know you, and no other, are my true soul. Tell me you don't feel this," he said as his mouth left her lips and trailed its way down her body, beginning with her throat and the sensitive spot inside her ear he'd discovered earlier.

Her responses shrieked, and she gasped at the sensations flooding over her. It was impossible to articulate anything with him attacking her body like this. "Terrill."

He recaptured her lips and her body arched up to meet his as he lay above her. The hardness of his body was solid proof of his desire and of his determination to have her. His kisses and the deliberately fleeting brushes of his hands heightened her pleasure, each touch exciting a part of her never before touched. "Deny this, Mara," he dared her as he continued his sensual assault.

She couldn't. The thought of clothing between them became unbearable. She felt wondrously wanton as she saw the look of vindication reflected in his eyes when he lowered his head to her exposed body, dusting kisses across its sensitive surface.

Mara couldn't breathe. He was stealing her will. All she could think of was her need to have him closer, part of her, complete. She had never gone this far, never been this close to anyone, but this yearning, this aching for something more – she couldn't deny it. She didn't want to. She kissed him back, wanting him to know what he was doing to her.

He opened his mind to her and showed her exactly what she was doing to him and what he wanted to do to her. "Mara."

She turned passion-glazed eyes to him. He lowered his mouth to hers and brought their lips together. "There will be a brief pain, but I promise you, it won't last."

She raised her arms and encircled his head. She nodded before bringing his mouth back in contact with hers.

He gently eased into her. As he broke through the barrier, she felt a sharp pain, and he stilled. He kissed her slowly at first, small teasing kisses that built upon themselves, growing in intensity and duration as her body adjusted to him. He left her mouth and his fangs lengthened as he brought them close to her neck.

She panicked when she realized his intent.

He retracted them quickly and Mara heard him cursing under his breath. "Mara, it's part of the bonding ritual between souls. I won't complete the ritual until you're ready. I promise. Open your eyes and look at me."

She didn't believe that was something she'd ever be ready for, but she found herself believing he meant every word he said. She opened her eyes, now a brilliant green with unshed tears. She nodded.

He lowered his head and kissed her. He deepened the kiss as he lowered his hand to her breast. His teasing touches and intense kisses were turning her insides to liquid. She felt something building then it quieted, strengthening after he shifted position. She gasped as he began to move faster.

"Terrill . . ." Her voice was a breathless whisper as she felt her body spiral tighter and tighter then suddenly fragment. She couldn't move. Still breathing hard, she didn't notice the tears trickling down her face.

He gently wiped them away, licking her saltiness from his fingers as he smiled down at her.

Mara felt him probing her thoughts. She slammed down a mind block so fast and hard it shocked him. It took everything she had to avoid bursting into laughter at his wounded expression.

Still overwhelmed by her emotions and what had just happened between them, she laughed nervously. "Terrill, ah, seriously, I'm not comfortable with you tromping through my head at will."

"After what we just shared you find my reading your thoughts more intimate?" Mara flushed at the words. He laughed. *It's okay. You can read my thoughts any time you like. They are open to you. I want you to know me, to trust me. I don't ask for much in return.*

She scowled and made an unladylike noise. The hell he didn't.

He smiled and tucked her hair behind her ears, parting the screen it made as it partially hid her expression from him. "How do you feel?"

She realized he was concerned not only about her tears and the new layer of intimacy between them but also about having forced her to take his blood. Mara examined herself and felt the traces of power from his blood amplifying hers. It wasn't threatening her well-being in any way she could identify. Instead, she felt her powers increased and wondered if it was appropriate to think about testing the new limits she perceived. She shared her thoughts with him and instantly received his reassurance and relief.

Suddenly she frowned.

What? he asked.

It's because of the shared blood, that's why the bond is getting stronger, isn't it? She glared at him.

Yes. It is the way of souls. With blood exchanges and time, the bond grows stronger.

You knew that would happen.

He stood and waited silently, a hand out to help her up.

She remained where she was, angry he'd seized the advantage . . . again.

He bent and scooped her up, carrying her off to the bathroom and a warm shower. *You would have done the same were you me.* He kissed her hard and gave her a hooded look before disappearing, leaving her to ponder his words and clean up in private.

CHAPTER EIGHT

Mara dressed slowly after the shower. She discovered she was sore in spots that brought a blush to her face. She was grudgingly grateful Terrill had allowed her a few minutes alone to collect herself.

You're not exactly alone, he whispered seductively.

Get out of my head!

I have coffee.

A bribe? she asked. But a good one she admitted with a laugh. Darn the man, he definitely didn't play fair.

You really expected me to play fair?

He met her at the bathroom door. The steam from her shower mixed with that of the coffee as he handed her the warm cup. He wrinkled his nose disparagingly at the contents as they walked through the house.

"I don't understand how you can drink that stuff. It smells awful, tastes even worse."

"I didn't think Vampires could eat or drink what mortals or Viajante do."

"We can, but our bodies expel it afterward. We can simulate eating and drinking when needed. You seem to actually enjoy it though. Do you need it as mortals do for sustenance?"

Mara looked at the early morning sunlight peeking through the curtains in the kitchen. She suddenly wanted to feel its warm rays on her face. "We need it to a smaller degree than mortals. It doesn't give us the same strength blood gives you, but if we go without it too long, we get weaker."

He opened the kitchen patio door for her. She looked at him curiously. He wasn't a young Vampire, his raw power made that obvious, but she wasn't sure about his resistance to the sun. The older Vampires got, the more resistance they built up, or at least that was what she'd been taught.

Mara's breath caught as they stepped outside. His deck had an absolutely breathtaking view of the mountain range. In the early morning sunlight, the peaks appeared to touch the sky and the clouds swirled around them like a veil fluttering in the wind, engaging in a playful game of hide and seek as the green mountain faces were exposed and then covered.

She inhaled the clean pine fragrance permeating the cold air. "It's lovely."

He smiled.

Mara watched him as he stood at the edge of the balcony, arms on the railing looking out across the expanse. He put his back to the view, leaning back against the sturdy rail, and watched her as she sipped her coffee.

"My kind can go in sunlight, as you seem to already know. Only the newly made, newly born, or young Vampires are in any serious danger from its burning rays," he said. "Most of us cannot tolerate direct sunlight without injury until hundreds of years have passed."

"Hundreds of years?" She put down her coffee cup, almost missing the table next to her chair. "So . . . any Vampires I see in daylight should be considered pretty powerful? Good to know." She picked the cup back up. "Wait, so just how old are you?" She hoped the question had come off casually.

He winked. "You're not afraid I'm too old for you, are you?"

She gave him a withering look and took a sip.

"I can easily walk in the sun. Actually, I could walk in the sun much earlier than any of my kind."

She wrapped both hands around her mug. "So that would make you how old?"

"I was born in 1651."

Mara choked and almost spit the coffee back out.

He laughed and took it back into the kitchen for a warm-up. Seconds later he handed it back to her and took a seat.

"Thank you."

He grinned. "Was it that I said I could do things many of our kind can't that surprised you or was it my age?"

Mara laughed. "And here I thought only women were insecure about their age."

He growled and she lost it completely. "It explains a lot, really," she choked out between fits of laughter. "Lord of the manor. Wow. Guess that really was an understatement, huh?"

"You youngsters have no respect."

"Sorry, gramps."

"Gramps?" He moved toward her, broadcasting his determination to show her just how persuasive a senior citizen could be.

She squealed and put her hands up in mock surrender.

"Too late." He lowered his mouth to hers.

By the time he had released her from his kiss, she could barely remember her own name. Mara took a deep shuddery breath. Okay, time for a change of topic. "Tell me about your childhood."

"Relatively uneventful. However, as a young boy I used to, umm, experiment a bit."

"Experiment?"

"What is one power you noticed about me that my kind wouldn't notice right away?"

She closed her eyes and thought about the times they'd been together – how he'd surprised her in the bar and then later in her home. Her eyes opened wide.

"You can shield yourself from my kind."

"And?"

Her mind continued to churn, processing the clues he'd purposely dropped. "If you can shield yourself from my kind, you may have developed the ability to shield yourself from other things, like safeguards, and maybe even certain elements?"

He nodded. "There were a few mistakes at first, some more painful than others. But yes, I've developed a few lesser-known skills."

"This shielding ability you have . . . your kind develops it over time?" Maybe she could learn to develop some of these powers too.

"Not quite how you think. It's more a tolerance. Vampires don't normally have shields, but they can build up a tolerance with increased exposure to things like sunlight. I've learned to turn tolerance into an ability to manipulate the environment in a variety of situations."

She was fascinated but found herself stifling a yawn. The drain of the previous night and all the day's excitement had caught up with her.

He grinned at her. "Viajantes need sleep?"

"We do better with rest. Like mortals, it helps rejuvenate and heal. You don't need it?"

"Not really. When we're wounded, we go into a healing sleep – deeper than mortal sleep cycles – but it essentially serves the same purpose."

She yawned again and he gathered her in his arms ignoring her protests. She relaxed against him and inhaled his masculine scent as he carried her back into the house. The kitchen door closed silently behind them. He looked at Mara in surprise.

"Sorry, habit."

As they entered the bedroom, he waved his hand, lighting several candles designed to soothe, and pulled back the covers, settling her down in his bed.

"I'll be right back," he whispered as he brushed his lips against her forehead. "I need to lock up."

Mara struggled against the layers of sleep threatening to claim her, but the candles he'd lit prevented her from surfacing and pushed her deeper into the healing sleep she needed. She'd let him have his way this time. But just this once, she told herself rebelliously.

CHAPTER NINE

Mara smiled. For once she felt well rested. Granted she didn't usually sleep until dusk, but given her present circumstances, coupled with the additional physical and emotional demands of the last few days, it seemed an acceptable lapse.

The day had started well. She felt herself color as she thought of Terrill and exactly why the day had started so well. While she still had some issues about their relationship and her dual nature to resolve, clearly, responding to Terrill physically was not among them.

Terrill made her take his blood again before he headed back to her place to pick up her things. They both agreed going back was no longer a safe option for her, at least not as long as she had unknown enemies stalking her.

Whoever was responsible may not have figured out she was part Vampire, but they certainly would wonder why Terrill was with a damaged mortal who needed transfusions or why she kept a stash of blood for him. It would be better to stay hidden and pretend she'd left the city. Anything else could easily turn undue attention on Terrill, putting him in danger too. She hadn't considered that risk before she let him head back to her place. Why hadn't she?

Let me go back? You didn't think of it because it was irrelevant. She felt him laughing at the idea of her attempting to stop him. *You worry too much, Mara; there's no danger to me,* he lowered his voice suggestively, *but I am pleased that you were worried for me.*

She frowned at the arrogance in his tone. Like she should even care.

He materialized beside her, and she scowled up at him as he gave her a knowing wink.

Even as arrogant as he was, sometimes she really wanted to let herself believe the illusion that this craziness between them could actually work. Then she would remind herself that she'd be crazy to trust in something so unlikely. The odds were stacked pretty high against them. No one would ever approve of the union, not even her family.

"Did you find anything?" she asked.

"Not exactly." He stroked his jaw, his expression pensive. "We both detected a Vampire presence before we got there, but did you actually sense one inside the house, around the blood?"

Her brow furrowed. "Now that you mention it, I never felt her presence inside the house. I was so focused on the fact that a Vampire was on the property, I didn't stop to analyze where the scent actually ended." But someone had obviously been inside her house. A mortal? "What do you think that means?"

He shook his head. "We weren't looking for mortal intruders."

"But it doesn't mean the Vampire who was there doesn't know about the blood. She could have easily read the mind of the mortal inside, right? Is she working with them? Did you pick up on more than one mortal when you went back today?"

He shrugged. "It's possible. If there was more than one, then there's something different about them – something that makes them hard to read. I've never come across anything like it."

Her eyes widened. "I have."

"The odds that a mortal might be working with my kind are pretty rare, but not impossible." It appeared that her words had just registered with him. He stopped and stared at her. "What did you say?"

She continued to stare at the floor distractedly.

"Mara, I can't keep you safe if you don't tell me everything."

She shared her memories of what had happened to her along the coastal highway. "Do you think we're dealing with the same people?"

"I don't know."

She could tell by his demeanor he was worried about why she'd been singled out twice. She was pretty worried herself.

"I think the stakes are much higher than I originally thought, especially if Claudio is involved."

Mara stared at him. "What do you know of him? Who is he? What is he up to?"

"We need to work on your defensive skills. He's a very skilled Warrior – one of our best."

Mara's eyes glittered dangerously at his authoritative tone. She'd survived in the company of Vampires, undetected no less, for quite some time without his help. He acted like she was some helpless little girl.

"You confuse luck with skill." He cut her off before she could respond. "You know how to be Viajante – how to fight that way maybe – but how well do you fight as a Vampire?"

The level of training she wanted had been denied to her in Sanctuary. They thought there would be less chance she would seek out trouble if she was undertrained. Regardless of the limits imposed on her, Yasmine had done her best to sneak in additional lessons.

"You'd teach me?" the excitement in her voice betrayed her interest.

"Yes, but I expect something in return."

"I can't teach you our weaknesses and strengths. I won't betray my people."

"Mara, we don't know who or what your enemy is. Even your parents had doubts. You're going to have to assume that some of your people will consider you their enemy once they find out the truth." She flinched. "They will find out, Mara. You know that at some point they will. Refusing to accept that possibility only puts you at more risk."

She didn't like that he was right. Determination glinted in his silver eyes and she nodded. "Only in self-defense. I need your promise, Terrill."

"I will not allow anyone to harm you, Mara. That is what I will promise."

"How did you just appear in the house earlier? I know Vampires move fast, but . . . wow. Can I do that? Will you show me?"

He laughed and she had the distinct impression it wasn't just at her eagerness to learn. Yeah, she must seem pretty transparent to him. So much for complex and alluring.

He turned her to look at him. "I like simple, and as to the other, I can show you how I feel if that's what you desire."

She quickly stepped away and headed toward the door. Why was it so warm inside? "Let's step outside, shall we?"

They exited the house and walked onto the deck facing the mountains. He left her at the end of the balcony and walked down its long length, stopping just before it curved around the corner. "Okay, now come here."

She focused and was at his side.

He shook his head. "No, you're thinking about it too much – like a mortal."

She put her hands on her hips and tapped her foot.

He grinned. "Stop thinking about the ACT of getting there, focus on the BEING there. Look in my mind as I do it." She blinked and he was at the end of the balcony she'd come from. "Try it again."

She took a deep breath and focused, centering herself and then envisioning herself next to him. She opened her eyes and found herself there.

"Better," he said and bent over to kiss her forehead lightly. "But try it again with your eyes open. You won't run into something that way."

Just when she finally felt like she'd gotten the hang of it, he changed the rules. "Ready?" he asked, and without waiting for an answer he grinned and leaped off the balcony, disappearing into the shadowy foothills.

She focused on where she'd heard him last and jumped, easily avoiding trees and other obstructions. She quickly crossed the distance between them, but he wasn't where she expected him to be. She heard laughter coming from above her in the tree and glared as he dropped down next to her.

"You have to use all your senses, Mara. Keep the paths open for continual adjustments. Never, never assume anything. Anything can – and will – change at any time. Forgetting that will get you killed."

She nodded. He gave her access to his mind, and she studied the techniques and experiences he laid open for her. Excitement lit her eyes.

"Let's do it again."

She gave him a few seconds' head start. When she knew he felt confident he was in control, she took flight, surprising him with her quick and quiet arrival.

"All right, let's make this more interesting – see just how good you really are. We're going to increase the limits of our little exercise. The mountain range work for you?"

She laughed in delight.

By early morning, she was exhausted but elated. Other than a few scrapes and bruises caused by certain stubbornly immovable objects that she wasn't entirely convinced he hadn't moved and put in her way to prove a point, she was relatively unscathed and overall pleased with her accomplishments. She'd even finally managed to beat him at his own game once.

He'd growled at her for cheating and reading his mind, but she could tell that he was more annoyed with himself that he hadn't thought of it earlier and protected his thoughts.

"Not bad, Mara," he said and ruffled her hair. "Let's get you some food and call it a night."

She grimaced at his protective streak. She dared him to a race back to the cabin and took off, reveling in her newfound powers. She was determined to give him a run for his money.

* * *

Mara had just finished her shower when Terrill stuck his head in the still-foggy bathroom. "You going to be decent soon?" he asked before handing her a towel.

She pretended not to notice the hungry look in his eyes. "We're expecting company?"

He hesitated slightly before nodding. "I meant to tell you earlier, but somehow got, er, distracted."

She hid the smile threatening to surface. "Don't think that bad-boy look of yours is going to get you out of trouble. I think company is something you probably should have mentioned earlier." She furiously scrubbed herself dry and dressed hurriedly.

This was a bad idea. She knew getting involved was a bad idea and others knowing, an even worse idea. It had only been a week. She'd hoped for more time. Once the secret was out, it would be over.

He was still standing there watching her when she looked up. "Seriously, I don't think this is a good idea. Meeting your kind? What purpose could it serve?"

"You're worrying over nothing. This will work. It's only Morgan and Caleb. You know them, right? I thought it would be easier to meet them first."

She nodded slowly, still confused about why they were coming and who else Terrill meant to introduce her to. She wasn't about to become some sort of exotic zoo exhibit, no matter how cute the keeper.

He laughed at her thoughts. "Mara, give them a chance. They'll be here in a few minutes and they want to see you."

She yelled after him to make some coffee. As she made to leave the room, she saw her reflection in the mirror. The confident-looking woman staring back at her wasn't the same girl she'd been before meeting Terrill. This woman appeared to know exactly who she was and what she wanted.

In spite of her nervousness, she had to admit she was relieved it would be Morgan and Caleb first.

They were already in the living room as she entered. Caleb and Terrill looked on with expressions of indulgent tolerance as Morgan nearly bowled Mara over, hugging her. "I'm so happy for you two!"

Mara laughed and detangled herself from Morgan's enthusiastic embrace. "It's good to see you too, Morgan." She looked at Caleb, who was still grinning from ear to ear. "You don't mind?" she asked him.

"Mind?" He looked at her like she was the crazy one. "We LOVE the idea that Terrill has finally fallen for someone. It's been way too unfair letting him poke fun at me all these years for giving in to this terror." He gave Morgan a huge smacking kiss before laughing. "It's about damn time." He shared a contented smile with Morgan. "We couldn't be happier it's you. Besides, I have the distinct feeling he'll have his hands full. It gives me a leg up on the teasing for once."

Mara tried not to laugh at the pained look that crossed Terrill's face as he handed her a cup of coffee and gestured for everyone to take a seat around the fire.

"We have a lot to talk about," he said.

Mara slowly sipped her coffee. It was a few seconds before she noticed Morgan's eyes on her and saw her friend's smile dissolve into a puzzled frown.

"Terrill," she asked, "isn't Mara one of us now?"

Mara and Terrill exchanged meaningful glances.

"Not exactly."

"But . . ."

Caleb silenced Morgan with a slight gesture, and Terrill rose to stand at Mara's side.

"Mara is part Viajante, part Vampire." Terrill locked eyes with Caleb. "And as you already know, the other half of my soul."

Morgan looked confused. "How can she be your soul if she's not completely Vampire?"

Caleb laughed and slapped his knee. "Viajante? You're kidding! Hell, I guess if you're going to break the rules, might as well go straight to the big ones. I'll be damned. At least that explains why you wanted us to keep an eye on her."

Mara stiffened. It felt as if all the air had been sucked out of the room, along with all the warmth. "Keep an eye on me?" she echoed as she turned to look at Terrill.

Morgan exchanged pained looks with Caleb. Too late, they realized that Terrill apparently hadn't wanted that little fact known.

"I asked them to keep an eye on you, Mara. They were following my orders."

Mara stood and backed away from him, her eyes wide. It was worse than she thought. "Your orders? They work for you?"

"My request then. Does one word really matter so much?"

"Yes."

"So it was okay for you to try and use them to protect yourself, but you object to my asking them to do the same for you?"

The accusation brought tears to her eyes. How could he turn this around into something she should be grateful to him for? "It's not the same." She had nowhere to go. She sat down and glanced over at Morgan.

Morgan smiled sympathetically. "Caleb and Terrill have been close for years. Terrill . . ."

"Mara, you lied to Morgan and Caleb," said Terrill. "You used them. I asked them to take advantage of that so they could get close to you, to keep you safe. If you have complaints, they are with me alone."

That he'd lied, and apparently had no issue doing so if he deemed it in his best interest, scared her. He was more ruthless than she'd given him credit for.

"So, part Vampire, huh?" Caleb asked.

"Mara has the ability to project whichever image she wishes. Once she knew you were coming, she instinctively reverted back to the mortal projection you already knew."

"You're Viajante? Why couldn't we sense that?" Morgan asked.

"Because I didn't let you," Mara said as she let down her shields and projected her true Viajante self. "I'm very good at protecting who and what I am."

Caleb reacted immediately, pushing Morgan behind him and unconsciously rising to take a defensive stance.

Terrill covered Mara just as quickly.

Mara immediately raised her shields, changing the projection to pure Vampire, and wiped furtively at the tears threatening to fall. What the hell had she been thinking? No way was this going to work!

Caleb's posture slowly relaxed and he shook his head. "Craziest damn thing I ever did see. Sorry, Mara. Just going to take a little getting used to, that's all."

Morgan slowly pushed her way past Caleb and gently moved Terrill away from Mara. She dropped to Mara's level on the couch. "Mara, honey, it's okay. Please tell me you forgive us. I don't want a misunderstanding to spoil our friendship. I don't care what you are. You're my friend and Terrill's soul. That's all that matters." She put her nose in the air in a mock haughtiness Mara found charming. "Guys have never been good at adapting on the fly. Us girls are going to have to be the sane ones, okay? Just be patient. They'll get it eventually."

Mara stifled her laughter as Terrill broadcast his opinion of Morgan's assessment to her privately. She slowly lowered her shields from full Vampire to project a more comfortable mix and relaxed as everyone became accustomed to it.

Morgan wrinkled her beautiful nose. "Is that really coffee? You actually drink that?"

Mara smiled and picked up her forgotten cup.

Caleb helped Morgan to her feet. "So coffee is the magic elixir of Viajantes. No wonder Starbucks is making a killing."

Unfortunately for Mara, it was precisely at that moment that she'd taken a sip. Much to the amusement of her new Vampire friends, she managed to inelegantly snort it out all over herself.

Don't you dare say anything, she admonished Terrill, knowing it was killing him not to make some smart-ass comment. She ignored the mess she'd made and ran to change before rejoining them on the balcony.

CHAPTER TEN

The next few nights with Morgan and Caleb passed in a blur of practical lessons in advanced fighting and tracking techniques. Terrill alternated between test subject and teacher, periodically disappearing to conduct some sort of surveillance.

No one seemed inclined to give too many details. But all three of them took great pains to separately reassure her of the necessity of maintaining a semblance of normalcy in their Vampire activities so as to not alert Victor of anything unusual.

She understood, but the unpredictability of their sudden appearances and unexplained disappearances were not only making her nervous but beginning to make her doubt whether she was truly part of the group or if they were deliberately keeping things from her.

"Mara, concentrate!"

Mara threw herself to the ground as the tree branch hurled at her by Morgan flew by, the smaller branches snagging her sweater as it passed. A few millimeters closer and it would have scored a direct hit.

Before she had time to dust off and disentangle the stray twigs from her hair, Morgan was by her side, helping her up and checking for injuries.

"Terrill's going to kill me. Thank god you weren't hurt! How did you manage to avoid it? And why weren't you paying attention in the first place?"

The torrent of questions continued. "Seriously, Mara, you have got to focus. I'm not holding anything back, and if you get any more distracted, you are really going to get yourself hurt."

Morgan was right. "I'm sorry," Mara said, "I haven't been able to shake this headache today. Maybe it's affecting me more than I realized." She shrugged it off and re-fastened the hair band that had been pulled loose by her unexpected tumble to the ground.

Morgan looked worried. "Headaches aren't common for immortals – not unless there's been a significant drain to one's powers – and we've only been at it for less than an hour. It's almost as if . . ."

Something in her tone made Mara stop messing with her hair and stare at her. "As if what?"

Morgan shook her head. "No, it doesn't make sense."

"Morgan!"

"We are warned about Viajante attacks, but I don't know the symptoms. So few survive to tell details – or else they're made to forget – so I couldn't say for sure that headaches are one of them."

"It's not a Viajante attack. I'm Viajante and there's no way I would be under any sort of attack by my own people that I couldn't detect. Besides, how could anyone, mortal or immortal, approach this place without Terrill detecting it?

Morgan sighed. "You're right. I know. It was a crazy thought. Maybe it's all the changes you've gone through lately?"

"Sure. That's probably it. I wouldn't worry about it." Mara hoped her voice conveyed a conviction she certainly didn't feel. Morgan had a tendency to worry, and while Mara really liked Morgan, she didn't need a nursemaid. It was bad enough that Terrill almost never left her alone as it was.

Mara led the way back to the cabin. "Where did Caleb and Terrill go again?"

"Victor called a meeting of all Warriors. It's uncommon, but not so rare as to be suspicious. Is that what you're picking up on? Something off about that?"

Mara tried to trace the source of the pain pushing on her mind, but it remained obscure. She shook her head. "No, it's not anything with Terrill. I'd know. This feeling is vaguer, harder to define."

Morgan nodded. "I don't feel anything that suggests Caleb's in danger either."

"You know, I'd love to learn how to communicate as you all do," Mara said. "I feel like I force the conversation out loud when we're all together. There may come a time when you can't risk that."

"It would be a good skill in case of a fight." Morgan sat down next to Mara. "Okay then. Obviously you know there are many ways we communicate. You and Terrill share the path of the soul, so what you communicate across that line, no mortal or immortal should be able to intercept."

"Actually, that's only partially correct. Viajante can read Vampire thoughts, maybe even their communication, but it's sort of a one-sided conversation. I can read more than one at a time, but it would take some time and focus to pinpoint the mental conversation between two in a crowd." Mara's brow wrinkled. She really should be practicing that more.

Morgan looked surprised to learn what Mara's kind could do, but her face cleared quickly and she laughed. "One thing at a time. Have you ever heard of this crazy thing called patience" Or maybe . . . I don't know . . . pacing yourself?"

Mara grinned. "Patience?"

Morgan shook her head in mock exasperation. "You mentioned that all Viajante can communicate on a sort of species communications line. Vampires also have one. Ours is limited by distance or weakness. Say in the event of an attack, if the wounds are terrible enough, it could limit our ability to communicate."

"The same is true for Viajante."

"There is also a type of family blood link like Terrill has with his parents. But there is another. One that can be made with any of our species, but . . ."

"It involves taking blood, doesn't it? Creating a special link?"

Morgan nodded. "Terrill and Caleb have done this. It is the way of many Warriors. They exchange blood with their second in command. It strengthens their abilities in battle, and lets them communicate without detection via the common link. I cannot hear Terrill's conversations with Caleb, but Caleb can relay information to me through our soul link."

"So this common Vampire link, do you think we can communicate on it?"

Morgan shrugged. "I think we have a better chance of that than getting the guys to approve of our exchanging blood."

Mara laughed. "I was just picturing the look on their faces if we were to do that. They would totally wig out!"

Morgan chuckled. "Yeah, right after they throttle both of us. I guess it's too bad they aren't here to stop us now, isn't it?"

"A shame," Mara sighed in mock disappointment. "But in the interest of peace and harmony, I guess all we're left with for today is the common path. How can I find it?"

"Concentrate on the Vampire part of you. Feel yourself embrace that side."

She found a strand leading out into the shadows of her mind where she rarely ventured. It led toward a faint light barely visible in the murkiness of her mind. Could this be it? She waited for Morgan to attempt contact. The light brightened, and when she heard her, it was so clear and unhesitating that her eyes flew open in surprise.

You can hear me?

Yes. How did we find the path so quickly? It's so clear.

I don't know, but it works. This is great!

Morgan suddenly placed her hands to her temples and her face paled. She abruptly severed their communication.

"Morgan, what is it? Are you okay?"

Morgan shook her head and took a deep breath. "I had no idea."

"Had no idea about what?" she asked with concern.

"I had no idea what had been bothering you all evening. No idea it was that strong. We should get Terrill."

Mara grabbed her hand, sending waves of reassurance. "No, we don't need Terrill. It's okay, really." She felt a little bit guilty pushing Morgan, but she needed time to figure out what was going on without being smothered.

Morgan's eyes looked glassy. "You're right. It's nothing you can't handle. Maybe we should call it a night."

Mara nodded. "I'm sure I'll feel better after some rest."

Morgan stood up. "Yes, all you need is rest." She turned back and made eye contact with Mara. "You should tell Terrill about this once he gets back. Promise me you will."

Mara smiled and made the sign of crossing her heart. "I promise." Morgan glared at her so she made the sign again, holding her hand up and laughing. Morgan finally left after eliciting another verbal promise from her to tell Terrill the instant he got back.

Mara wandered around the house, knowing it would still be several hours before Terrill returned. What was happening to her? She wished she could talk with Yasmine about it, but she'd promised not to contact her aunt until she was ready to return.

She thought about what Morgan said about a Viajante attack. No way. Still, she couldn't help feeling the compulsion to contact Yasmine. But Yasmine was in Sanctuary, wasn't she? Would she even be able to make contact? Did she dare?

She fingered the amulet her mother had given her. Nicolette had told Mara it helped warn of danger. She held it in the palm of her hand and focused on Yasmine. The sense of urgency leaped through. That settled it.

Yasmine? Can you hear me?

She heard a faint reply through their familial bond. *Mara is that you? Are you safe?*

Mara felt a numbing cold blast through her and waves of pain caught her in their midst. She smelled blood and her stomach lurched. It wasn't real. A terrifying realization set in. It may not be real for her, but it was for Yasmine. *Where are you?*

We were attacked. Dabir's dead. Yasmine's voice sounded emotionless, like she had died herself.

Yasmine in danger, her soul dead? What the crap? No, this couldn't be happening. Mara opened her senses like Terrill had taught her and pushed into Yasmine's mind, looking for clues as to where she was.

Mara let her vision blur and searched deep in the shadows. The image of a building slowly took shape, black with years of filth and soot from a long-ago fire in this derelict district of abandoned properties.

She'd passed through the area on one of her daylight familiarization drives of the city. It was close to the docks. She remembered the overpowering stench of refuse from overflowing dumpsters mixing with the seaweed and algae that clung to the pier understructure. A toxic perfume of automotive and chemical waste dumped unchecked into the water from broken and long-neglected sewers lining the road added a decidedly nauseating touch. The area was so uninviting even the dregs of mortal society avoided it. Of course, that would be where Yasmine was.

Mara didn't stop to think of the tongue-lashing Terrill would give her. She just acted. She armed herself with the small knife Terrill had given her, grabbed the keys, and started his car. She raced down the mountain toward the city and Yasmine. *Yasmine, hang on! I'm coming.*

No, Mara, don't . . .

Mara tried to reestablish communications with Yasmine, but couldn't. She blinked, refusing to dwell on whatever might be preventing her from getting through.

She parked the car and took care to disguise her appearance. She projected a mortal façade but took special care to obscure her presence and blend into the shadows as much as possible as she approached the building. She doubted there would be anyone around to give the alarm, but didn't know what sort of technology they might have employed.

She tapped the knife tucked securely in the sheath at her ankle before staring coldly at the building in front of her. She crossed the street and avoided the scattered street lights illuminating grease-stained patches of broken pavement and abandoned shells of vehicles long since cannibalized.

She slowly opened the door. A dank, musty smell surrounded her as she wound her way inside the dark interior, seeking proof her aunt was truly there. Her internal alarm was in full shriek, but she couldn't afford to turn back. Yasmine was counting on her. She tried to separate the sound of cockroaches and rodents scurrying about from any other sound that might indicate danger. A slight motion and groan caused her to pivot. It took seconds for the image in front of her to sink in. She was looking at a badly-beaten woman shackled to the floor. It took a few seconds more for it to register that this was her aunt. She swore under her breath at her own stupidity and slowness and rushed to her side.

Yasmine, are you all right? What happened? Who did this to you? The torrent of questions poured out as her fingers raced, struggling to free Yasmine from her bonds.

Why was her skin so cold? Yasmine seemed to be too weak to help with her own escape. Her hands were shaking, and Yasmine seemed to flinch and cringe with every motion Mara made. Damn! She hated that she caused her aunt more pain as she pulled and twisted at the manacles, but she had to free her. She dropped her arms from the restraints that didn't seem to be responding and turned instead to the gag.

Too late she realized that Yasmine's frantic movements weren't from pain, but a desperate attempt to warn her of the danger behind her. A warning that came too late.

Mara felt an oppressive presence cloak her as a needle plunged into her neck. Her eyes widened in shock and she dropped to the floor. She attempted to stand, blinking at the darkness choking her vision, leaving her little more than a blurry sea of bouncing colors and shapes. Even her limbs stopped responding and turned to stone. At least gargoyles were given the dignity of a planned pose – not this version where she lay sprawled on the floor, defenseless and vulnerable.

She remembered the knife as it was pulled out of its sheath and sent clattering onto the cement floor, well out of her reach. Terrill was right, she couldn't fight for crap. The darkness continued to slide over her like fuzzy saran wrap, pinning her in place, pulling at her eyelids, weighing them down. She refused to give in.

Terrill!

Already the dancing shapes and shadows were dimming before her heavy eyes. A brutal kick sent her flying and she gasped, her ribs burning where a booted foot had made contact. She didn't try to move, it hurt too damn much to do anything except concentrate on breathing. The last image she had was the look of extreme pleasure on Claudio's face as he squatted down next to her. She groaned and closed her eyes. He slapped her face so hard she swore she'd have a mark there for eternity. She couldn't even muster up the strength for a decent glare of hatred.

"Nice to finally meet you, Mara."

He lightly tapped her cheek, the one he'd just smacked. Mara saw him smile as she winced at the contact. It was too damn hard to focus. He rose above her, the toe of his boot poking at her ribcage, a gentle reminder to behave. It worked. She didn't dare try to move.

"You had to know I'd find you again, didn't you?"

CHAPTER ELEVEN

No! Terrill subtly took stock of the room and its occupants as he struggled to maintain his composure. That he knew what had happened to Mara had to remain secret. Hell, Mara had barely been able to send him the images she had. Victor, the cowardly bastard he was, had finally made his move. It really shouldn't have surprised him that Victor would use Mara against him. He never had been much for direct conflict.

Even so, fury and the promise of retribution surged through him. He struggled to regain his iron grip over his emotions. He quickly mastered his fear for her safety and replaced it with a singular determination to find her. Replacing his guilt for not keeping her safe wasn't ever going to happen.

Part of him hoped Victor would start something. He grinned a purely malevolent grin. He thought of the enjoyment he would get from ripping Victor apart, limb by single limb. His eyes narrowed. All Victor had to do was say the wrong thing.

Terrill scanned the room and found Victor deeply engaged in conversation with a few of his protégées. Terrill's lips curled in a smile both dangerous and feral. If he confronted Victor now, over a girl, it wouldn't be enough for the High Courts.

Terrill signaled silently to Caleb that they needed to talk.

He reached again for Mara and found only black, cold space. In spite of his resolve to feel nothing, the emptiness yawned back, and dread quickly coated him in an icy blanket of sweat. He refused to believe she was lost to him. He straightened to his full height and placed Victor in his sight. Screw protocol, it was time Victor realized just who he was dealing with.

Victor saw him coming and smiled. Terrill knew instantly that Victor was well aware of Mara's situation. No way would he have that much confidence otherwise. It must really please him to have taken control of something of Terrill's. There had always been animosity between them. Terrill had initially chalked it up to a lack of self-confidence, but Victor's cold and triumphant smile highlighted just how deep the hatred went and how determined Victor was to beat him.

"Any news on the eastern front?"

Always pleasant, Caleb had said of Victor in the past, just like a damn spider sitting patiently in its web. It lured you in with its passivity, smiling at you with its beady little eyes until it watched you falter, and then, bam! It attacked.

"Nothing significant." Terrill kept his voice cold and detached. That was the sort of thing Victor hated. He expected deference, something he normally only got the pretense of from Terrill and his family. "It would be wise to go further east though, skirt the edges of Viajante territory and verify the boundaries haven't been disturbed. It's been too quiet. I was planning a trip to look into it." His tone became harder, challenging. "Unless you recommend an alternate course?"

Victor narrowed his eyes and nodded curtly. "Not at all. It sounds wise. But I must admit I am surprised to hear you advocating for travel. I had thought you had acquired a new interest here in town. Mara, I think her name was?" He stopped, pretending to consider. "So quickly bored with her?"

Terrill's voice took on the coldness of steel, hard and unrelenting. "When has anyone ever interfered with my duties?" he asked as he locked eyes with Victor, daring him to say something. "As to my intentions with the girl, let's just say that I find it unlikely I will lose interest anytime soon. She should be found interesting by any others."

They smiled coldly at each other, a deadly game of cat and mouse. Terrill knew he had all but thrown down the gauntlet by his public statement.

"Will you be staying for the special court session before leaving?" Victor inquired politely between clenched teeth.

Terrill wondered how much those polite words had cost him when his body language was clearly seething to respond to the challenge Terrill had laid down.

"I've never shirked my duties before. Why should that change now?" Aware they were drawing an audience, he inclined his head slightly toward Victor. "I trust you'll excuse me." Without waiting for acknowledgment, he turned and walked away.

He felt Victor's eyes burning holes into his back. He ignored it and stepped out into the night air where Caleb waited for him. Terrill relayed what little he knew about Mara's abduction. He could feel Caleb's shock.

I'll get hold of Morgan, Caleb said. *Maybe she has some idea of where Mara went. She told me Mara had a headache so they called off training early. I didn't think anything of it.*

You two didn't think anything of leaving her alone?

What would you have done? Left here and gone back? Appearances are everything right now, man, you know that. She was safe back at your place. It never occurred to me she'd leave your place without protection.

Terrill ran his fingers through his hair. It wasn't fair to take his frustration out on Caleb. *You're right, but it should have occurred to me. She thinks she can handle herself.*

And now with all the extra training she's been doing . . . Caleb finished what they were both thinking.

Terrill nodded. *Exactly. She thinks she can handle anything now. I never told her it was too dangerous for her. I assumed she'd stay where I put her.*

Caleb laughed. *Bro, you're both too pig-headed to realize that neither one of you is about to let someone else set barriers or dictate boundaries.* He stopped laughing, his face once again serious. *We'll get her back.*

Terrill clenched his fists. *Awfully damn convenient we were summoned here now, isn't it? Almost as if Victor wanted us out of reach.*

Caleb turned to face the inner room and nodded as he leaned back against the rail. *Victor has suspicions, sure, but he can't know everything. I think the most significant part of all this is that he considers you such a danger, he needs to make special provisions to prevent you from interfering with his plans, whatever those are. Then again, it could just simply be that he hates you so much he'll do anything he can to hurt you, and anyone you care about.*

The guilt was like a sucker punch to the stomach. Terrill sighed. *Talk to Morgan. Once we get out of here, we'll have to move fast.*

He broke off contact and tried again to reach Mara. Nothing. His eyes turned a dangerously dark gray. Victor had no idea the monster he had just unleashed. None. But he soon would.

* * *

Mara awakened slowly and fought her way through layers of freezing cold. The cold was so intense it actually hurt to breathe. She made a conscious effort to control her chattering teeth and failed miserably. Best she could tell, she was in some sort of container with her hands and feet bound. The cramped quarters didn't give her much room to move – not like that was an option anyway.

Her people had never settled in cold places for long, but as immortals, nothing short of death by fire could truly hurt them. A lot could incapacitate them and require time for healing, but she had never guessed the reason why her kind avoided the brutally cold climates before now. Why hadn't the Shaman ever talked about the cold before? It couldn't be new knowledge that it inhibited or slowed down powers. She should have been taught about this from a young age.

She struggled ineffectively against her bonds and reached out to Terrill. The path was somehow blocked. She couldn't even see it glowing faintly. She felt her strength weakening and tried the path to Yasmine. Hopefully, that one would work.

I'm so sorry, Mara. I hoped you were safe and away from all this. Why did you contact me? You promised you wouldn't!

Mara heard the tears and self-blame in her aunt's voice and it stabbed at her. Yasmine had always put Mara's welfare above her own. This wasn't Yasmine's fault. Mara was the one who had broken her promise and still, Yasmine acted as if that too had been her own fault.

Mara cautiously took a deep breath. The cold scraped her raw throat as she strained to complete the action. *They've been after me for some time now. I don't know if they've figured out everything about me and who I know yet. I'm the one that's sorry they dragged you into this.* She softened her voice. The next question wouldn't be easy for Yasmine to answer. *What happened to you and Dabir?*

Yasmine didn't use words. Instead, she projected the battle. They had been attacked by Vampires. Through Yasmine's vision, Mara saw Dabir go down. The pain her aunt felt at his loss was intense, something Mara easily shared. Dabir had been part of her life almost as long as Yasmine had been. Could the attack on Yasmine and Dabir have been a ploy to draw Mara out?

Why didn't you contact me after the attack?

I didn't want to risk you. I still don't.

Mara borrowed some of Terrill's favorite curses, using them liberally under her breath as she remembered the vivid bruises and cuts she'd briefly glimpsed in the dark. She felt fury and helplessness rise within her. *How is it that we can communicate? It's cold as hell here.*

Yasmine laughed bitterly. *As it is here. They do this for transport or extra security.*

So?

I've been able to build up an immunity. But you, well . . . Mara could hear the smile in her aunt's voice. *You've always had some of your parents' special gifts. Maybe an increased tolerance is one of them.*

Mara grinned wryly. *Well, I'll take whatever advantage I can get right now. Do you think they suspect?*

If they did, we'd both be out cold. They may think you're still out with the drugs. We need to be careful. If they find out . . .

She clenched her jaw. *Where are they taking us?*

North. If they take us back to where I was held, it will still be a few hours. Rest now while you can. We'll be there soon enough.

Mara wondered how she was supposed to sleep with every inch of her being acutely fixated on the damn arctic temperature in her coffin-like container.

A jarring shook Mara as the container was abruptly lowered onto the floor. She heard a lock disengage and the container opened. Before she could react, a fist smashed into her face and her head whacked hard against the bottom, disorienting her. Arms reached for her. A syringe was again plunged into her flailing arm, sending the world upside down and back into a blurry blend of grays and darks. The next thing that registered was concrete as they unceremoniously dumped her onto the cold hard surface. Someone attached a shackle to her foot. She winced as its weight bit into her ankle.

Why couldn't this be a bad dream? She certainly felt loopy enough. She tried to right herself, but an increased sense of vertigo and a condescending laugh were her only rewards for her dismal efforts. Damn, not exactly what she'd been hoping for. She heard the sound of a heavy door closing and a lock clicking ominously in place. She tried to focus and open her eyes but felt herself slipping away again.

Mara, can you hear me? Terrill asked. *Mara!*

She heard his voice as if across a great distance. It sounded so tiny, so far away. She shook off the fogginess, instantly regretting it as the slight movement caused her head to ring.

Yes, I can hear you.

Mara, answer me!

I'm here. I hear you. The pounding in her head amplified as she sent the words down their private communication path. She wasn't reaching him. What was wrong? Had she lost her ability to communicate on any path?

Yasmine, can you hear me?

Thank god you're all right. You didn't answer earlier, I was so worried!

Mara made another effort to sit. She tried to pull her fuzzy thoughts together. So not all communication was inhibited, only that with Vampires. Interesting. She thought back to the shot they'd given her. What the hell was in it anyway? Like she was really going to let some nasty cocktail slow her down. She drew the path between Terrill and her more brilliantly in her mind, sending pulsating beams of power through the shadowy divide. Somehow – and she didn't know how – she WAS going to get through.

Terrill.

It was weak but he heard it. *Why didn't you answer me earlier?*

Any other time and she would have teased him about his attempt to be all big and bad, but it was too much work to concentrate on anything except the most basic connection.

Some sort of drug. I can't maintain contact. Her voice came in fragments. *Go north. Yasmine in trouble. The cold. It's too . . .*

* * *

Mara, we're going to find you. Now that we have a direction, we're coming for you. I promise. All he heard was silence. *Mara?* He ran his hand through his hair distractedly.

Victor has his eye on you. Terrill felt his father's presence at his side.

"Victor, shall we get started?" Lauris's voice was solicitous, but it carried the unmistakable ring of authority as it rose over the crowd. Lauris was a powerful member of the court. Even Victor couldn't afford to alienate him.

Victor smiled thinly and indicated for Lauris and Terrill to precede him into the antechamber. Terrill and Lauris exchanged looks, insisting Victor precede them. Once he turned his back to them, Lauris laid his hand on Terrill's shoulder. *Gabriella wanted me to tell you not to worry. We'll get her back, son, and those responsible will pay.*

Terrill narrowed his eyes briefly. *Yes. Yes, they will.*

CHAPTER TWELVE

After coming to, Mara ran through the chain of events that led her to her less-than-desirable position. She inserted a few of Terrill's favorite phrases and added a few new ones in her assessment of her actions – or correctly, her failures. Now Yasmine was in danger because of her. It was time for answers.

You asked me to conceal the true events of that night from everyone, even the Shaman. We even concealed my difference from them, from Dabir, from everyone.

She felt Yasmine hesitate. *I wasn't sure what to do at first. I mean, when I realized what had happened and what that meant you had become. Honey, they killed your parents, killed your sister, and you were left like them in so many ways. I was afraid any reference would remind you of the violence of that night. I couldn't let anyone find out. I didn't know how else to protect you.*

I always thought you were afraid I would become like them – a danger to our people. Mara couldn't prevent the hurt from creeping into her voice. Yasmine's approval had always been important to her. She reminded her so much of Nicolette.

Yasmine answered her quickly. *Mara, any doubts I may ever have held ended the second I laid eyes on you and took you into my home. You had a hard time as a child, but you trusted me. I was more worried I would do something to cause you to lose faith in me – in our people. Afraid something might lead to . . .*

Lead to turning against you. Mara absorbed her words. Yasmine believed them. Mara felt that. But she was surprised by the self-doubt Yasmine had in her abilities to raise her niece.

Yasmine, you were, and still are, the one I have been closest to since that night. She raised her head keying in on something unrealized until that moment. Yasmine wasn't questioning what she had done, but what she hadn't. Mara wiped away her tears. *There is something else you were worried about. You promised my mother something. What?*

Yasmine laughed dryly. *You always were perceptive. It's a wonder I was able to keep it from you this long.*

Keep what from me?

You're right. It's time I told you – time you knew. When we were little girls, your mother and I were separated. I've never regretted anything more in my life than my failure to find her. There is a lot you don't know about her and what she suffered because of me.

Yasmine, you were a child yourself. How could you have protected her? You could barely protect yourself. I know she never blamed you. She only spoke of you once, and her fear was that she'd failed you!

Mara knew Yasmine had heard her, but Yasmine continued as if she hadn't. *Something happened to our parents and we were left to fend for ourselves. England wasn't a kind place for orphans – especially not then – and never for little girls. We didn't know anything of our heritage or what powers we had. We were living as mortals, working odd jobs for food, begging, even stealing if we had to. One day I was found and taken away. I didn't know it at the time, but the people who took me away were Viajante, and they spirited me out of there as quickly as they did because of a Vampire threat I was naturally oblivious to.*

I was frantic to find Nicolette, but I didn't know if I could trust them or not. So I said nothing. I finally broke down and told them about her. They brought me back to try and find her, but we couldn't. I made them search for days. It was only after another Vampire entered the city that they forced me to leave. Nothing I said changed their minds. We sailed for the Americas, and I think my heart broke as the miles separated us.

Mara nodded, feeling Yasmine's pain and her helplessness that she had lost the one thing that mattered to her.

I was raised Viajante, later learning that I had the special talent to become a Seeker. I couldn't understand why I was chosen to pursue a path I had failed at as a child. I still don't. I never stopped looking for your mother once they let me leave Sanctuary.

You did find us, Mara reminded her, *and you saved my life. My mother would have been so happy to know it was you that found me. You were there when she needed you most.*

No, Mara, if I had been, your family would still be alive. Nicolette had a hard life. The things she shared with me before I took you away . . . I've never spoken of them.

Mara sat motionless. *What do you mean by the things she shared with you? I saw her die. She died before you got there.*

No, honey, she didn't. Not quite.

The horror of it hit Mara. She'd escaped out the window and left her mother to die in the fire that had consumed their home. Oh my god! What sort of daughter was she?

Mara, stop it! You were too small to help her. She knew that. She didn't want you to live with any guilt. There was nothing you could have done. She knew she only had minutes left. She was dying, and there was no way to bring her back. She put everything she had into convincing you to get out and to safety.

Mara struggled to understand. A stream of tears burned unchecked down her face. *She . . . she pushed me to get out?*

Yes, baby, she did. Before the smoke, before she fell asleep for the last time, she showed me things. Mara, you have another sister out there – a half-sister. She would be older than you. I don't even know if she's still alive.

Mara's eyes widened in shock and she fell back against the wall in surprise. Not sure she was capable of coherent speech, she forced a single word out. *How?*

Before she went to Ireland and met your father, Fredrich, she had already given birth. Mara heard the bitterness in Yasmine's voice and steeled herself. *She'd been raped, but she'd survived the abuse and escaped. Her only thought had been to protect the life of her unborn child. Once she gave birth, she left the baby, a girl, on the steps of a church known for its generosity and escaped across the water to Ireland. She was so weak from the abuse and then the labor, she almost didn't make it. She told me something pulled her there. That was where she found the missing part of her soul, Fredrich, and where you were later born.*

What happened to her baby?

Nicolette was never able to find her. She thought she did the right thing at the time. She couldn't take care of her, but in her heart, she always regretted that decision. She and Fredrich searched, but they weren't able to locate her. Had I any other choice I would have gone back to look, but your mother made me promise to protect you first. That meant putting as much distance as possible between us and the ones who attacked your family.

Mara tried to take it all in. Vampires had chased her aunt out of England as a child, leaving her mother behind by mistake, but the attack on her family had been deliberate. They had planned to destroy her entire family, including her. Now, Vampires working with mortals she had observed earlier had captured Yasmine to once again get to her. Why were they all so damned determined to kill or capture her?

Yasmine, how did they find out about me? They went after you and Dabir after they tried to get me on the way into LA. I've already met the one behind the attack on my family, but I don't think he recognized me. Who are these people that keep coming after me? And why now?

She felt Yasmine's protest to her having been in the proximity of her sister's killer. *I don't know. I think it's safe to say they've obviously known about you for a while. You left Sanctuary and have been in their city for some months now. It's a great question. Why didn't they attack earlier?*

Maybe they had to try again because their earlier plan didn't work out so well.

Mara smiled in satisfaction for having thwarted their plans. *Where were you when attacked?* she asked Yasmine.

A young Viajante couple had gone missing. Dabir and I were sent out to investigate. She was expecting soon and insisted the baby be born in her homeland. They were heading toward the Mojave Desert Sanctuary. Their kin contacted us and told us they never made it there.

Someone must know us very well if they counted on that disappearance to get to you.

What are you saying?

Mara couldn't believe what was going through her head. *Viajante are in league with this organization. It's the only explanation.*

Mara imagined Yasmine shaking her head.

Why? How would any of our people do anything to hurt our own kind? Help Vampires? Yasmine asked. *It goes against everything we are.*

I don't know, but this group certainly includes Vampires. I ran into a particularly nasty one named Claudio who seemed especially glad to see me today.

Mara.

She didn't need to see her aunt to read the worried expression she knew would be on her face. She smiled. *They have no idea what they're dealing with.*

Yasmine's sniffle turned into a choked laugh. *You always were arrogant, weren't you?*

Mara laughed, truly feeling better for the first time since her capture. *Yeah, well maybe a little. There are a few things our captors don't know about that they'll wish they had known later.* She wrung her hands together nervously. *Ah, Yasmine, there are a few things I still need to tell you about though.*

Mara suddenly froze in place. Something about their situation had changed. The temperature in the room started to drop quickly.

Yasmine answered her unspoken question. *They're leaving. The Vampires. They drop the temperature to control us better when they can't be here. The cold gives the mortals a sense of power. These mortals though . . . Mara, there's something different about them. I can't control them for very long else they realize it and they get angry.*

Mara's mind whirred and a wicked gleam flashed in her eyes. If the Vampires were leaving, that meant there was a chance they could escape. She still had a few tricks up her sleeve. She rubbed her hands together in anticipation.

Yasmine, if you can get over me being part Vampire, I've got an idea that's going to blow your mind. Mara didn't try to hide the note of triumph in her voice.

Yasmine laughed. *So what's the plan?*

CHAPTER THIRTEEN

Mara scrutinized the heavy shackle attaching her ankle to the floor. There was some sort of locking mechanism they'd enabled when they put it on. A key was the only way to take it off clean. The seam where they'd locked it didn't budge as she directed her powers at severing or twisting the metal. She scowled and changed tactics, running her fingers down the links testing for any sort of weakness she could exploit. She'd hoped the links were made of something different than the shackle. No such luck. She wasn't a metallurgist, but if nothing responded, it could only mean one thing. The metal wasn't earth-born. Maybe meteorite. Crap. Viajante powers were limited to manipulating earth-based elements.

The chain continued into what looked like a carelessly made layer of concrete covering the otherwise smooth slab beneath her. She ran her hand over the rough, slightly-upraised surface and a grin slowly broke through the grime covering her face. There was something they may have forgotten about in their haste to construct this little playhouse. Odds were, they hadn't spent the same level of effort below ground as they had above.

Her eyes narrowed in concentration as she directed a pin-point stream of wind at the surface of the floor surrounding the link. The concrete material slowly dissolved, exposing more and more of the links to her inspection. Mara kept the circle small. Just wide enough to free the links, but not large enough that it would be noticed. She let the wind disperse the larger chunks. She kept the sand close so she could fill in the hole after she broke through.

Mara!

She flinched guiltily. She still owed Yasmine answers. Information on how she planned to get out wasn't all her aunt was waiting for.

I have a plan, but to make this work I'm going to have to do something we both find repulsive. Yasmine, I've never crossed that line before. I'm not even sure I can now. Just the thought of it literally scared the crap out of her. She couldn't let Terrill close to her because of what had been done to her, yet she intended to do to another the very thing that she feared most. *I don't know what's going to happen after that. What if I can't come back?*

Yasmine sent her strength through their bond. *Nothing about you is evil, Mara. I don't think embracing that side of you means you have to surrender your control or that you automatically become evil.*

Mara swallowed hard and took a deep breath. She hoped Yasmine was right.

How long do we have before the mortals come? It seemed likely that Yasmine's torture had not been at the hands of Vampires, but she had to know for sure.

They usually don't waste much time – just long enough to ensure they're truly alone. If it's after dark, Raul probably has duty. He particularly enjoys being in control. With someone new here, he won't be able to resist. What are you going to do?

I've learned a few additional tricks since last we saw each other. She didn't mention the role Vampire blood running through her veins played in those tricks. Yasmine probably wasn't ready to hear that yet. Hell, she still wasn't sure she was.

Mara was close to the bottom of the chain. A few more seconds . . . The dust cleared and Mara was able to see the base clearly. It wasn't the same metal as the links. Someone had gotten sloppy and it was gonna cost them – big time. She felt the metal's resistance give as she slowly unraveled the welded seam at the base. She lifted the chain free of the hole and tested the resistance before placing it back.

Yasmine sent her a warning. Company was on the way. She filled in the hole with the dust she'd saved and painted a defeated look on her face as she sat facing the door and waited.

Wow. The aura of violence Raul exuded was so strong it preceded him into the chamber.

She examined the barrier protecting his mind. Yasmine passed her what she'd discovered about the few weak spots in their defenses. It wasn't much, but if she was lucky, she wouldn't have to do much more than feed him the illusion that she remained helpless – until he got within range anyway.

The sound of the locking mechanism disengaging was loud in the darkness. She was momentarily blinded by the glare of his strong flashlight as he entered. It was disorienting after the almost total darkness of the last twenty-four hours. She nearly forgot to maintain the illusion of captivity. You need to be more careful, she chastised herself.

"Well, well, well, what have we got here?" He stroked the bulge at his crotch and licked his lips before leisurely circling her in anticipation.

It was his smell that hit her hardest. The rush of adrenaline in his system seeped out his pores, a sickly sweet smell overlaid with dried semen. Clearly, Mara hadn't been his first date of the evening.

He stepped closer and reached out to touch her hair. Mara held herself immobile. He lunged forward and grabbed the ends, twisting harshly and snapping her head forward so hard she groaned.

Before she could react, the flashlight smashed into the back of her head. She made contact with the floor in a flash of pain and surprise. Crap. Should have expected that.

He used his sweaty body to glue her to the floor as his chest heaved in excited pants and grunts of excitement that got even more frenzied. He captured her hands with one of his and groped at her breasts with the other.

Her struggles to avoid his wet, rank mouth seemed to arouse him more, and he made no attempt to hide his intentions as he ground his body against hers. His grasping fingers left a trail of bruises and scratch marks in their wake. He slid his hand down her stomach, slamming it up against her core, causing her to twist in revulsion as his fingers sought entrance through her clothing.

He laughed. "Yeah, baby, move for me."

"Get off me, you pig!" Mara reared up and spat on him.

He wiped the spittle off, drying his hand against his jeans. He backhanded her so hard that her head bounced off the concrete. She felt a trickle of blood from her nose where he'd made contact.

He released her hands and thrust her shirt up, his hands crushing tender flesh as he attempted to remove her bra. He gave up momentarily and focused his attention further south. His breathing became ragged as he struggled with the waist of her pants.

Mara felt a moment of oh-so-satisfying gratification as she observed him pause before following his eyes to the shackle and chain piled loosely above the concrete. It should have been stretched taut. He looked down at the point where it attached to the floor and then back at Mara's face. She saw the first signs of irredeemable panic dawning. Oops.

Mara's eyes crackled with emerald fury, and she used her full body weight to pounce. Her momentum threw him backward and put him in intimate contact with the hard floor. She growled as she pinned him. Her fangs lengthened, and she winked at Raul's now terrified face before plunging them into his neck.

Before this, she'd wondered if she would be able to do it when the time came. But now? The rush was so sweet. She found herself almost greedily lapping up the blood, forgetting the tainted nature of the source – just feeding. Pure power from the kill slowly eclipsed her concept of wrong and right.

Mara!

Yasmine's panicked voice startled her. What was she doing? She released him, not bothering to stop the flow of blood running down his neck, and got to her feet. She felt a little shaky knowing how close she'd come to losing control. She shuddered as she watched blood drip from her mouth onto the floor. Unconsciously, her tongue ran over her lips, catching the remaining drops.

Stop it! she told herself.

Disgusted, Mara looked at the wasted piece of humanity crumpled like tissue paper at her feet. Her feeding had opened a blood link and the protective barrier to his mind had been severed. She'd seen what he'd done to Yasmine and to others.

She squatted beside him and picked up the flashlight. Sure he'd die from the bite, but . . . She raised the flashlight high.

Mara, no! You're not like him.

He's going to die anyway – and he hurt you. He deserves it.

I know he does, but he's already paid, Yasmine said. *Let it go.*

Mara slowly lowered her arm.

She spotted a ring of keys on Raul's waistband and snatched them off. She removed the offending manacle before running out of the room after Yasmine. Mara quickly released her, but Yasmine was weak from her prolonged captivity and needed Mara's help to stand.

"We are going to have company soon, aren't we?" Yasmine asked.

"Yes."

"I'm not going to like this company, am I?"

Mara looked at her, hoping her aunt could take the leap of faith she wanted her to. She took a deep breath. "I know it sounds crazy, but he's my soul, just as Fredrich was Nicolette's. I didn't believe it at first, but he and his people are risking everything to help me. They won't harm you."

"His people? Ah, Mara, are his people what I think they are?" Mara gave her a tentative smile. "You're kidding, right?" Yasmine shook her head, her eyes wide. "You're not kidding, are you? Of course, you're not kidding. Why am I not surprised? I always said you were insane."

"I'm still getting used to it myself." Mara grinned. Yasmine's face mirrored the grin her niece wore.

Mara looked around with newly determined eyes. "I need to find some answers. Raul had info about this organization – some society linked to this place – and I need to know what they're up to."

"Mara, we have to get out of here. The Vampires always come back. It's still dark out. It isn't safe."

Terrill's presence filled the room. Caleb entered right behind him, covering his back. "No, Mara, it certainly isn't safe," Terrill said as his eyes bored into hers, "and you have a lot of explaining to do."

Torn between the irrational desire to throw herself into his arms and her desire to protect Yasmine, she teetered between both, finally holding herself still and returning his stare with one of her own.

He shifted his attention to the battered woman Mara supported. "This must be Yasmine," he said, picking the information from Mara's mind, "We need to get you out of here. Introductions can wait." He turned to his second in command. "Caleb?"

"The safe house?" he asked.

Terrill nodded. He turned back to Yasmine, forcing eye contact. "Can I trust you will do nothing to endanger him?" He'd asked the question indifferently, but Mara had no doubt he wouldn't hesitate to remove a threat to his friend's safety or any perceived threat to it, regardless of how Mara felt about it.

Mara sent him a scalding look. He ignored it. *On this, I will not compromise.*

Caleb will not be in any danger from either of us, Mara promised, silently urging Yasmine to trust her and her companions. Yasmine took her cue from Mara and nodded.

Caleb stepped up from behind Terrill into the light and saw the damage done to Yasmine for the first time. His face softened. "You've suffered much." He held out his hand. "Mara and Terrill will follow shortly."

Yasmine looked at Mara, who once again nodded her reassurance. "I trust them with my life," Mara confirmed.

Are you okay? Mara asked her aunt.

Is it stupid that I still call out to Dabir, even knowing he is gone?

Mara smiled in sympathy. It had been natural to seek her soul. She didn't have any idea how well she would have reacted had it been her in that situation. She squeezed Yasmine's hand and released it. *Trust me, we'll be right behind you.*

Yasmine hesitantly held out her hand to Caleb.

For several moments after they left, Mara and Terrill remained silent, facing each other. Terrill moved first. *You're safe.* He shared his need to run his hands through her hair, to touch her face, and showed her the desire that had been beating at him to see her unharmed or seek vengeance against those who had harmed her.

I knew you'd come.

His eyes glared gray fire. The abduction must have really rattled him. He still looked angry.

I almost didn't. Why wouldn't you communicate with me? He ran his hand through his hair. *Damn it, Mara, why the hell did you leave the house without me?*

Mara's vision blurred behind unshed tears. He really had been worried! She threw her arms around him and kissed him. *I'm okay, really.* She felt him probe her mind, trying to pull out what had happened and she didn't fight it.

He stepped back, his expression black. *You shouldn't have left. Not without telling me what was going on. I should have known better than to trust you could stay out of trouble for a few hours. Clearly, I need to reconsider chaining you to my side for your own safety!*

Although his words were harsh, Mara knew they weren't meant in anger. *They know about me, Terrill. Some Society. I need to find out what's going on. We need to look at any records they left behind, and we need to be out of here before Claudio returns.*

Mara, he growled the word, *we're leaving. A confrontation with Claudio is NOT what we need right now!*

I know, but we'll never have another chance like this. I'm staying until I have answers.

He cursed under his breath and she smiled in satisfaction. She was going to get her way.

Seconds later he was chasing her through the dark labyrinth of halls as she wove her way through the filthy interior.

Mara wants to do some exploring before we return. Terrill sent the message winging through the night to Caleb.

Are you kidding? And you're going to let her? You're out of your ever-loving mind! I'm coming back.

No, not until Yasmine is safe.

Fine, he said. *Stay out of trouble until I get there. I mean it, bro.*

Terrill smiled. *No problem.*

* * *

Mara followed the path provided by Raul and was drawn to another cell-like room. The lingering violence vibrating through it actually caused her to retch. Terrill dragged her out of the room. She took a deep breath and stepped out of his embrace. *We're running out of time. We need to split up.*

No. We're leaving. Now. A few minutes with Victor and we'll have our answers. His eyes gleamed in anticipation. *It's lucky for that mortal you took care of him before I could.*

Mara rolled her eyes. *Bloodthirsty much, aren't you? I don't doubt Victor's helping them, but he's not running this. We're missing something.*

Terrill looked skeptical. *Fifteen minutes, Mara. That's it. And you call immediately if you find anything.* He grasped her chin in his hand and forced her to look at him. *Any hint of trouble, Mara, I mean it. ANY hint.*

She grinned up at him. *What sort of trouble could I possibly get into with you here?*

He growled and she kissed him lightly before taking off down the hall.

CHAPTER FOURTEEN

Mara raced through the passageways, searching for the clues she'd taken from Raul's mind. The air was thick with remnants of better-forgotten emotions. She tried to block out the awful mix of violence and fear coating the walls as she sailed by. She paused outside the open doorway to a small viewing chamber with what looked to be a two-way mirror separating it from another room she'd not yet discovered the entrance to. The feelings it provoked had her senses tingling as if electrified. She swallowed the apprehension gathering inside her, took a deep breath, and entered.

Greasy fingerprints decorated the glass, and she looked in disgust at the drops of dried fluid on the floor that needed no explanation. She refused to imagine what the spectator had gotten so excited about. She used her foot to kick apart the trash piled carelessly around the room and came to a satisfying halt as she made contact with something solid. Finally! She knelt down and carefully picked up the smashed laptop buried among half-eaten meals long since discarded.

A rat scurried away, scolding her for depriving him of his meal. "Relax, little guy," she said as she smiled and moved away from his smorgasbord. "I'm not after your food." He looked at her as if considering whether or not to believe her before darting forward and pouncing on the hamburger her foot had uncovered.

She chuckled and returned her attention to her discovery. The screen was broken but she used her powers to turn it on and extract the information left on the hard drive. She smiled grimly. They'd probably tried to erase it, but her people had some amazing abilities to pull information off any electrical interface.

It was actually pretty cool how they did it. It didn't matter if the medium was active or not, they tapped into the electromagnetic currents attaching themselves to the equipment once they used their powers to charge it up. It was kind of like a virtual spiderweb invisible to others. The manipulation of electrical currents really wasn't that much different from manipulating other elements. They all emanated from a power found in nature.

She flinched at the images starting to pour into her as she handled the equipment. Once she had gotten everything she could off the computer, she used the same electrical wave slipstream to transfer them to an electric connection she could later access.

She moved to the corner of the room and dropped the laptop on the floor then poured energy back into the computer and melted it into an indistinguishable hunk of twisted metal. Satisfied no one could pull its sick conclusions or twisted research from it ever again, she headed back toward Terrill.

She blinked. Her eyes swept the large room before her. The faint odor of sulfur and soot rose from a barrel in the far corner. This didn't look familiar. She must have taken a wrong turn. She approached it cautiously. She struggled not to throw up as a nauseating sweet smell mixed with a more metallic one. Her eyes widened in horror when she realized what it was. Burnt flesh and hair. She held her breath. Something forced her closer. The smell clung to her nose and she found herself forced to take giant oxygen-starved breaths through her mouth.

Several fragments of paper floated out of the top of the barrel, miraculously escaping destruction. Mara picked up the pieces.

Embedded in the corner of one was a partial symbol. She felt an immediate sense of déjà vu and strained to remember where she'd seen it before. The last two days' events flashed lightning-fast through her mind.

When she'd arrived and the container opened ... the fist ... she'd seen a tattoo on that forearm. Damn. The image appeared smudged in her head, almost hidden or camouflaged. Why was it so hard to see? She focused harder on the symbol. There were two symbols, not just one. Then she remembered. Raul. Queasiness had never stopped her from pursuing anything before, but she found herself suddenly reticent to re-enter the room where he'd died. She winced. No, she needed to be honest with herself. The room where she'd killed him.

Mara, are you all right?

Duh ... of course Terrill would have picked up on that. *I'm fine. Just have to check on one more thing.* She reoriented herself and changed course, heading to the room where she'd left Raul.

You're fifteen minutes are up.

She ignored him and the jarring disquiet eating at he, the closer she got to her destination. She shook her head. This place was starting to give her the creeps. She entered the chamber and crouched down over the awkwardly sprawled body. She shuddered. Even in death, he exuded sickness.

She made herself lean over him and turn over his right arm, ripping away the sleeve to bare his forearm. There it was. This was the mark of the Society that had been sent to find her. The characters 净血 were Chinese for Pure Blood. Why were these mortals so obvious about their affiliation, scarcely hiding their intent behind such clear symbols? And what sort of a Pure Blood organization mixed with other species? Before she had time to analyze further, the door slammed shut. Cold air blasted into the room. She heard the ominous sound of the lock engaging. Crap, not again.

Terrill!

Terrill materialized opposite Claudio. "Claudio, so nice to see you. You saved me the trouble of looking you up later."

Claudio sent him a withering look as he turned away from the door to face him. "Terrill, Terrill," he clucked his tongue and shook his head in mock sadness. "You always did have a problem seeing the bigger picture. Once again you have no idea the significance of what's going on here or what you could be a part of. They will deify us once they learn what we have accomplished!"

"Immortality is no longer enough for you? You now seek worship and adoration?"

An angry response twitched across Claudio's mouth before he bit it back and offered a placating smile. "And you would risk everything over the life of a Viajante?"

Terrill merely stared unblinkingly at him.

"You did realize she was Viajante, didn't you?" Claudio asked. "Don't tell me she fooled you with that mortal façade of hers. I know they have some abilities to control minds, if not controlled first, but you?" He smiled and flexed his arms in front of him then stopped and mocked slapping himself on the head. "Oh, I get it! She convinced you she was your other half? Your soul? A Viajante? Really? I have to admit, I'm shocked as hell you fell for it." He appeared to examine his fingernails as he waited for a response.

"She fooled you once before though, didn't she, Claudio?"

Claudio glared as he clenched and unclenched his fists.

Terrill moved forward, forcing Claudio to choose between moving away from the door or allowing Terrill to close the distance between them. Claudio chose the former.

"Who are you working with? I never took you for the scientific type."

Can you see the lock or controls? Mara asked. *If you can focus on it. I can link with you and help move it.*

You'll have to do it silently while I keep him distracted. Are you all right?

Yes. The cold's getting a little, ah, uncomfortable, but nothing I can't handle. Terrill, I wouldn't want to be in here much longer though, she grudgingly admitted.

Claudio hissed. "The Society is growing. Soon there will be no one to stop us from reaching our goals."

What goals? Mara asked Terrill.

Not now, Mara!

Terrill sighed his expression one of sad commiseration. "Ah, but how strong can you really be, Claudio? You lost her twice. Left her in the care of mortals. Mortals she was able to escape from. Your Society seems to have a few weak links. And your partners? Not overly impressive, I'd have to say."

"Escaped? The past matters little. She is quite well taken ca—" He flicked his eyes to the chamber where he'd imprisoned her.

At that instant, Mara launched herself from behind the now unlocked doors. She attacked and sank her teeth into his shoulder.

Before Terrill could reach her, Claudio flung her off with a vicious snap and sent her crashing into the wall behind him so hard the fury of his incensed growl rang in her ears. She hit with a thud, sliding down its smooth surface before collapsing in an undignified heap. Dazed and bloodied, she struggled to get to her feet, scrambling for purchase among the debris littering the floor. She strained to focus on the battle unfolding in front of her.

She watched the two Vampires square off. Claudio was strong, she realized – almost an equal match for Terrill. She reached out tentatively for Terrill's mind.

Don't worry, he said. *Claudio's strength lies primarily in his ability to ambush or surprise his victims – something not possible here.*

Even so, Mara didn't feel reassured. She cautiously moved around the two Warriors circling each other in a dangerous and deadly dance. If she could just get a better position, she might be able to help Terrill.

"What's the matter, Claudio, afraid to pick on someone your own size?"

Claudio ripped the metal door off its hinges and sent it flying toward Terrill. Before Mara could call out a warning, wood and metal fragments from the room behind Terrill quickly followed.

Terrill easily deflected the missiles. "That's the best you've got?"

Claudio paused and cast a murderous glance at Mara before turning his attention back to Terrill. "What do you think?" Even as the words left his mouth the damaged door Terrill had deflected was once again airborne and headed straight for her.

Too late Mara realized she hadn't left herself a way out and she backpedaled furiously, biting down on her lip as the door hammered her into the wall like a lumpy nail before she was able to refocus enough energy to push it away.

Claudio used Terrill's distraction to seize the advantage. Mara screamed as he drove his hand into Terrill's chest, clawing at his heart and trying to tear it from his body. Linked to Terrill, Mara felt the shredding of tissue and cracking of bone as Claudio dug through his ribcage and clutched greedily at the heart. The pain was excruciating.

Terrill smashed his fist into Claudio's jaw, the satisfying sound of bone shattering audible above the scuffle. Claudio hissed and spat blood before curving his lips in a gloating smile of delight.

Mara felt Terrill's strength diminishing as the blood drain increased. She had to get Claudio away from him before he lost any more. She struggled to get to her feet. Her muscles bunched and she prepared herself to attack.

Like an angry wind, Caleb ripped into their midst, colliding with Terrill and Claudio. The impact severed the limb ripping at Terrill's heart from Claudio's body and snapped his neck.

It took a second for her to realize that the bloody rush of bodies that had just rolled past her like tumbleweeds meant it was really over.

Caleb removed Claudio's hand from Terrill's chest and flung it at the now motionless body. He carefully leaned Terrill against the wall.

"What, you couldn't wait for me? Had to save all the fun for yourself?"

Terrill smiled wanly at him. "You always were a show-off." He looked around anxiously. "Mara?"

She fell forward from her forgotten crouch and clambered up clumsily. She made it to his side just as he started to slide down to the floor. "Damn it, Terrill!" Disregarding her own injuries, she used her tongue to close the wounds she could, slowing down his blood loss. The pool of blood rapidly forming around him had her heart racing. She wouldn't lose him – not like this!

Caleb looked shocked to discover the extent of Terrill's wounds. "It's bad. We need to get him back to Gabriella."

Mara shook her head. "He won't make it that far." She laid him down on the floor and placed her hands on his chest.

"What are you going to do?" he asked suspiciously.

"I can heal his wounds, but he's going to need your blood. At least until he can hunt again and get his strength back."

"Why can't he take yours?"

"I need you to take care of Claudio. He can't be allowed to recover."

Clearly torn between his desire to help Terrill and the knowledge that something would have to be done quickly before anyone else appeared, he nodded and slung Claudio's body over his shoulder. He picked up the severed arm and left to destroy the evidence.

Mara sent herself into his body, repairing the damage as quickly as she could. Like a surgeon, she mentally stitched together the torn tissue and muscle. She couldn't stop all the blood loss while she healed him, only slow it. She worked as fast as she could to repair arteries and veins. Once the bleeding was contained, he'd be all right. Finally satisfied she'd done all she could and that he would recover, she collapsed next to him.

Mara, we need to get you out of here.

She snorted. *Get ME out of here? You're in no shape to do anything. I'm the one taking care of you.*

Even with her eyes closed, she felt Caleb's return.

"Is he going to be okay?" Caleb asked.

She nodded slightly, the effort to do so suddenly seeming gigantic. "He needs blood."

Caleb took his place at his friend's side and cut open his wrist for Terrill to drink, stopping him only after he'd taken enough to survive.

Mara.

She stirred restlessly. He sounded stronger. That was a good sign she thought to herself as she sighed in relief.

Never place yourself in danger again!

She opened her eyes and muttered something uncomplimentary back. He smiled.

"I see she's taken well to your particular style of discipline," Caleb said, barely suppressing his laughter. "I'm certain this experience will cure her of acting independently, don't you think?"

"Shut up," he said warmly. "Let's get out of here."

Caleb looked like he wanted to disagree with Terrill's plans to carry her, but held his tongue as Terrill stood. He struggled to maintain his balance with Mara in his arms. Neither one spared a glance behind them as they launched themselves into the night sky.

CHAPTER FIFTEEN

Mara awoke and stretched slowly, the ache of her muscles less than what she'd expected. She didn't see Terrill. She hoped that meant he was no longer angry with her and had started some new project.

"I wouldn't count on it."

He had fed and was back at full strength. She stood up quickly, unwilling to remain at a disadvantage. She winced as muscles tightened and pulled against bruised skin. He was at her side instantly. She smiled at his protective streak. He wasn't really so tough after all.

"Yasmine?" she asked.

He ran his hands down her face, parting the vibrant red curtain of hair framing it. "She's fine. Anxious to see you." She nodded and threw on the clothes he'd provided for her. "As are my parents."

She stopped in mid-action, her shirt not yet covering her. She pushed her head through in slow motion and freed her hair from its confines then turned to look at Terrill. "Your parents?"

He gave her one of his wicked grins.

She groaned. "I'm imagining that I'm not quite what your parents were expecting, right? Should I be worried?" He didn't answer. "Terrill!"

He just smiled that damn bad-boy smile of his and blew her a kiss as he left the bedroom. "Guess you'll have to get dressed to find out. Hurry up. I'll be back for you in a few minutes."

Still fuming at his infuriating superior attitude, she finished changing and tugged a brush through her unruly hair, grimacing as the tangles caught and ripped small knots out.

She opened the door as Terrill appeared outside its frame.

"Ready?" he asked.

He laughed at the less-than-thrilled expression on her face and kissed her. As they headed through the house, he silently shared the ribbing he'd already gotten from Caleb.

So . . . I'm not the only one who thinks you're the big bad wolf? she asked.

Grrrrrr.

She laughed and let him lead her into the great room where the others had already assembled. She recognized the couple standing near the fireplace as those she'd seen talking with Terrill at Victor's party. Like Terrill, his father exuded power. His brilliant blue eyes missed nothing. Mara could tell he accepted nothing less than the entire truth from whomever he dealt with, and that he was used to getting it. Great. Well, at least she now knew where Terrill got it from. She turned her attention to the woman at his side. Deceptively petite, the power she masked let Mara know she too was a force to be reckoned with. Her smile implied she was aware of Mara's thoughts.

"Mara, allow me to formally present my father, Lauris, and my mother, Gabriella."

Mara stepped forward to greet them, half-expecting Lauris to prevent her from getting too close. That he made no physical move to do so seemed more from a desire to please his soul than to act as his instincts directed. She found herself pulling up her shields in response. She amplified her Vampire façade, hoping to make them more comfortable.

Gabriella gently laid a hand on Mara's arm. "That isn't necessary." She smiled at Mara. "Your birth name, Amara, is such a beautiful name," she said, "but Mara suits you as well."

"Thank you." She let Terrill pull her back against him. "If you will excuse me, Yasmine's waiting for me."

They nodded and Mara turned and headed toward the opposite end of the room, her connection to her aunt providing a mental map. The door opened as Mara approached and Morgan exited. She smiled and squeezed Mara's hand before heading toward Caleb.

Unable to contain her concern long enough for Yasmine to appear, Mara called, *Are you all right?*

This has to be one of the weirdest long-term hallucinations I've ever had. Yasmine laughed softly. *Am I really in the midst of a Vampire lair?*

I'm afraid so. Mara chuckled as she closed the door behind her and threw herself into Yasmine's arms. She was acting more like Morgan than her normally more-reserved self, but she couldn't help it. "I'm so glad you're okay. You are okay, aren't you?" She stepped back and anxiously examined her aunt for injuries. She was relieved that it looked like the worst had started to heal.

Yasmine patted her hand in reassurance. "Yes, Mara, I'm fine."

The lack of blame in her voice made Mara feel guilty and she hung her head. "I'm sorry it took so long to get there. I should have known something was wrong and tried to make contact earlier. Maybe I could have done something before the attack . . ."

Mara saw the sheen in Yasmine's eyes as she vehemently shook her head. "Mara, there's no way you could have done anything to stop it." She composed herself and forced a smile. "We need to find the way ahead. You have information the others need. I think that's where we should focus, don't you?"

Mara nodded. They all needed answers. Their lives might very well depend on it. Together, they returned to the others.

"Yasmine," Gabriella said, "we know you've been through a great deal already, but your observations and experiences . . ." She smiled gently in encouragement. "It takes great courage to do what you are doing and to trust us – those who you believed the enemy."

Yasmine nodded. "You've all been so kind to me, a stranger and also considered an enemy. I'm still trying to take it all in. Mara and I are ready. We just need a place to plug in a laptop."

Mara looked at their puzzled faces and back at Terrill's as he set it up on the table. "I can pull energy from any object, but a charged one helps amplify the results. I want a medium strong enough to show you all what we're facing."

Gabriella led them to the formal dining table and everyone took seats.

As she sat down next to Yasmine, Mara looked over at Terrill, who dimmed the lights in anticipation of her request. She powered up the computer.

A startled sound left Morgan's lips as the image on the computer screen was mirrored on the wall. Mara laughed and winked at Terrill as Yasmine placed her hand on Mara's arm and the image quality intensified. Gabriella looked at her speculatively. "All your kind are capable of such?"

Mara shook her head. "We all have powers to cause others to see things. Those are mental projections into the mind, not visible outside the mind to others. This is a sort of extension of that. We can tap into electronic nets and circuits and pick up virtual information. But combining the two takes a little more practice. This started as a trick when I was little and Dabir and Yasmine wouldn't let me watch the shows I wanted to. I sort of tapped into the TV and projected it into my room."

Yasmine chuckled affectionately. "She always was a handful."

Was? Terrill asked.

Mara nearly bit her tongue in an effort to avoid from sticking it out at him.

Lauris stared at Yasmine's hand on Mara's arm before returning his eyes to Yasmine's. "So how does it work? Is your physical contact with Mara feeding her power? Somehow enhancing the projection?"

"Lending power or manipulating currents is as normal to us as breathing," Yasmine said. "We learn to survive as a unit and help each other. Mara is more than capable of holding the image or performing other functions without my help, but my assistance makes it easier and costs me little."

"Wicked cool," said Caleb. "So, Mara, if we keep you around for football season, we won't need a big-screen TV, right?"

Mara hid a smile as Morgan socked Caleb. "You're worse than a child!" Morgan whispered.

Mara's lips twitched.

Are you ready? Terrill asked.

She drew in a deep breath. *Yes.*

"Let's get started," Terrill said.

Pictures flashed on the wall as she sifted through the scraps of information she'd downloaded. Colors and words whirled across the projected screen in a drunken cornucopia of notations, coded transmissions, and symbols as she sought to organize the random numbers and letters into something coherent. Her brow furrowed in concentration as she tried to decipher the riddles.

"Mara, was there anything else you saw there that you didn't download that might help sort this all out?" Gabriella asked.

Mara was startled for an instant then remembered the powers Terrill said his mother had. She nodded. Instantly the Chinese symbols she'd discovered on Raul's forearm were scorched into the wall.

Morgan looked anxiously at the characters and then back at Mara. "Those will come out, won't they?"

Mara laughed and cast a chagrined look at Yasmine before answering her. "Yes, they will. The first few times I tried it, the results were . . . a little more permanent than I'd planned."

Lauris got up and walked over to the characters, staring at them intently as he traced the figures. "Pure Blood." He looked at Terrill. "And you're certain this is an alliance between Vampire and mortal? Not Vampire using mortals?"

Terrill nodded. "It appears that way. Mara ran into both a couple of months ago before she came into the city. That time Claudio killed the mortal he was with in front of her. And again, Claudio was involved in her capture. The mortals may be the ones doing the research now, but they are definitely in league with the Vampires."

"Their minds were protected," Mara said. "I couldn't read them easily – not without them discovering it."

Terrill pushed away from the wall and unfolded his arms as he approached. "So the mind blocks are to protect them from Vampires or to prevent the Vampires from discovering something, but . . ."

Lauris moved back toward Gabriella.

"The time you couldn't contact me," Terrill said as he placed his hand on her shoulder. "What was different?"

"I'm not sure. I could talk with Yasmine . . ."

"Because they were not specifically targeting Viajante communications," Yasmine broke in.

Caleb drummed his fingers on the table. "These mortals were working with these Vampire cats, but obviously didn't trust them. They designed mind blocks and somehow found a way to inhibit communication." He looked at Gabriella and Lauris. "But how?"

"It could have been the shot they gave me," Mara said. "But that doesn't explain why a Vampire would give me something to prevent me from communicating with other Vampires, unless the Vampire thought it did something else. Maybe something told to them by mortals? Maybe that's what they were hiding?"

"Who's behind all this?" Lauris asked. "Is it Victor or not? Why would he risk a confrontation with Viajante over a mortal alliance? Could this Society be sanctioned by the High Court?"

"Not likely," said Terrill. "The courts are generally too wrapped up in political struggles to let an actual war disrupt their petty power plays. And why make an alliance with mortals? Not exactly the strongest power play."

"There is something more we haven't talked about." Mara stopped and looked at Yasmine, who nodded slightly. "We think Viajantes are involved."

The others exchanged shocked looks.

"Viajante and Vampire working together?" Morgan asked.

"As we are?" Mara smiled. "It may not be that far-fetched. Or it may be that each knows nothing of the other's involvement. But the way they got to Yasmine and what they knew about us, Viajante collaboration is the only explanation we can come up with. Add that to the fact our communications were uninterrupted and it doesn't leave too many other options, does it?"

"The question I have is why," Yasmine said. "What are they trying to do? Or what are they trying to prevent?"

"The name," Morgan said. "The answer is in the name. Pure Blood. Maybe the mortals are trying to purify or distill their blood. Taking from Vampire and Viajante to create something they can use. Perhaps to enhance their abilities or their defenses against us. Maybe they seek to create something new."

"How can they even know about us? Immortals work hard to hide their existence from mortals," Caleb said, "but I suppose some do know about us. We don't exactly live invisible lives."

Mara rose from her seat. "I guess that's one option." She crossed the room to the wall and waved her hand to flip through the data projected there. "Here's some sort of scientific formula."

Yasmine looked up from the keyboard and at the information reflected on the wall. "But if the mortals are seeking to do this, how are they getting Vampire and Viajante cooperation? Neither species is stupid enough to willingly assist mortals in creating a weapon to destroy their own species."

"Victor may be a lot of things," Lauris said, "but stupid and wanting the end of his own kind, he's not."

"Maybe he doesn't know everything about the mortals either," Terrill said. "They've taken significant steps to protect themselves. Maybe whoever's been dealing with Victor has been successful in keeping their true purpose from him. They may believe what they are contributing will destroy those they're collaborating with. Claudio hinted at something hugely significant. Maybe that's what he believed too."

Caleb looked at the information projected in front of him and then back to Mara. "So why go after Mara?"

They were all startled by Gabriella's laugh. She pointed at Terrill. "Because he wants her."

Terrill appeared to consider it. "If Victor was approached by this Society, he may have helped simply because it gave him an opportunity to get back at me. But this opportunity only presented itself recently."

"And they came after me before we met."

"Exactly. They had an agenda. You. They went to Victor to get to you." He chuckled. "They used him."

Lauris and Caleb also looked amused at the thought.

"Mara, what have you told them about your family?" Yasmine asked.

Terrill started to step closer to Mara but she waved him away. By the sudden silence in the room, it was obvious Terrill had already had this discussion or at least a partial one.

She faced the other couples. "Victor was responsible for the deaths of my parents, and until recently I thought him responsible for the death of my sister, Celeste."

Gabriella spoke softly. "It's clear that Victor is somehow involved in this Society. We need to be careful."

What do you mean by 'until recently'? What happened to Celeste? Yasmine asked her.

Mara paled. She'd been so overwhelmed with Yasmine's news she hadn't told her what she'd discovered. She relayed what she'd learned as the conversation flowed around them.

Terrill nodded. "We'll keep an eye on him, but there are other threats, maybe even greater ones in play that now require our attention as well."

Yasmine's hand trembled.

Are you okay? Mara asked her. *I know it's a lot to take in, but she's out there and we're going to find her. Victor isn't going to prevent it. I won't lose her again.*

Yasmine placed her hands back in her lap and smiled. *I just can't believe it. Imagine finding her after all this time.*

Mara returned her attention back to the discussion.

"We need to discover more about this Society and its goals," Terrill said.

Mara nodded. "It may take some time to decipher these codes and determine what the formulas are for – find out if they're any good or not."

Terrill shook his head. "Maybe it won't be so difficult. Yasmine, what can you tell us about the Viajante couple that disappeared – the ones you left Sanctuary to go after."

Yasmine appeared startled to be the focus of attention. Mara watched her with concern as she collected her thoughts. "Kali and Augustine were heading back to her family home. They wanted to be there when—" She gasped and turned pale. "Mara, it can't be because—"

"What can't be? Don't keep us in suspense," Caleb burst in.

Mara faced him. "Kali was pregnant. I think she was who I sensed inside that building, in that room where . . ." Now she needed to pause and collect herself. "She's the Viajante that I detected had been killed there." She snuck a glance at Yasmine, who was so pale a ghost would look like a Hawaiian Tropic model next to her.

"But why take them? Are they related to you?" Caleb asked.

Gabriella stared at Mara. "What aren't you telling us?"

Mara locked eyes, knowing her bluff had been called. It was time they knew. "They wanted someone like me – a mix – and they sought a pregnant Viajante to experiment on in order to get it."

Terrill took her slightly shaking hand. "When my parents were attacked, I was bitten and almost killed. My mother helped me convert my cells to a form both species accepted. It was the only way I could survive."

"I didn't tell them anything beyond Victor's responsibility for the death of your parents. You need to tell them the rest," Terrill said. "They'll understand."

She inhaled a jagged breath. "After we were left for dead, Victor showed up. He attacked my mother and his attack released Celeste, my sister, from my mother's masking spell. Victor saw her and took her away with him, leaving the rest of us to burn. I never knew what happened to her until I saw her portrait at his house the night of the ball."

Morgan brought her hand to her face. "Angelica?"

"Yes," Mara said and swallowed painfully. "Victor must have turned her. I think she knows nothing of her background or the circumstances of her upbringing. I intend to find her."

Lauris's expression was icy. "If she is your sister, Victor has much to account for. Knowledge of her existence and yours would explain the interest this Society has with you."

"We don't think they knew anything about Mara – at least not until recently," Yasmine said. Mara heard the self-doubt in her aunt's voice. "Mara and Nicolette did such a good job faking Mara's death, we believed ourselves successful at fooling anyone who might have come after her," Yasmine continued. "We prevented her from leaving Sanctuary until she came of age, protecting her even more by creating more distance between any remaining rumors and myths."

"It no longer matters when they knew or how they found out," Terrill said. "Our only option now is to assume they do and to act accordingly."

Lauris crossed his arms and leaned back. "I guess the question still comes back to who's playing who? Are the mortals seeking to play both sides or are they merely the pawns of one? And if so, which one?"

"We haven't seen or heard of anything like this before among our kind, but we don't maintain close ties with the other courts other than the normal hierarchical requirements." Caleb frowned. "If there are Vampires in on this, perhaps our disconnected communications are exactly the sort of thing these mortals are counting on."

"Mara, when they captured you, what did they do with you?" Gabriella asked. "Yasmine may or may not have been the bait to snare you, but what were their plans for you? And why didn't they act on them immediately?"

Mara saw where she was going. "Because they were waiting for something or someone first."

Gabriella nodded her approval.

"But they didn't expect Terrill and Caleb to come after you, else they would have increased their fortifications, right?" Morgan asked.

Mara shrugged.

"Who were they expecting?" Yasmine asked. "Who were they waiting for?"

Terrill shook his head. "Claudio would never have been working for Victor. He held him in as much disdain as we do. There must have been someone else powerful pulling the strings."

Gabriella suddenly stiffened, her eyes glazing over as she stared, sightless, out the windows behind them. Her voice sounded strangely hollow as she spoke. "Something approaches. Something dangerous."

The males exchanged glances and silently assessed defensive options and prepared to move the females to a safer location.

"How long?" Lauris asked.

"Now."

They turned in shock as Yasmine threw open the French doors and disappeared across the threshold into the now ominously silent night.

CHAPTER SIXTEEN

Mara leaped out of her seat and beat Terrill to the door by milliseconds. He pushed in front of her, shifting her behind him and to the left of the door with a velvet fluidity she hadn't expected. Caleb and Lauris exploded onto the patio behind him. Their exit was met by a deafening clap of thunder. Torrential rains drenched the landscape without warning and Mara jumped as the horizon was suddenly ablaze with wiggling tentacles of electricity streaking prophetically across the skies.

Through the downpour, Mara saw Yasmine sprint down the stairs into the expansive garden. Where was she going? Mara looked at Terrill and saw the same question engraved on his face. He gave her a look designed to ensure her capitulation to his edict to remain in the house. With that, Caleb and Lauris spread out silently in flanking positions and disappeared into the rain and dark.

As if. Mara took off after Yasmine with Gabriella and Morgan in close pursuit. Her concern for Yasmine caused her to revert back to accepting her Viajante limitations instead of concentrating on her Vampire powers, and the pursuers soon caught up with her.

"Mara, stop! We need a plan." Morgan tackled her. She slipped in the mud but refused to release her hold while they struggled. Mara stopped moving and nodded. Morgan reluctantly released her. "I need to be there. You have to let me. I can't explain it. Something horrible will happen to Yasmine if I don't get there first."

Gabriella touched her arm lightly. "Yes, I can sense that. But you still need to be careful."

Mara grinned at Gabriella's calm. "Has your spidey-sense ever been wrong?"

Gabriella laughed. "My what?"

Mara stood, pushing her now mud-soaked hair out of her eyes. "Spidey-sense. Like Spider-Man? That's what I call my special little insights."

"You have a very interesting way of talking. Spidey-sense," Gabriella chuckled. "I think it's good Terrill has found you."

They heard Yasmine cry out and Mara's heart almost froze. She found her feet already in motion, sliding for traction. Her mind struggled to catch up as she ran full tilt toward her aunt. This time she didn't forget her new Vampire powers.

She reached the clearing quickly, easily outdistancing her companions. Something warned her of danger and she skidded to a halt too late. She found herself suddenly airborne. She slammed into the ground several hundred feet away before she realized just what she'd stumbled into. The faint electric charge and ozone smell in the air quickly gave it away. She rolled quickly to the left and rocked back into a fighting stance as she surveyed the situation.

Gabriella and Morgan had seen her attacked and had fallen back into protected positions. Morgan communicated their plan to back her up if needed. She didn't yet see Terrill but knew he was there, using his powers to shield himself from detection. The sheets of rain blanketing the night certainly helped, but it was the unpredictability of the lightning that threatened exposure.

She moved carefully, hugging the ground, and used her best camouflage skills to inch forward, still not sure who or what they faced. She discovered that even her new Vampire speed didn't completely protect her. She grunted and flinched in pain each time her position was discovered and a burst of wind or electricity slammed into her. She'd almost reached the cover of a small clump of trees before a particularly savage strike hammered into her, spinning her like a child's toy before smashing her against the ground.

She groaned, unable to concentrate on anything but the pain as her body involuntarily curled itself into a ball. She felt another strike coming and painfully dragged herself out of the line of fire. The smell of singed hair indicated just how close her attacker had come to scoring another direct hit.

Damn it, Mara, get back!

I can't! And I won't.

I can make you! Terrill threatened.

Mara shook her head, sending water spraying as she hunched over, panting from the last near miss. *Not this time you can't.*

He sent the impression of strangling her unconscious and locking her in a tower on some far away remote island. One he thought she wouldn't be able to get out of.

She grinned. *Yeah, as if.*

He gritted his teeth in frustration.

Keeping him focused on me gives you an advantage.

Be more careful then, he admonished, mentally sending her instructions on how to do that.

She gave him the impression of blowing a kiss then crawled forward. He growled out loud.

The night shadows seemed to twist and contort in front of her, moving as if animated by some macabre puppeteer. A strange sense of disquiet slithered down her spine. Who controlled the elements, the night colors, and the shadows? Could this be the Viajante collaborator they sought? Whoever it was had incredible masking skills. She shared her suspicions with Terrill, knowing he would forward it to the others orchestrating the counter-attack.

Damn. She'd lingered too long in one place. She felt the crackle of power building and lunged right. The attack caught her by the ankle, and the pain caused her to bite her lip. She pulled her foot into her and placed her hands over the injury and attempted to ease the pain while rolling to avoid the next attack.

Immense shadowy shapes swirled and twisted angrily, obscuring her view ahead, but she knew she was close. She focused on the forms in front of her and used her mind to push past them, bending them in such a way she could see through the rain bouncing off the hard ground to her target. Her eyes widened at what she thought she saw.

Your shields! Terrill shouted.

Surprise had left her vulnerable to the attack. The force of the strike pitched her through the air again, her body actually completing a full rotation before the ground caught her in a bone-crunching embrace and heaved her away so that she flopped around like a disjointed ragdoll before finally rolling to a stop. She groaned as the impact knocked the wind out of her and cursed herself for being so stupid.

Mara knew Terrill would use the attack on her to launch one of his own. Through eyes opened to slits, she watched him move in a blur of speed, his attack beautifully choreographed to coincide with those of Lauris and Caleb. Even the deadly intent with which they struck wasn't enough to bring down their attacker. Mara tried not to look at Yasmine lying motionless on the ground.

Gabriella and Morgan helped Mara to her feet. They heard a cry. Finally, it looked like the attacker had taken a serious blow and was going down.

Mara took off running. She directed her energy at all the combatants equally and flung them backward with a force she didn't know she had. Not knowing how long that would stop them, she flew at their attacker, intent on protecting him with her body.

Groggy from the power hit they had just taken, Terrill and the others shook off the aftereffects and slowly approached her.

It's Dabir, Yasmine's soul. He must have somehow survived and followed her here.

Mara turned to look at Yasmine checking Dabir for injuries. Don't let her have been too late.

He attacked us, Mara. He attacked you too, or did you forget that? Terrill asked. *Come to think of it, you attacked us too. What the hell were you thinking?*

Mara watched him unconsciously touch the newly forming bruise on his hip that he'd gotten on impact. Even in the pouring rain and covered in mud, he looked damn good.

Give me a chance to talk with him, she pleaded. *He's family.*

He motioned to the others to halt their advance and take up defensive positions while she did.

Grateful for his understanding, Mara turned to a now-conscious Dabir staring at both her and Yasmine in disbelief. The rain mixed with blood trickling from a nasty cut to his head painted a surprising picture of weakness, not something she'd ever associated with Dabir before.

"I must be losing my mind, first finding Yasmine, now you." He touched Yasmine's arm, looking deep into her eyes before turning his gaze to Mara. "Those were Vampires I fought, right? Vampires? What's going on, Mara? Why are they holding you?"

Yasmine gently stroked his face as his head lay in her lap. "It isn't what you think. They rescued me."

Judging from their intent expressions, Mara could tell Yasmine was using their link to try to catch him up on everything that had happened.

Dabir lifted his hand to wipe away Yasmine's tears then turned his attention back to Mara. "You have other answers for me?"

Mara grinned at the demand in his voice. He was going to be fine. "Only if you're ready for them."

He nodded and grimaced as they helped him to his feet. Terrill appeared at her side. "I guess I owe you an apology," Dabir said stiffly to Terrill.

"We have much to talk about," he agreed.

They returned to the house slowly, cautiously crossing the now-muddy gardens while the rain continued unabated. Yasmine supported Dabir as he limped painfully across the threshold and into the house. Once out of the rain, Lauris directed them toward a bedchamber.

Mara lingered behind on the balcony with Terrill, watching the couples enter and the byplay or lack thereof between them.

They are to stay in a different area of the house? she asked, noticing that the quarters Yasmine and Dabir were directed to were not where she had found Yasmine.

A precaution, Terrill answered without remorse.

She watched the rain transform itself into a light drizzle before dissolving into clouds. Terrill tugged at her hand and she followed him inside, leaving tentative rays of sunshine peeking through the remaining clouds. She inhaled the soft scent of fresh rain on the wind and cast one last look down the passageway Yasmine and Dabir had taken.

CHAPTER SEVENTEEN

I f the atmosphere had been considered tense the night before, it was damn near electric now. Mara fought to keep her frustration with the situation to herself.

She looked at Yasmine and expected to see some of the happiness she'd felt upon Terrill's arrival after her own capture mirrored in her aunt's eyes. She frowned, noticing instead the tense set of her lips. It looked like she was trying to keep herself from crying.

Mara tried to imagine what she'd be going through if she'd thought Terrill dead. Even with as little time as they'd been together, it would be ugly. She couldn't even fathom how much more intense it would have been if she'd known Terrill as long as Yasmine had Dabir. No wonder she looked like a basket case.

Terrill entered the room and locked eyes with Mara. He was suspicious of Dabir and he didn't bother to hide it. "I assume you've had a chance to rest and are up to this," he asked Dabir. Mara barely concealed a sharply indrawn hiss at his tone.

Terrill kept his eyes focused on Dabir, who responded only with a slight incline of his head. His expression of distrust matched Terrill's.

Lauris's subtle motion drew her attention to Gabriella. She appeared to be in distress. Mara threw a layer of tranquility over

Gabriella's emotions, muting the intensity, and monitored her for any sign it had helped. Mara knew only too well the burdens that came with being so finely attuned to the thoughts and emotions of others. And she only had a fraction of the powers Gabriella did. She should have been more considerate.

"Thank you," Gabriella whispered.

"I ask that you all try and keep your emotions under control." Lauris stood and placed his hands on his soul's shoulders in a protective gesture. "We have things we need to clear up that concern us all. There's no room for distrust and anger among ourselves."

Gabriella's soft voice picked up where he left off. "I need to be able to concentrate."

Dabir looked confused for a moment, and then his expression cleared. "She's a seer, sensitive to emotions, isn't she?" He straightened, like Mara, also striving to calm the environment. "I understand and I apologize."

Mara's thoughts circled back to the attack on Yasmine and Dabir. Something wasn't adding up. She turned to Dabir. "Dabir, what happened the day you two were attacked? Yasmine told us about you heading out after the missing couple and about the attack, but how did you survive?"

The more she thought about it, the more confused she was. She was thrilled he'd survived, but why had Yasmine thought him dead when he wasn't? The bond between like souls was incredibly strong. She felt Terrill watching her as the troubling thoughts galloped through her mind.

Oh, shut up already, she told him.

He half-heartedly attempted to contain his smirk. *So, I'm not the only one with questions? Good. Never accept anything on blind faith, Mara, no matter who it comes from. Trust, but verify.*

She felt immediately remorseful for doubting Dabir. He'd practically raised her, for Pete's sake! What was she thinking? Terrill was a Warrior. He'd survived on his instincts for centuries.

Naturally, he'd be suspicious of everybody. That didn't mean she had to be. She waited for Dabir's reply.

When Mara turned her attention back to Dabir, a fleeting look of disdain marred his features before disappearing as if never there.

"We were ambushed," he said. "It was extremely well planned and they were prepared for us. I was left for dead with Augustine. One of the Vampires stayed behind to take care of us while they took Yasmine away. I didn't realize she was still alive at first . . ."

He looked directly at Yasmine and squeezed her hand. "Yasmine never saw them destroy me. It must have been the drugs. I was knocked out for a short time, but they didn't get the chance to finish the job."

Yasmine looked like she was trying to remember something and a slightly confused look passed over her face before her features smoothed out and she nodded.

"He's right, I didn't actually see it happen. I guess the horror of what I expected them to do combined with what they told me about throwing the bodies into the fire. I eventually came to believe I'd seen it happen." She rubbed her forehead in a distracted motion.

Dabir patted her hand. "Needless to say, they'd miscalculated. I killed the one they left behind and then escaped. I searched for clues as to where they'd taken Yasmine, but couldn't find a trail." He clenched and unclenched his fists. "Nothing has ever tested my faith like that feeling of helplessness did when I realized I could do nothing to find her. I don't ever want to feel that again."

Yasmine's eyes shone with unshed tears. Even Mara felt her eyes cloud at the obviously strong emotions flowing between them. Not ready to accept her own feelings about Terrill and how she would have handled it, she steadily avoided his inquisitive gaze.

Dabir continued. "I went back to Sanctuary and we mounted a search." He shook his head in frustration. "No one found anything. I had a vague sense of a southerly direction, but nothing more. After a while, the search was disbanded. The elders felt there wasn't enough to go on and fearing additional attacks, didn't want to let me go out on my own."

"What?" Mara asked, "The elders forbade you from going?" Her brow wrinkled in puzzlement. She had never heard of any such edict ever having been issued before. Surely they were just acting on Dabir's behalf, worried about his emotional state at the time, right?

Dabir grimaced and looked hesitant to continue. "I'm sorry, Mara, not all of them were opposed. Only one, but he was able to sway the others."

Mara gasped, instantly knowing who among the elders would have that ability. "Sinjon? But why? How could he ever seek to keep souls apart, allow Yasmine to be abandoned?"

Dabir shook his head. "I think he believed he acted for the benefit of those remaining in Sanctuary over the few."

Mara noticed that he hadn't released his hold on Yasmine's hand.

"I think he feared further pursuit would result in all-out war."

Mara was grateful that Dabir was as strong as he was to defy Sinjon and the elders, or else he would never have continued to hunt for Yasmine. "How did you finally find her?" she asked.

"I didn't have any luck for the longest time, but when you escaped that place . . ." His face twisted into an ugly scowl. Yasmine must have shared with him what had happened during her captivity. "She called out to me and gave me a trail to follow."

Terrill turned his iron-gray gaze on Yasmine. "You didn't know anything about his survival until last night?"

Yasmine shook her head. "I was as surprised as you when he appeared." She gulped away tears. "I hadn't tried to contact him after it happened except that one time. Had I known . . ."

"Why didn't you contact her and let her know you were all right?" Morgan broke in. "Mara told us that the connection between souls among your people is like it is between ours. Once you found her, why didn't you communicate?"

"I didn't know who she was with and what sort of control they had over her. I came across some sort of Society connected to her capture and that of the young couple we were tracking, but I wasn't able to learn more than that." He looked down at their intertwined hands before looking up again. "I didn't know if she was still my Yasmine. I couldn't risk anything that would give away my presence, and thus my only advantage, before I could make my move."

Something isn't right about this, Terrill said to Mara, his face expressionless. "Yasmine," he asked, "did you know it was him when you ran into the garden?"

Yasmine detangled her hands from Dabir's and rubbed her forehead again. "No, not exactly," she said hesitantly. "I knew I needed to be out there. He must have called to me, but I don't think I let myself understand who called me or why. I truly thought him gone. Maybe I wasn't able to understand where my heart drew me."

Dabir recaptured her hand. "Yasmine, I am sorrier than you can ever know that this has been so painful for you." He stood and formally addressed the group. "I am grateful for the assistance you provided to my soul and to my niece." He frowned. "Although I do not understand that part quite as well." He looked expectantly at Mara, impatiently awaiting the explanation she'd promised the night before.

Terrill moved to stand behind Mara. "Mara is my soul."

The look of shock that crossed Dabir's face pained her to watch. "Your what?" he managed to choke out.

"My soul," Terrill repeated calmly. "Yasmine knew of Mara's condition as a child so I assume you must have too. It was Mara's condition that saved Yasmine and brought her to me."

Dabir snapped his mouth shut, turning accusing eyes back to Yasmine, who avoided his gaze. "I guessed but was never certain. That information was not shared." He took a deep breath and released it. "Forgive me, the concept remains somewhat alien to me. With all that has occurred, I am still processing. I have not handled it as well as I would have liked."

He got up from his seat and approached Mara. Terrill positioned himself in front of her. Dabir continued to stand there and stare him down. He slowly stretched out his arm to Mara in a peace gesture. She placed a hand on Terrill's arm and rose to move around him. She let a suddenly awkward Dabir embrace her.

"I wish you happiness, Mara," he said. "It's just surprising to me that after the attack on your parents you would . . ."

Terrill less than gently pulled Mara from Dabir's embrace and back against his own. Mara felt the anger coursing through him, even as the shock of Dabir's words started to register. She tried to conceal her hurt. How could he think such a hideous thing? Aware of Terrill's intentions, she spoke quickly.

"This is between Terrill and me. And as far as the attack on my family, my relationship with Terrill does not influence my pursuit of justice in ANY way. I have absolutely zero intention of turning from that path, nor has Terrill sought to dissuade me. In fact, he supports it and offered his help."

Dabir quickly glanced around the room. "Then I must apologize for my thoughtless words. I never believed you would abandon your quest for justice, but given the circumstances, I felt I had to ask. You understand?"

She nodded, but his accusation knelled bitterly in her ears.

Lauris stood at the head of the table. "Perhaps we ought to call it a night, let Dabir rest, and let everyone get some air before talking about the future." He lowered his voice and continued to hold Dabir's gaze. "Yasmine, perhaps you could take Dabir back to the quarters we've prepared for you? We've had it restocked with food and any other comforts you might require."

Dabir narrowed his eyes. "We are to be guests here indefinitely?"

Lauris's unblinking gaze didn't waver as Yasmine appeared at Dabir's side. "You are welcome to come and go as you wish. Unlike my son, I would not revoke the offer of hospitality based on rash words alone. We offer safety within a territory controlled by those who would destroy you for no crime greater than your presence." He paused, seeming to reflect for a moment. "I would have thought you'd welcome the chance to even the score against those who hurt your soul."

Dabir bristled but seemed to recognize the wisdom of Lauris's words and nodded almost reluctantly. "Yes. I would welcome that opportunity. Of course. We thank you for your gracious hospitality."

Yasmine said her goodbyes and led him from the room. She sent Mara a look pleading for patience.

Mara couldn't resist the pain in her eyes and lowered her head slightly in acknowledgment.

CHAPTER EIGHTEEN

Mara looked around the room, expecting the meeting to break up. One glance at the granite mask on Terrill's face made her realize how wrong her assumption had been. She sat back down. "We have more to discuss?"

Mara felt anger vibrating through Terrill as she took his hand, and she pivoted to look at him.

If he ever makes stupid-ass remarks like that again to hurt you, I won't be responsible for my actions.

He's my uncle! Well, sort of.

He stared at her. *And?*

Caleb whistled under his breath. "So, is he always like that?"

Still off-balance at Terrill's vehemence, she turned back around and shook her head. "Dabir's always been, well, a little old-fashioned. We just threw him a heck of a twist. I'm sure he didn't mean to come off as he did. He'll come around." She heard the hint of persuasion in her voice and wondered exactly who she was trying to persuade.

"We still have other things to discuss," Gabriella said. Her voice redirected attention back to her and thankfully, Mara thought, off herself.

"What's so important that we need to talk about it now as a group, but . . ." she paused, realization lighting her eyes, "but we needed to wait until after Dabir and Yasmine left to do so?" She looked at Terrill for answers but got silence. She glared at him, furious for spreading his suspicions and siding against her family.

No one said anything and Mara realized that Gabriella was waiting for the fury sparking in Mara's eyes to die down before she continued. Mara released a deep breath and gestured for Gabriella to proceed.

"There's nothing I will say that cannot be said in front of them, Mara. I just needed the tension to dissipate so I could make sure I saw things clearly." She smiled. "You're already a little difficult for me to read as it is. A little extra clarity is not necessarily a bad thing, is it?"

Mara smiled wryly. She was being childish. "What is it you see, Gabriella?"

"I thought you couldn't see the future about Mara," Terrill said.

"I still get hazy indications more than concrete predictions, but I can see more now that you are together." She made eye contact with Mara. "It's like when you told me you had to get to Yasmine back in the garden. I couldn't see the reason why, but I could see that you were predestined to be there."

"So you see directions more than predictions?" Mara asked. That actually explained a lot.

"Exactly," she paused and looked at Lauris and Terrill before continuing. "And the direction I see most clearly now is east."

"We are to go beyond the boundaries into Viajante territory?" Terrill asked.

"Yeah, like we aren't rocking the boat enough here with our own kind, and now this Pure Blood Society. Might as well add tromping through Viajante territory to the plate as well."

Morgan frowned at Caleb's sarcasm. "Gabriella, who's to go east? All of us or just Mara?"

"Mara goes nowhere without me."

Lauris nodded. "Of course not son. I don't have to have Gabriella's special powers to know your fates are intertwined."

"Why east?" Mara asked. "There's a Sanctuary in the Mojave Desert, but you already know that. Am I supposed to join them? Or do I travel back to my home Sanctuary?"

She thought she'd hidden her concern about how her kind would react to her now that she traveled with her non-Viajante soul, but Terrill's hand taking hers was proof she'd failed. She smiled at his understanding.

If I didn't know what you were thinking, what sort of soul would I be to you?

I still don't like you crawling around uninvited in my head.

Would you rather we crawl around back in our room? He sent her a few naughty images and she fought the need to flush. She hoped the others weren't paying too much attention. *Knock it off!*

He raised her hand to his lips and smiled that wicked smile she liked so much before letting her go.

"I only know the direction is east," Gabriella said. "It's still a little cloudy, but I get the impression of something remote, the seat of ancient magic."

"Our people have many sacred places in the desert." All eyes turned to the door as Yasmine and Dabir reentered the room. "We felt a need to rejoin the conversation. What were you saying about the Mojave?"

Mara hid a grin at her aunt and uncle's ability to return undetected.

Explain, Terrill demanded.

Our Seekers have masking abilities. She shrugged. *They need it to be successful at their job. What my mother did for Celeste was extremely difficult, but with a lot of practice and skill, others could learn it. Of course, it's much easier to mask your own presence than someone else's.*

You masked yours and created the illusion of another being you. How common is that?

Well, let's just say that other than Yasmine, no one really knows it's even possible.

"Gabriella says we're to go east, to the desert," Mara said as Dabir and Yasmine took seats. She turned back to Gabriella. "Is there anything else?"

"I'll show you." Gabriella closed her eyes and made a link with Mara. She focused Mara's vision among the swirling mists between the shadowy desert and mountain shapes. It was so small Mara almost missed it. Growing in a clump of rocks was not the cactus or desert flower she expected to see in such terrain, but instead a delicate rose. The rose disappeared and was replaced by a black stone, something like obsidian or onyx. Gabriella's eyes snapped open and she looked at Mara. They shared a smile.

"Viajante put great stock in mystics and visions," Dabir said. "I had no idea Vampires did as well." He looked curiously at Gabriella. "How were you able to show Mara your vision?"

"If a path is available, I can show the vision of that person to them," she said. "It doesn't always work, but they can usually see enough to clarify it."

"What did you see?" Dabir asked Mara.

"Mainly mist and shadow," Mara said. "We saw the desert, but among the normal desert plants and blooms was a lone rose, small and delicate." She looked at Terrill. "Something not natural to the area."

"A symbol of some kind," Terrill thought out loud.

"Or a name," added Yasmine.

"Of course!" The others exchanged startled looks when Dabir spoke. He looked triumphant at having figured it out. "Many of our elders depend on the Shamans for insight into the spirit realm, how Sanctuary is to work, impending dangers, that sort of thing. Very powerful Shamans never really settle down in one place and become part of the Council of Elders, they continue to wander."

"Wait," interrupted Yasmine. "There is one such Shaman whose name means rose. Could that be it?"

"Shaba!" Mara gasped. "Shaba's shown up throughout my life. She took a special interest in me when Yasmine brought me to Sanctuary, and over the years, that's never changed."

Yasmine nodded. "She's the one who made sure the elders let me go on that last mission to find your mother." She shook her head. "It was like she knew I would find you. If there's anyone among our people with whom we should now talk, it would be her."

Gabriella nodded. "In my vision the rose turned to a stone – a stone like that in the amulet Mara now wears."

Heads turned to look at the necklace Mara unconsciously fingered. "My mother gave me this."

Terrill stood. "There's no time to waste. Mara and I travel east tomorrow."

"Wait," Dabir interrupted. Mara looked at him, surprised at his objection. "It makes more sense for Yasmine and me to take her. The presence of a Vampire among our people would be hard to explain."

Yasmine hesitated but a second before nodding in agreement. "Mara's been disguising herself her entire life. Getting in and out of Viajante territory will be easy for her." Yasmine looked apologetically at Terrill. "You won't be as easy to disguise or explain."

His eyes darkened to a steely grey. "I'll say it again. Mara goes nowhere without me."

"What if Yasmine and Dabir were to locate Shaba and then bring you both to her?" Morgan let the idea sink in. "They could set up some safe place, maybe outside Sanctuary where it would be safer for all of you to meet."

Mara looked hopefully at Terrill. It sounded like a good plan to her. "Terrill," she said, "you have the ability to hide your presence from my people, but have you ever tried it against such a large number as Sanctuary would present? Morgan's plan makes a lot of sense." Then she turned to Dabir and Yasmine. "What do you guys think?"

"It sounds logical," Dabir said reluctantly.

Mara tapped her foot and waited.

"The plan has merit," Terrill grudgingly admitted, "but you two shouldn't travel in and out of Vampire territory without an escort." He exchanged a look with Caleb. "We'll accompany you to the border and back." He looked directly at Dabir. "Those are my conditions."

Dabir smiled thinly. "Of course. It is for Mara that we go. If her soul would offer protection within his territory, it would be churlish of us to refuse."

Terrill stared at him a few seconds longer then curtly inclined his head. "Then we're agreed."

"Are you all right to travel?" Mara asked Dabir.

He grinned. "When have a few scratches ever stopped me before?" Mara smiled in relief. This was the Dabir she knew and loved.

The rest of the night passed in a flurry of preparations. They finally all drifted off to their separate sleeping quarters as early morning dawned.

Mara stood by the window and watched color slowly seep into the grey and black horizon. Hesitantly at first, then with greater confidence, ribbons of pink and yellow silk wove their way through the darkness. It was beautiful.

She should have been relieved when Terrill told her Dabir and Yasmine had made it through Vampire territory without a problem, but she couldn't shake the impression that something wasn't quite right with Yasmine. Of course, she had been through a lot lately. It was probably her imagination.

While they were gone, Mara dedicated her time to working on improving her powers with Morgan and Gabriella. A little over a week later, Terrill announced his departure to bring them back. She'd felt antsy and out of sorts since they'd left. Not that patience was actually one of her virtues anyway.

"You look like a caged tiger anxious to pounce," Morgan said. "Don't you ever relax?"

Mara laughed. "I guess I'm a bit nervous about what they found out."

"A bit nervous? Understatement!"

They both turned as Yasmine and Dabir entered the room. Terrill and Caleb appeared shortly after.

Any problems? Mara couldn't stop herself from asking.

Terrill winked. *None. I told you not to worry.*

"Welcome back," Lauris greeted Dabir and Yasmine. Mara watched him assess everything about their appearance, seeking his own confirmation that it had indeed been an easy return into the city.

"You didn't run into any patrols?" he asked Terrill.

Terrill shrugged nonchalantly. "The eastern border is my territory. We hadn't expected any."

"And Shaba?" Mara asked.

Dabir smiled at her impatience. "She waits for us now at one of her sacred spots outside Sanctuary. She seemed especially interested in meeting your chosen one."

Mara's eyes widened. "You told her about him?"

"She already knew. She wants you to bring him," Yasmine said.

"She knows he's Vampire?" Mara asked incredulously.

"The subject didn't exactly come up," Yasmine hedged. "We thought it best you explain. But knowing Shaba . . ." she shrugged.

Mara nodded. Yeah, knowing Shaba, anything was possible. "When do we leave?"

Terrill stared at Dabir. "You had no issue getting her to agree to meet us? There was no resistance in Sanctuary to the idea of her leaving?"

Yasmine smothered a laugh, and Terrill sent her a dark glance that sobered her immediately. "Sorry, I just tried to imagine someone telling Shaba what she could or could not do." Her voice gentled. "We don't tell Shaman anything. We respect their autonomy and their decisions. Whether we agree with them is irrelevant. They do as they wish. They always have."

Dabir nodded. "We managed to talk with her in private. We'll take you to the meeting place. If there are any problems, we'll be close. Our plan was to spend a few days in Sanctuary and return."

Terrill looked at Mara. *You're ready for this?* She nodded. He sighed. "We leave tomorrow."

Mara lightly tapped into his mind and felt Gabriella's need to communicate with him. *You would add something?* she heard him ask.

I sense your hesitation, but this meeting must take place, regardless of the danger you fear. This Shaba holds information Mara needs, and as her soul, you need it as well. I don't sense any deception but trust your instincts. They haven't failed you yet.

Happy now? Mara asked.

The look of shock on his face was priceless.

You heard all that? How?

Mara had the good grace to look the tiniest bit ashamed for eavesdropping. *I can hear your thoughts, and it wasn't hard to pick up on who you were communicating with. Gabriella, Morgan, and I have been practicing.*

He didn't appear too happy to hear it.

We'll talk about this later when we're alone. If that's possible anymore, he all but growled.

She bit back her desire to stick out her tongue. Damn spoilsport. Instead, she settled for narrowed eyes and ignored him as he became engrossed in security discussions.

CHAPTER NINETEEN

M ara sighed in contentment. The sounds and smells of the city faded away and the tranquility of the desert seeped into her. The more distance they put between the city and themselves, the more excited she became. Twice already Terrill had sent her quelling looks to check her flight. She smiled as she recognized Terrill's presence in her mind again.

Anxious to get there?

I don't want to waste the time we could be spending with Shaba.

Mara stopped abruptly and nearly ran into Terrill who'd stopped in front of her. She scented a change in the atmosphere.

"We'll be there when you call for us. Sanctuary isn't far," Yasmine said.

Mara embraced her and watched them depart. She reached for Terrill's hand. *Ready?* Her voice quivered just the slightest bit.

Baby, I'm always ready.

She groaned painfully and swatted him on the arm.

Terrill waited for her as she shook her hair back out of her eyes. They slowly picked their way through the night to the stone outcropping Yasmine said Shaba had designated for their rendezvous.

She smelled the fire burning long before she saw the eerie flicker of flame-cast shadows dance against the stones. The herb smell was a comforting mix of pine resin and desert sage. The Shaman often used it to invoke the spirits or for purification or cleansing ceremonies. She shared the knowledge with Terrill as they stepped into the light.

"Mara, I've been waiting for you." Mara let the rhythmic cadence of the deep voice wash over her. "And such interesting companions you keep now." Shaba chuckled in her throaty voice. "You, Terrill, come where I can see you."

Terrill reluctantly did as she bid. Mara watched his approach with interest.

He seemed surprised by the tiny stature of the woman in front of him. Mara found her fascinating. The biggest thing about her was her hair. It fanned out halo-like in a riot of coal-black curls. Smooth, coffee-colored skin framed penetrating black eyes huge with contained wisdom. Her brightly colored robes swirled around her as she moved, dwarfing her small body, but doing little to conceal the immense power radiating from within.

"Never judge a book by its cover child," she scolded him.

It's like she's reading my thoughts, he complained to Mara. *Almost laughing even.*

He scowled when Shaba cackled as she walked away from them. Mara shrugged and tried not to laugh. *I did mention that Shaman have powers above our own, didn't I? I'd just go with it.*

He grunted. *You accept. I'll question.*

Shaba turned back to face him and focused the full measure of her five-foot-nothing stature on his over six-foot one. She didn't seem the least bit intimidated at being close to him, a Vampire, regardless of whatever powers he might possess.

She sniffed and wrinkled her nose at him. "Well, you have confidence, and no small degree of arrogance either. I'll give you that. Handsome, smart, and strong as well, humph." She looked at Mara fondly and nodded. "Yes, I can see why you were drawn to him."

She shifted her gaze back to Terrill. "But you. . ." she said waving her hand at him. "You have no idea what you set in motion when you called her to you." She ignored their stunned expressions and gestured for them to take seats around the fire on the rugs she'd spread there.

What did she mean when she said you called me to you?

He hesitated.

Shaba laughed again, interrupting their private feud before it could fully develop. "Not often caught without words, are you now? Come, come, sit. We have much to discuss and the night flies quickly." She took a look at the long shadows stretching between them then made some sort of a hand motion Mara recognized as a ward against evil. "Some things are better said with the protection of daylight," she muttered to herself.

Terrill scowled and shared his displeasure at Shaba's words with Mara silently before taking a seat across the fire from her.

Mara heard the chanting start quietly in her mind. It built gradually in intensity and volume. She watched in awe as the flames started to dance to its hypnotic beat.

Her connection with Terrill allowed him to experience what she did. He wasn't comfortable with the magic Shaba wove. Mara guessed he was used to being in control of spells, not subject to their control. *Terrill, can you please trust me?* Mara asked as he studied the tiny woman completely wrapped up in the ceremony of her own making.

I do trust you. It's all others I distrust, Terrill said. *I've sworn to protect you, Mara, but there's only so much I'm willing to tolerate and less I'm willing to risk – you least of all.*

There's no risk here. Don't insult Shaba and what she does for us. She lowered her voice. *Terrill, please, she has the information we need. We need to know what she knows about the prophecy and what the Society wants.*

He exhaled and stared into the flames. "Shaba please tell us about the prophecy."

She tapped her staff on the ground in a rhythmic beat as Mara motioned for Terrill to be patient. "Yes," she said, "the prophecy provides some answers. It tells of a time when one of the others will call across the shadow divide to his other half, his soul. It says that she will answer."

She opened her eyes and focused on Terrill. "You called her to you." Her eyes glazed over as she peered into the darkness like she saw something invisible to both Terrill and Mara. "Your awareness of her as your soul has been growing for some time, but you fought against it."

She stopped at the dark expression in Terrill's eyes. "Even had you given in to it, it would not have stopped the chain of events that brought her to you." His eyes maintained their steely glint, but Mara saw him start to accept the truth Shaba offered.

"What happened is what made Mara what she is, and what she is now is what the prophecy meant she would become. This is what your enemies fear."

Mara's eyes widened. It was supposed to have happened?

"Your mother recognized this. She knew you were the chosen one." Shaba's hand went up, forestalling Mara's denial. "No, child, she did not fight the end, she fought for your life. She gave hers so that you might fulfill your destiny."

"I believe she learned something of the prophecy along her travels and believed you held the key. That is why your parents avoided all contact with others. They didn't know who they could trust. They could not have predicted an attack, but they did everything they could to give you the best chance for survival they could."

Tears spilled from Mara's eyes. She looked at Terrill. He nodded in reassurance and dried her tears with his thoughts.

Shaba observed the undercurrent between them and nodded in approval. "Yes, your bond is strong, but will it be strong enough . . ."

"Strong enough for what?" Terrill asked, suspicion still unconsciously lacing his tone.

"The calling and the joining – this is only the first part of the prophecy. Much of what else it is and what it means has been lost."

Shaba shifted position and they swiveled around to see what had caught her attention. Shadows twisted and contorted in the inky blackness. They appeared to be writhing purposefully to avoid Shaba's gaze, but were also intent on working their way closer to the fire and the immortals surrounding it.

Have you ever seen anything like this? Terrill asked Mara.

No.

Her gaze flicked back to Shaba. Shaba's eyes narrowed and she muttered a few undistinguishable phrases under her breath. The shadows cried out, a piercing and frightening sound, and fled to a position where they could no longer be seen. Somewhere out of the reach of Shaba's voice, Mara figured.

Shaba slumped down a little from the expended energy. She waved off Mara's attempt to help and straightened. "Someone of great power wants the information I give you. I can hold them off a while longer, but he may be powerful enough to succeed in tricking me into giving it if we tarry too long."

I didn't know how strong they were, Mara said. That Shaba had concerns said tons.

Are we facing an elder? Terrill asked. *Another Shaman? How else would they know about ancient magic like the effect of cold and now the use of shadows?*

I don't know, but now we know about them. I don't think that was part of their plan. We'll be okay.

One look at Shaba confirmed that she'd somehow followed their silent conversation. Shaba smiled.

"Shaba, what is the rest of the prophecy? Why is it so feared?" Mara asked as she continued to cautiously monitor the shadows skulking just outside the boundaries Shaba had set.

She looked like she'd been expecting the question. "The calling sparks the gathering of the four, the corners, and then the second joining."

Terrill frowned in confusion.

"Viajante have a strong connection to the earth," Mara explained. "The four corners are just what they sound like, the four polar directions. Each one symbolizes not only a direction, but a natural element: earth, wind, fire, and water."

Shaba nodded. "The prophecy sends its call first to the south." She gently touched Mara's face. "You. The south is represented by the symbol of fire. The call then changes direction and goes north to its polar opposite. You've already found your north guardian. Or perhaps it is more correct to say she found you."

Mara raised her head and looked into Terrill's inquisitive eyes. "Yasmine. She is the earth and the balance, both of herself and of me. In our culture earth represents both dependability and stability. The role she serves in our society is also a balancing one. She brings back the lost ones, restores their balance, and ours."

"But who represents the east and the west?" she asked Shaba.

Shaba stared into the fire.

Terrill's voice rang out against the crackling of the flames. "Your sister Celeste must be one of the remaining corners."

"Yes, Celeste," Shaba said. "We thought her gone, but her role here among us is yet incomplete."

But which one is she? And who was the fourth? Mara turned back to Shaba, the question on the tip of her tongue, but was distracted by the gathering shadows. They seemed more numerous, stronger, and somehow more determined this time.

As if sensing the same thing, Shaba spoke. "There isn't much time left and my answers also run dry. I can tell you only that the discovery of the fourth will lead you to the third."

Terrill rose to his feet. "I don't like this. Whoever's directing this little shadow party is starting to piss me off."

Mara stood and helped Shaba to her feet. Shaba patted Mara's hand. "Go now, child. I can hold them off. They'll lose interest once their opportunity for mischief is over."

"But what about the prophecy – what does the coming together of the four corners herald? What is the second joining? What about the Society that hunts us?"

Shaba positioned herself as an obstacle the shadows would have to cross to get to Mara and Terrill. She raised her arms and the sands before her moved to do her biding, building a curtain of silt that obscured the shadows' view and forced them to slow their advance.

"I don't know about this Society, except that they seek to prevent the prophecy. It's about the blood, the prophecy. The tie is in the blood and the blood is life. New life, Mara. New for both species. Find the center. That's the catalyst. It's what binds the corners, finds and grounds them. It's what starts the past."

She pointed a long thin finger at Terrill, her bracelets jangling melodiously as she did. "You must prevent the destruction of the line. Mara is the key, and you are the key to her protection."

She squeezed Mara's hand one last time before disappearing into the whirlwind of sand she'd created. Mara felt Shaba step back into her mind before the hem of her robes vanished. *The blood that protects, the blood that ties, also seeks to destroy. The strongest danger comes from within the circle, child. Watch for the danger within.*

Mara didn't have time to think about Shaba's last words as Terrill dragged her away from the circle and the dark forms threatening them. Once they cleared Shaba's retreat she was able to see dawn rapidly approaching. She hadn't realized how long they'd been gone. They redoubled their efforts to put distance between themselves and daybreak.

CHAPTER TWENTY

As soon as they entered shelter, Mara wheeled on Terrill and pushed him. "Why didn't we stay and help Shaba fight? I could have handled it. We could have learned something about our enemy. Damn it, Terrill, she didn't mean protection that damn literally!"

Terrill stood impassive against her verbal assault. A half-smile crossed his face as she fumed and paced.

Mara finally halted and huffed. "Okay, what?"

He grinned broadly. "I hadn't had the chance to say anything yet. Someone didn't let me get a word in edgewise."

Mara glared at him, hand on hip and foot tapping.

"Mara, have you ever seen anything like that before? The shadows, I mean."

Mara's foot froze in mid-tap. Of course she had. Some of her kind had the ability to control the colors and semipermanent apparitions like shadows. She knew Dabir could, and she knew Terrill did too because of Dabir's attack that first night. But just because he could didn't mean he was the only one. It was a rare talent that few mastered, but the important thing was that there were others.

She quickly dismissed the disturbing possibility Terrill raised. It wasn't even an option. Terrill's suspicious nature was making her paranoid.

She realized Terrill was again intently watching the inner battle within her and she waved off her concerns. "Some of my people have that ability," she said. "Vampires can't do that, can they?"

He shook his head silently.

"Dabir can do it," she said.

"I know."

She felt her blood pressure rising. "You don't think . . ."

He shrugged and she sighed. She wouldn't be changing his mind anytime soon. At least she knew better.

Mara rose early the next evening. She turned to find Terrill's half of the bed empty. She should have known better than to assume he'd still be there. He probably was talking with his father and Caleb. She smiled. Well at least she was beginning to understand him. She'd jumped in the shower, dressed, and was brushing her hair when a knock sounded at the door. Morgan and Gabriella let themselves in.

"I assume the guys are all talking?" Mara asked with a wry grin.

Morgan laughed. "You know how they are. They have to protect us silly little females from big bad man business." She rolled her eyes. "As if we couldn't handle things ourselves."

Gabriella shook her head. In her typical business-first way she redirected the conversation. "How was your trip? Did you find what you were seeking?"

Mara shrugged. "Only part of it," she admitted, disappointment strong in her voice. "Maybe you all can make something more out of it. I really wish Yasmine was here. She has this way of helping me see the truth."

"They'll be back in a couple of days, right?" Morgan asked.

Mara smiled. "Yes. I guess I really miss the tranquility of Sanctuary and the way things used to be sometimes." She looked up at Gabriella guiltily, realizing that she probably sounded ungrateful or worse, unhappy.

Before she could voice her concerns, Gabriella cut her off with a wave of her delicate hand. "No need to explain, we understand. Missing home or your people isn't a sign of unhappiness." She smiled gently. "It's the memory of those precious moments you treasure that protects you when times are more difficult."

Like Yasmine, Gabriella too seemed gifted with the ability to understand her, Mara mused. She brightened as she heard Terrill enter the room.

"Let me guess. You got nervous about the thought of us girls together so you broke off your important powwow with the guys to make sure we were staying out of trouble and not talking about you." He narrowed his eyes and sent her the impression of growling. She grinned back, unrepentant, as they exited the room.

Terrill shook his head and followed them into the room where they'd gotten into the habit of meeting as a group. Mara had sarcastically labeled it the war room, but to her surprise, the name had stuck.

There was silence around the table after Mara and Terrill recounted the events of the previous evening. Mara looked over at Terrill, a little nervous about how the others would react. As usual, Terrill displayed no outward signs of unease or discomfort. She envied him that ability.

Looking cool and detached is not the same as being so. This affects me as well. Especially considering I'm the one who started it. That's something I'll have to live with for eternity.

She heard the bitterness in his voice and his unspoken concern that he'd brought her into danger against her will. He truly believed he'd put her at risk just to satisfy what he considered his own selfish needs.

It's not true. If we weren't meant to be together – and Shaba confirmed we were – you wouldn't have been able to bring us together. Anything that happened as a result of that coming together is not your fault. The prophecy has intertwined in our lives and is something neither of us could have known or planned for. She softened her tone and took his hand in hers under the table. *Would you honestly never have called for me had you known about it? Would you have kept us apart?*

He hesitated, but Mara knew he wouldn't lie to her, not about this. *No, I would have still called for you. I just don't know what I would do if something happened to you because of it,* he admitted reluctantly. She smiled as he squeezed her hand.

Terrill tore his gaze from hers. "So, what haven't we considered?"

Caleb stroked the stubble on his chin. "Shaba said it was about the blood, right? You Viajantes don't generally talk about blood much. Why now? Could that be what those Pure Blood guys are all about?"

"Do you think they're after Mara because they know about the prophecy?" Morgan asked, as her eyes flew to Mara's face.

Mara and Terrill locked eyes and he nodded in encouragement.

"Based on what Shaba told us, that much is certain. They've failed to prevent the first part of the prophecy – Terrill and I coming together. I'm not sure what their next move is. If it's to control the . . ." She cleared her throat hesitantly. ". . .the potential results of our union. Or if they seek a way to prevent that or to keep us from finding the others." She shook her head in confusion. "We just don't know enough to be able to predict with any degree of accuracy."

"Maybe both," Gabriella said as she closed her eyes in concentration. All eyes turned back to her. "I don't think they know exactly what they're dealing with. It seems they know of the prophecy and that you're involved, but Shaba said most don't understand the whole thing."

She looked directly at Mara. "I think you're correct that it might be related to the child you will someday carry, but I sense that it also has something to do with your sister."

Lauris nodded, also looking deep in reflection. "What I found especially interesting was what your Shaba said about the elements. Your people seem deeply grounded in them. Many of our kind have forgotten the old ways."

Terrill looked at his father in surprise.

Lauris noticed and smiled. "Yes, son, Vampires used to be more in tune with the elements, even controlling them. There are some families with strong abilities to do so, but not many have persisted through the centuries. Ours is one of them."

Not only Terrill sat in stunned silence. Mara stole a glance at Morgan and Caleb. They too looked captivated by what Lauris revealed.

"Much of the original history of our origins and how we relied on elemental magic has been relegated to myth and fiction. The emphasis now is placed on structure and organization. All reference to the mystical was systematically cut out as our leaders lost their abilities or the desire to maintain those abilities.

"Your little experiments as a boy?" Lauris looked at Terrill. "Don't doubt for a moment I would have allowed you that freedom had I not been absolutely certain you couldn't seriously harm yourself." He looked fondly at his wife. "Now convincing Gabriella that it was okay . . . well, that was something else altogether."

Already aware of Gabriella's protective nature, Mara smiled as he chuckled at the memory.

"Mara, what do you think Shaba meant about the center?" Terrill asked. "That which ties it all together."

Mara shook her head. "I don't know, but I think Yasmine might. She's always been more in tune with the hidden meaning behind words and thoughts."

"What's the latest speculation about where Victor disappeared to?" Terrill asked.

Mara felt like she'd just had the wind knocked out of her. Yasmine, Dabir, Angelica, were any of them safe? What did he mean, where was Victor? What was he doing? She didn't even attempt to mute her emotional response to the news.

Did you forget to mention something to me?

No, he said. *Just because we don't know for certain where he is doesn't mean anyone is in danger.*

She was furious. He was damn lucky she'd never developed the power to cause damage with a single look. Damn lucky.

Lauris watched the byplay with amusement and swallowed his grin by clearing his throat. "We've been told he was summoned back to the High Court in Europe. No one seems to know more than that. If they do, they certainly aren't saying."

Caleb nodded. "There are a lot of rumors out there. Talk of rival factions within the city and unrest outside our borders. A lot of confusion about why they sent for him, and why now."

"I've been asked to step up to assume some of Victor's guardian duties here in the city," said Lauris. "I will continue with his original plan for Caleb and Terrill to step up patrols of the eastern border and, if we are lucky, get a little insight into his operations." Lauris smiled at her surprise. Terrill's family really was powerful.

"Of course, if I'm in charge, who's to question decisions I make about what's best for our protection?"

Terrill stared at him, apparently understanding his father's intent before Mara could. "I don't like you putting yourselves in danger for us."

Lauris snorted in derision. "It's for me to determine the nature and extent of the risk. Your quest serves ours. Besides, the intent of a patrol of the eastern borders is met, even if it extends beyond the border, is it not?"

Gabriella placed her hand on Lauris's arm. "Everyone has a role to play. This is ours." She smiled at her soul. "Doubt not our abilities, son. We can easily handle any problems here."

Terrill nodded reluctantly. "Caleb and I will continue to learn what we can about Victor, his intentions, and the Society while we wait for Yasmine and Dabir to return. After that, we head east."

"Angelica," Mara interrupted. "I need to know about her too. Where she is . . ."

Caleb and Terrill's eyes met in instant understanding. "Apparently she never returned to the boarding school Victor enrolled her in after her holiday vacation," Caleb said. "We've put out discrete feelers for her current location."

Mara looked at Terrill in shock. "Does that mean she's in danger?"

The Vampires in the room exchanged amused glances. "Not necessarily. She's been known to do this before. If she is playing hooky, we want to get to her before Victor."

CHAPTER TWENTY-ONE

M ara felt the coldness seep into her skin and rubbed her arms unconsciously in an effort to warm herself. The air around her was void of color, dark as death, and there was a musty odor of something damp or decaying. Where the hell was she?

As if in silent answer to her question, she felt the layers of darkness covering her lift, exposing a dim light ahead of her, barely visible through the dense fog and shadow. Cautiously, she moved toward it.

Ouch! She pressed her hand against the spot where her leg had made contact with something. The sticky substance between her fingers was evidence she'd cut herself. She touched the spot again and found it no longer tacky. Good, only a minor scratch.

Intent on avoiding other potential obstacles, she slowed to a snail's pace as she made her way toward the brightening light. She shielded her eyes and looked back at the darkness. A cave? She didn't remember having entered a cave.

She looked at her clothes, hoping for answers. No shoes. Well, that was certainly helpful. Her feet were already wet from the dew shimmering on the lush green plains all around her. In fact, rolling green and sunlit sky were all she could now see.

She saw a faint path of foot-beaten grass leading over a knoll away from the cave and felt compelled to follow. Her feet moved of their own volition. Before she knew it, she'd crested the rolling hill.

She closed her eyes and inhaled the crisp fresh air. It tasted faintly of salt water. The sea must be somewhere close. She used her superior hearing to locate the muted sound of surf in the distance. Something felt oddly familiar. Another mystery.

She opened her eyes and was surprised to see ruins dominate the landscape before her. She turned around in confusion. Where had the rolling hills gone? The world seemed to spin again and she was inside the ruins, a strange chanting softly echoing in the background.

Mara tried to follow the motion of shadowy figures that darted between the stones in an infuriating game of hide and seek. She gave up and turned back to the circle of stones. Three figures now stood there, bathed in white light. She couldn't see any features, yet it felt like they watched her. They moved in a deliberate fashion to take the corners opposite her, just as Shaba had described.

Darkness blindfolded her and she cried out in frustration. The innocuous rustling of cloth on cloth slithered ominously against the pulsing castanet that masqueraded as her heart.

"Who's there?" She whipped around to the left as the slithering sound moved closer. "Identify yourself!"

Still unable to see, Mara kept her fingers on the column of rock closest to her, hoping to prevent transport to another location before she could figure this one out. She jumped at an unexpected sound to her right.

"Mara?" a familiar voice called.

Mara bolted upright and gulped in a frightened breath. She was still in her sleeping chamber, Terrill beside her, asleep. She touched the sheets in disbelief and tried to calm her pulse, still rocketing out of control. She knew who the disembodied voice belonged to.

She shivered. Viajante rarely dreamed. Nightmares, while rare, were not completely unknown, and she'd certainly had her share as a child after the attack. Maybe this one had something to do with the prophecy. If she could fall back asleep, she might learn more. She lay back down and turned to her side to curl up against Terrill.

A sudden pain on her thigh forced her to shift position. She moved the covers to get a better look. Her eyes widened. Holy crap! She saw the cut from her dream. But it had been a dream, right?

Gradually her mind released its hold on her and she fell into a dreamless sleep, one so deep she wasn't aware of Terrill's arising.

Mara spent the next night working on her fighting skills with Morgan and Caleb. Each took turns planning ambushes and conducting defensive drills. She wasn't about to admit it, but by sunup, she was exhausted. She'd hoped Yasmine and Dabir would arrive before daybreak, but they'd decided on a daylight return, eliminating the need for an escort back into Vampire territory.

I'm sure they're fine. Terrill's words brushed against her nervous mind like a comforting balm and she felt some of her tension subside.

I know, I know, it's just . . .

You need to talk with her about Shaba.

Mara nodded, still amazed that he could read her so easily.

It's my responsibility to be able to do so, cara mia. That is what it means to be one's soul. He followed his words with his presence, materializing beside her.

When had she come to need him so badly? Her feelings, she feared, were distracting her from the dangers ahead. She shouldn't be here with him when her sister and her family needed her. Her parents had sacrificed themselves for her. They deserved justice.

Mara, Terrill interrupted her self-ruminations firmly, *you're following your heart. That could never be a betrayal of your parents. They would want your happiness and safety.* He lifted her chin so that she had to meet his eyes. *They would have wanted you to find love too.*

A love like theirs, she whispered softly.

He nuzzled her neck. *Yes,* he repeated, *a love like theirs.* He kissed her. *There's nothing for you to feel guilty about. Those against you and what the prophecy represents are not your people. Your people, be they Vampire or Viajante, are the ones who will stand with you for justice and for the future, whatever shape that takes.*

The sides are no longer the black and white of my childhood. So much more is gray than I expected.

And grey is bad? he asked.

She raised her green eyes to stare into his silver ones, and her lips twitched into a mischievous smile. *I'm beginning to like the color quite a bit, actually.*

"Is that right?" he asked as he closed the distance. "So tell me, what else are you starting to like?"

"How about I show you?" she murmured suggestively. She had hardly finished speaking before she was whisked away to the bedroom.

Mara awoke with a start again. It was the same dream as before. She absentmindedly rubbed the bruise from the other day. It still hadn't completely disappeared. Strange. She looked down at Terrill, sleeping peacefully, and smiled. She really was lucky to have found him.

She didn't want to wake him, so she slipped quietly out of bed and got dressed. It was still early afternoon, but maybe the sunlight would help clear her troubled thoughts. She slid the locks closed behind her with her mind and softly padded down the hallway to the kitchen for a cup of coffee before heading out.

She was delighted to find Yasmine in the kitchen waiting for her. She took the proffered mug and followed her outside. The sunlight felt amazing on her chilled skin and she basked in its warmth for a few moments.

Mara took a deep drink from her coffee. Yasmine liked it the same way she did, nice and strong. She looked over the rim at her aunt. There was still something off about her appearance. She raised an eyebrow in query.

"I love the sun, seeing it the last few days made me realize how little of it I've seen lately," Yasmine said. "You know what I mean?"

Mara smiled and lifted her face to the sun. "I've turned into a bit of a night owl myself." They shared a laugh. "I am so glad you and Dabir found each other again," she said. "I couldn't imagine going through what you did – losing him and then finding him again." She smiled grimly. "I don't think I could . . ."

Yasmine immediately moved to comfort her. "You'd be all right, Mara. You're stronger than you think. Besides, it's not going to happen. That's what family is for." She shuttered in mock distaste. "Even if it now includes a Vampire."

"Hey!" Mara playfully swatted her and they both smiled.

"Why are you up so early?" Yasmine asked.

"Anxious to talk with you, I guess." She looked around before continuing. "I've been having some odd dreams," she confessed.

Yasmine's eyes widened.

"I thought as much," Mara said. "You're having the same one, aren't you?"

Yasmine nodded.

"What do you think it means? Shamans have visions, but we both know I'm not one of those, and last time I checked, neither were you, so?"

Yasmine shrugged her shoulders. "Have you talked to Terrill about it?"

She shook her head. No, she hadn't spoken to Terrill about it. "I didn't know how to explain it. Besides, he'd only worry and make a big deal out of it."

She stood and leaned against the warm balcony railing. "We need to find Celeste. The dream concerns her and the prophecy. I won't allow anything to interfere with me finding her or fulfilling the prophecy. My parents died because they believed in it."

"Mara, you have to tell him about the dream."

"No, I don't. We don't know what it means yet. Promise me you won't talk with him – you or Dabir. Promise me."

Yasmine nodded hesitantly. "All right, Mara. I won't say anything for now. But you need to think about what's going to happen when this comes out, and you know at some point the dreams and everything else . . ." She pointed at their hidden birthmarks. "It's going to come out. It'll be a lot harder to explain why you kept it secret after that happens."

Mara sighed. She knew Yasmine was right. "I know, but what we need right now is for everyone to focus on finding my sister. If the prophecy's right, she's the key to finding the fourth."

Yasmine's confused look reminded her she hadn't yet filled her in about their visit to Shaba. Crap! She'd been so obsessed with trying to figure out this dream thing she'd nearly forgotten. She used their private communications path to fill her in and the hours passed quickly as they caught up.

Yasmine seemed to think that the center was a location. A location that bound the four corners. As much as they tried, they couldn't figure out where it was. "What bound the corners together," Shaba had said. Fragments of her dreams kept intruding into her waking thoughts, but they didn't provide any additional clarity either. She almost welcomed the distraction Terrill's appearance provided.

"You weren't where I left you," he said. His voice held only a partial teasing note. She smiled at the censure in his tone.

He growled and leaned over her, mockingly nipping at her neck in retribution.

"Where's Yasmine?" he asked.

"Out in the garden," she indicated the direction with a turn of her head. "Dabir came out just before you, and they went off together."

"I don't like waking up and you not being there," he repeated, capturing her mouth.

She muttered something incoherent when he released her, still dazed from the intensity of his kiss. Yasmine and Dabir's return prevented further conversation.

CHAPTER TWENTY-TWO

Mara emerged refreshed from the shower, ready to face the long night of training ahead. The plan was to work with Dabir and Yasmine on close combat skills, something they'd been reluctant to show her until now.

She ignored the fatigue tugging at her and squared off with Yasmine, each of them holding the freshly cut staff defensively in her hands. For every thrust Mara made, Yasmine quickly parried, following with an offensive of her own. The thwack of wood on wood echoed through the forest.

Mara wiped the sweat off her brow, and Yasmine took advantage of the lapse to launch a particularly complicated sequence of offensive jabs, scraping the skin off the tops of Mara's fingers as she struggled to hold on to the pole now slick with her own sweat and blood.

"Damn it!" Mara hissed as she lost her grip. She quickly transferred her free hand to the other end, joining them together to swing the staff in a golf-like motion. As it completed its sweep of Yasmine's feet, Mara rolled with it to her land on her own feet behind her aunt.

It hadn't tripped her, but Yasmine grunted under the effort of jumping the obstacle she hadn't been expecting.

"Not bad," Dabir said. "Try and maintain control of your weapon at all times. That part was sloppy." Mara muttered under her breath. He was always so critical.

"No, he's right," Yasmine said as she pressed forward. "I almost had you."

Mara could tell from the determined set of her chin that Yasmine intended to end their mock battle. She didn't need to look behind her to know Yasmine was forcing her toward a tangle of roots protruding from the base of the larger forest trees. If Yasmine could get her opponent to lose her balance, she'd have the advantage. Well, Mara wasn't about to make it easy.

She timed it so their poles made contact. As soon as Yasmine pulled back for her next strike, Mara used the powers her mother infused within her to project the image of immobility as she invisibly flashed behind Yasmine, rustling leaves in her wake.

Staff already in motion, Yasmine realized too late what Mara had done and swung at empty air. The effort toppled her forward. Before she could rise, Mara straddled her from behind and pointed the staff at her neck. "Checkmate?"

Yasmine buried her face in the leaves, groaning in mock defeat, even as her body convulsed in laughter.

Mara laughed in delight and helped her up. She turned to Dabir, expecting at least a grudging thumbs-up for her efforts. Instead, a sharp mental explosion stabbed into her consciousness. Pain swamped her senses and dropped her to the ground. Hard. It was as if the souls of dozens of her people had cried out. She gingerly raised her head. Yasmine was beside her on the ground, not even attempting to rise. Even Dabir had taken a knee against the onslaught. Terrill materialized at her side within seconds and the other Vampires quickly filtered into their training area.

"What is it?" Terrill asked her.

She tried to shake her head, to prevent him from probing her mind, but moving her head intensified the pain so much that it felt like shooting glass. "Pain, a lot of pain. But not mine. My people. Viajante."

Slowly the pain abated to a level she could function through.

Mara saw Terrill and Caleb exchange concerned glances. Dabir recovered first and helped Yasmine to her feet. Terrill turned to him. "What was that?"

He rubbed his temple and squinted. "It's Sanctuary - our Sanctuary. A call for help. An attack." His voice sounded tight, accusing, as it echoed through the early dawn air.

Terrill's eyes hardened, but Mara's gentle touch on his arm made him relax his aggressive posture.

"I thought you couldn't communicate across great distances," he said.

"We can't," Mara said, "but our Shamans have made protective links among our people that exceed the abilities of any one or two of us. Only they could be responsible for such a distress call."

"Then we go to your people tonight," he said.

She closed her eyes against the pain. "No, now." Her voice was barely audible, but they all heard it.

"Mara," he said as he stroked her hair gently, "we have to finish the patrols we started or it will get back to Victor that something is amiss. We'll leave as early as we can tomorrow."

She looked at Dabir and Yasmine. "I'll go with Yasmine and Dabir," she said defiantly.

"Over my dead body."

Damn his protective streak! This was different.

No, it's not. Do not try my patience, he said between clenched teeth. *You will not win.* He turned back to Dabir. "When do you leave?"

"As soon as we can. our skills will be needed." He locked eyes with Yasmine, who sighed and nodded sadly.

"Rest first if you can. Take whatever supplies you need. We'd rather you waited until Mara and I can join you but understand if you cannot."

Dabir looked at him solemnly, warrior to warrior. "We dare not. We'll rest for a few hours and then set out." Mara and Terrill said their goodbyes and promised to follow the next day.

* * *

It was like a police state. If it wasn't Terrill keeping an eye on her, it was Caleb or Lauris. Mara chafed under the male edict not to immediately follow.

Mara looked at herself in the mirror. The dark circles under her eyes were back and shadows lingered in her normally clear green irises. The last time she looked this exhausted was before she'd accepted Terrill's blood. She knew he was concerned. Out of sheer spite, she'd rejected his offer to provide for her last night. She rubbed her temples and attempted to erase the dull ache that had started behind her eyes the night Yasmine left.

It didn't help that she didn't sleep much anymore. Her rest was now haunted by the dream whose riddles she couldn't decipher. They were getting more vivid, more insistent. Each night she awoke to find more proof that her dream world and the one she lived in were on a collision course. Even Morgan and Gabriella were beginning to look at her suspiciously. Either that or lack of sleep really was making her paranoid. She pinched her cheeks to get a little color in them, splashed water on her face, and went out to face the others.

Caleb and Terrill were arguing in undertones but stopped when she entered. So . . . they weren't going to tell her anything. She rested her gaze on Terrill. "When do we leave?"

"Tonight." He stared at her and Mara knew he was trying to figure out what was happening to her. It was easy to see the concern in his mind, but she wasn't willing to talk about it.

Her casual mind probe caught an increased level of tension between Caleb and Terrill she'd never seen before. She swung her eyes back to Terrill, the cause of the tension between them suddenly clear. "Caleb and Morgan aren't coming."

He stiffened and his eyes darkened. Everything about his body posture warned her not to interfere with his decision.

"I think it's a bad idea." Caleb halted as Terrill fixed his laser-like vision on him. He threw up his hands in disgust. "I'm just saying, it's smart to have backup close by."

Mara saw Lauris watching the interplay between Terrill and his second.

"I agree with Caleb, but," Lauris chimed in, holding his hand up as Terrill started to object, "I also see the wisdom of entering with a smaller footprint. I leave you all to sort it out. Call us if you need anything."

Terrill sighed. Mara sensed that he wanted Caleb there, and she knew that he greatly respected his father's opinion as well. She touched his mind again lightly, not wanting him to know she was there. He was concerned about whatever he'd promised Dabir about bringing reinforcements. He was afraid his continual distrust of Dabir was driving a wedge between them. He saw her recent withdrawal as a result of his actions.

"Give us a chance to check it out first," Terrill said, "but be ready."

Caleb nodded.

Before they left Morgan pulled her aside. "If you need anything, contact me, okay?"

Mara promised that she would and smiled. The bond between them had grown stronger. She would miss Morgan's companionship immensely. She'd even gotten better at communicating without sound too, a lot of that due to Morgan's persistence.

* * *

The devastation was appalling. Never had she seen such wanton destruction and loss of life. She'd read about mortal wars, but immortals did not do this. Her eyes burned with tears and smoke, and her grief threatened to choke her.

Terrill held her, his eyes a stormy gray as he surveyed the damage. They'd made an impressive image as they entered the village. Mara had removed the safeguards to Sanctuary almost as an afterthought rather than the hugely significant thing it once would have been. When they met Yasmine and Dabir at the Elder's Circle, Terrill was sure it looked to some as if the village had been handed over to conquerors. He was thankful Mara was so lost in her pain that she appeared temporarily oblivious to that and to the suspicious looks cast their way by the survivors. Terrill however, was not oblivious to it. He wasn't going to allow anything to happen to her. "What happened?" he asked Dabir.

"We got here and the village was already under attack. Yasmine and I spread out, doing what we could to help, but it was too late for most."

Terrill listened stoically to the bitterness in Dabir's voice. There was nothing he could do or say that would excuse his species for this senseless action. He understood the pain and betrayal Mara's family felt. "How did they get in?"

Dabir pushed a shock of black hair out of his face. His eyes hardened. "A traitor."

Yasmine took Mara's arm, gently prying her away from Terrill. "Honey, they are saying it was Sinjon."

Mara's face blanched and she shook her head in negation. *Sinjon was one of the few, like Shaba, to accept me. He trained me when others hesitated. He was like family. I can't believe—*

Mara, Terrill said and squeezed her hand, *we knew there would be surprises, things we wouldn't want to find out.*

No! Not this. Not Sinjon. Something isn't right about this.

She stared at Dabir in disbelief, her eyes demanding proof. "He's like family. How?" she asked.

Dabir sighed sadly. "I found him conspiring with a Vampire – one of the attackers," he said. "There's no way they could have gotten inside Sanctuary without assistance, Mara. You know that."

"No way would he be in league with them. Maybe he was forced, attacked by the Vampire or tricked. Could you have misunderstood? Are you one hundred percent sure about what you saw?"

Unable to meet her eyes, Dabir dropped his gaze. "I'm sorry, Mara. Before I could find out more, he attacked me. The Vampire escaped and I had no choice except to act in self-defense."

"He's dead?" Terrill could physically feel the disbelief and pain in her voice. He also noticed that their presence had attracted attention. More witnesses meant higher tension levels, and neither boded well for them. There was nothing more they could accomplish that night.

"Mara, let's go," he said. He ignored her lack of response and lowered his voice to talk with Yasmine and Dabir. "We'll seek shelter close by and be back tomorrow at dusk. We can talk more about the attack then and hopefully figure out what it means."

Dabir nodded in agreement and placed a comforting arm around Yasmine.

Mara stepped forward to say goodbye to Yasmine and was only saved from hitting the ground by Terrill's strong arms and quick actions. He temporarily pushed his concern about her weakness out of his mind and whisked them out of Sanctuary to a location where he could deal with her alone, without interruption.

CHAPTER TWENTY-THREE

Mara awoke to a persistent dripping. The sound itself was quiet, some water source deep within the earth, far from her, but the echoing amplified each drop, doubling and tripling the effect until she could no longer determine the origin or how far within the earth she was. Terrill had sought shelter in the massive limestone cave systems traversing the remote territory. But where was he? Even as the question formed in her mind, she found her eyes drawn like magnets to Terrill's angry ones.

"Did you think I couldn't feel your weakness beating at me, demanding my attention? What aren't you telling me?"

Mara lowered her eyes certain he'd already seen the guilt swimming in them. He was right about her hiding things. But as uncomfortable as she was about keeping it from him, she kept drawing back to Shaba's warning. But Shaba had said they were meant to be together, right? So how could **he** be the threat? Their fates were intertwined. She couldn't fool herself into believing she had the ability – or even the desire – to deny that truth any longer.

"Mara?"

"They started right after we left Shaba," she said quietly as she watched the censure build in his eyes once he realized just how long she'd kept him in the dark.

The rock he was tossing up and down as he waited for her answer pulverized to dust in his hand. Her eyes widened at his reaction. She heard him exhale slowly, an angry hiss of air like a tire emptying after being struck by a sharp object.

"Exactly what started right after we left Shaba?"

Oh boy, this wasn't going to end well. Yasmine had been right. Mara took a deep breath. "The dreams." She saw confusion combined with anger in his eyes and stopped. It would be far easier to show him. She used her powers to replay the fragmented dreams that haunted her sleep.

Terrill blinked and stared at the dark cavern around him, as if slightly disoriented. "These dreams are not a result of any environmental factors where you are or have been. I'd swear I literally tasted the salt air. Do—"

Before he could finish phrasing the question, she spoke. "No, my people do not dream like this. Your people don't either, do they? Not even your mother?" She really hoped he might say yes and explain some of what was going on, but she was pretty sure she already knew the answer, and she wasn't going to like it.

He shook his head and frowned. "I don't understand exactly how it works, but the visions my mother has don't come through her sleep. They're part of her conscious hours." He captured her eyes with his, moved to her side, and took her face in his hands. He touched her chin tenderly, pushed the hair back from her eyes, and leaned forward. He stopped when his mouth touched her ear. "When were you planning to tell me about this? Why don't you trust me?"

She gasped at the accusation and faint layer of hurt she heard in his voice and moved to escape him. He didn't allow her any room, just held her in place and forced her to meet his gaze.

The problem was that she wasn't really sure why she'd done it herself. She swallowed convulsively and lifted her eyes to his. "I honestly didn't know what to make of it at first."

He relaxed his hold infinitesimally, leaning back to give her the impression of more space. "At first?" he said, his voice shaded with sarcasm. "That's all you have to say? What happened to you in these dreams got brought back into reality. How the hell is that not something unusual or serious, even for you?" He looked incredulous that she would continue to deny the importance of the dreams. "What if you had gotten seriously hurt in these dreams? Did you even think about the consequences? And what about my second question?"

"I wanted answers before I told you about it. I honestly believed that the next dream would be the one that led to answers, and then the next, and before I knew it, I was sucked into this cycle of finding out just enough to keep looking for more."

"That's the biggest bunch of crap I've ever heard and you know it. Do you actually believe the words coming out of your mouth?" Before she could respond his voice got darker, almost menacing, and she shivered. "Partial truths I will no longer accept from you, Mara. You are my soul. Perhaps if the ceremony were complete, you would not find it so easy to continue to lie and omit these types of things."

Her green eyes widened fearfully. She knew what he meant about completion. and she'd believed him when he said he wouldn't push her until she was ready. Was he changing his mind? Would he force her? Take her blood?

She felt the surge of testosterone and male satisfaction that rose in him at her nervousness. "So, now, you begin to take me seriously?"

"Terrill, I . . ."

"No, don't." He pushed up angrily and turned his back to her before taking a few steps away.

The few seconds his back was to her passed like years. She didn't realize she'd held her breath until it escaped in a huge sigh as he squatted next to her. "Is that everything you have to tell me?"

She shook her head. "Only one last thing. I'm not alone in the dream. Yasmine's there and two others we cannot yet see clearly."

"We?"

Great, now she'd implicated Yasmine in this conspiracy to keep him in the dark. Me and my big mouth. "Yasmine and I. We talked about it right before she left with Dabir the other night. That morning you saw us catching up." She raised her chin defiantly. He couldn't expect her to trust him more than her own family, could he?

He cocked an eyebrow and returned her stare.

Well, okay, so maybe he could expect it. It didn't mean he was going get it automatically, like every time, did it?

"So," he continued smoothly, his voice deceptively soft, "you two have been having dreams about a meeting of some kind. Have you figured out where it is? Or did you plan to go there first and then tell the rest of us?"

She attempted – poorly she had to admit – to hide her irritation with his superior attitude. She shrugged her shoulders. "We haven't figured out very much yet. Just a general direction."

He sat waiting patiently, a mockingly indulgent look on his face.

All right, now he was really beginning to piss her off, even considering his threat. So maybe she'd neglected to mention a few details. It's not like she'd lied or put anyone in danger for Pete's sake. They hadn't set off on mission impossible by themselves, so what was the big deal? "East," she said, "where we were all planning to go anyway before the attack. I didn't see the need to bring it up since we were already headed that way anyway."

"The big deal," he whispered in her ear, "is that you are my soul, Mara, and souls share everything. When you hide things from me, you make a mockery of that word, a mockery of our bond. And the big deal, Mara, is that doing so is something I take VERY seriously."

She shivered at his silk-over-skin words and tried to convince herself the goose bumps that had suddenly risen were because of the cold and exhaustion and not because of what she'd heard beneath his words.

"Mara, you need to trust me. I can't fully protect you unless you trust me, or until we complete the ceremony and trust is no longer an issue between us." He held himself immobile, waiting for her answer. "Mara . . ." he whispered.

She felt tears of real emotion dangerously close and nodded slightly. "I do trust you." She closed the distance between them. The instant their lips met she was lost.

She gave in to his need to replenish her. She knew she needed it, but it was the need he had to give her strength that hit her hardest. His lips found her neck and she stiffened, then relaxed, as he touched the surface with feather-soft kisses before returning to her mouth. He wouldn't force the completion of their union until she was ready, regardless of her provocation. Well, at least not without additional provocation.

Curled up next to him, she allowed the security and tenderness he offered to calm her – let it erase the horrors she'd seen. She enjoyed the first dreamless night she'd had in a long time.

When they exited the cave the next evening, Caleb and Morgan were waiting at the entrance. Terrill must have contacted him while she slept as there wasn't much that needed filling in.

"So, the four of us striding in there is probably not going to go over too well, is it?" Morgan asked. Mara heard the slightly nervous note masked by the flippancy of her voice and exchanged glances with Terrill.

Terrill smiled grimly. "We'll have to trust Dabir and Yasmine to run interference for us," he said. "Last night, getting in was easy. Mara let down the safeguards. But I think it's safe to assume we got through without incident due more to chaos than anything else. They'll be on their guard tonight, and four Vampires entering their territory is going to send sensors spiking off the chart."

Mara raised her eyebrow at him.

"Three and a half?"

Mara knew he was trying to be funny, but all she could think about was what had happened here and what could still happen. This was her home territory and she was responsible for their safety.

Not that it would be home much longer once her people found out the truth about her and her relationship with Terrill.

Terrill touched her face. *You're not responsible for our safety, Mara. We're more than capable of taking care of ourselves and of you.* He made her look at him. *You can't blame yourself for what happened here. It wasn't your fault. You don't even know if it has anything to do with the prophecy.*

I know, I know. But . . . She ran her hand through her hair as she turned to stare off into the starry sky.

Terrill moved so that he was back in her line of sight. *But what?*

If something should happen to any of you, I would go after my own people. My own people, she scoffed. *I don't even know what that means anymore.* She looked up at him in confusion. *What sort of monster does that make me?*

He kissed her forehead and raised her chin with his hands so she could only see his eyes shining with affection for her. *The way I see it, you'd be protecting family and friends from those who would kill based on species alone. I know of no other such noble monsters.*

Before she could respond, the air crackled with a new tension, signaling the approach of a Viajante. The males immediately took defensive positions, able to clearly ascertain the direction of approach. Almost too clearly, Mara thought to herself. The Viajante that approached them was making no attempt at subterfuge and she was pretty sure she knew why.

CHAPTER TWENTY-FOUR

Y asmine," she called out quietly. Everyone stilled, waiting for
an answer but refusing to let down their guard. Trust, but
verify – Terrill's motto in practice.

"Yes. May I enter?"

Yasmine sounded calm, but Mara picked up the faint impression
of worry.

At Terrill's nod, she answered. "Yes, Morgan and Caleb have
joined us."

Almost immediately, Yasmine appeared through the mist. Mara
stepped forward and they embraced. "What news?" she asked.

Yasmine turned to face the group. "Dabir organized a gathering
of the Council of Elders." Mara heard the crack in her voice. "What
remains of them." She raised her eyes to meet Mara's concerned
gaze. "The Council knows about you and Terrill. They would have
words."

Mara's face paled.

"We're going with you," Caleb said.

Morgan nodded. Before Mara could protest, Morgan raised her
hand to cut her off and stepped up to Caleb's side. "We're in this
together." She looked at Caleb and they grinned. "We might have an
interesting counterargument or two to offer. Besides, do you two

really think there is a chance in hell Caleb's going to allow you to sideline him? I mean, really?"

Mara couldn't hide her smile.

"All four of you entering will complicate things," Yasmine said.

"It's a complication we're going to have to work through," Terrill said. "Does Dabir know?"

Yasmine communicated the change of plans to Dabir and nodded. "He does now." *And he's less than thrilled,* she told Mara privately.

What's the problem? Mara asked.

His influence with the Council has weakened and with the high emotions of the others, he's worried about how it will go over.

Mara nodded. It couldn't be helped.

Terrill indicated Yasmine should go first, followed by himself and Mara, with Morgan and Caleb bringing up the rear.

Yasmine looked over the group. "All right then, let's get this over with."

There was no breeze. – none at all. Mara couldn't remember a time when the air had stood so still. It was as if it too held its breath as they entered. They passed additional sentries and Mara felt the heat of dozens of eyes blast anger and hatred at her for her presence among the enemy. She recognized some as those she'd gone to school with and the realization stung. At least the majority of the population seemed asleep and unaware of the meeting the elders had approved during the heart of the night.

Terrill sensed her nervousness and stepped closer, partially for reassurance, but also as a not-so-subtle indicator to their observers that he stood as her protector and they'd have to go through him to get to her.

She sighed. She'd always known her partial acceptance was temporary. Since the beginning there had been questions and distrust. How had she survived an attack that killed her family? What had really happened? She'd heard the whispered questions her entire life. She'd spent most of it deluding herself into believing they had finally stopped wondering and had grudgingly accepted her. Now, even that flimsy illusion was gone.

You worry too much. Shaba was here when you were a child, and she believed in you, right? You said she was well respected.

Yes, she said, *but the keyword is 'was.'*

Mara, Morgan whispered, *I am picking up on a lot of angry thoughts right now.* Mara saw Caleb move closer to Morgan, also scanning the area for danger.

"Mara," the soft-spoken ancient on the raised dais said as he motioned for silence. "You've come back to us, but different."

He stared at her in silence, and Mara felt his presence move through her mind, probing for answers.

Terrill used his bond with Mara to slam down a mind block, temporarily forcing the elder out of her mind and back into his own body.

The elder looked surprised, then his eyes crinkled and he laughed out loud.

From the reaction of the onlookers, laughter was not something they'd expected. Confusion and curiosity began to replace the previous feelings of hostility.

"You were right, boy. Shaba did send word to me, but you just provided me even more information than she."

Dabir whipped around to stare at the old man.

"Did you hear anything of Shaba coming back after she met with them?" Dabir asked Yasmine. Yasmine shook her head.

Guess Shaba didn't give him the 411, Morgan joked. *Awful touchy, isn't he?*

I didn't realize he was normally in contact with so many elders. Mara shrugged.

Who is this man? asked Terrill.

His name is Pavo, Mara told Terrill in an awed voice. *I've only seen him once before. He is one of our most ancient. Very powerful. We knew of him – that he made his home here among us – but he maintained his distance. I never knew why. Still don't.*

In the instant of her communication with Terrill, Pavo's piercing black eyes bored into hers, triggering Terrill's protective instincts.

Terrill's aggressive body posture didn't sit well with the Viajante gathered and once again things threatened to erupt.

Pavo lifted his hand and signalled for calm. To Mara's surprise, she actually felt a calming influence enter her. She was shocked to see the same influence working on the Vampires in her group.

I've never seen anything like it either, Terrill said, voicing the answer before her question had even formed.

Clearly confident that he held the attention of all present, Pavo began to speak. There would be no sidebars during his speech, such was his power.

"An ancient prophecy foretells of the joining of the two species." He paused as the murmuring of the crowd rose. He held up his hand for silence and instantly they complied. "It is also true that this prophecy was kept closely guarded. Few of us with knowledge of it remain, fewer with understanding. The time for keeping secrets is no longer."

Mara looked up at him quizzically. "Yes, my child," he answered her. "You are the chosen one."

Rumbles of discontent began again. Pavo waved it off and looked directly at Terrill before addressing the crowd. "Little was known of the chosen one's soul, only that he would be found across the shadow boundary. He would be powerful, powerful enough to bring her to him. And having done so would bind her to him, swearing her protection above all others." He looked at Terrill and nodded. "This too I have seen."

Dabir cleared his voice. "What has the prophecy to do with the destruction of our Sanctuary? Was this also predestined? The result of the prophecy?"

Dabir's questions captured the attention of all Viajante present. The Vampires among them stiffened defensively. Mara knew they were blameless in the attack, but like them, she was unsure how Pavo would answer.

Pavo shook his head sadly. "No, there is no correlation between the prophecy and this attack. Unprovoked and senseless it was. The intent behind it remains shrouded in a bloody mist." He turned his obsidian gaze back to the Viajantes gathered. "What is clear to me is that these Vampires here were not behind it. I sense their intentions clearly. They would have prevented it had they known."

He shook off the almost trance-like state he'd worked himself into and addressed the Vampires before him. "Your journey has been interrupted by this tragedy, but it must continue. What you seek concerns us all. You must seek the second joining. The answers lie not here among our ruins, but among others."

At Mara's sound of protest, he waved his hand. "No, child, Sinjon would not want you to linger here. What is done here is done."

He indicated for Dabir to approach. "You and Yasmine will accompany them on this journey." Dabir lowered his head in acknowledgment and Yasmine came forward from her position to the right of Mara, obviously humbled by the trust in them Pavo had shown.

Pavo spoke to Mara privately but allowed Terrill access to his words through their soul link. *Be careful and make haste. Danger fast approaches. To remain here longer is not to remain safe.*

Yasmine took the lead again and Dabir the rear, ensuring their safety as they left. Mara wasn't really worried about an attack – no one would dare within Sanctuary – but even with the innocent verdict they'd just gotten from Pavo, there might be some tempted to once they left. Terrill's continued vigilance evidenced his agreement with that sentiment.

Once they cleared Sanctuary, Mara felt the tension pounding at her slowly diminish. She breathed a sigh of relief and then smiled at the irony. Once upon a time, Sanctuary had been the only place she'd felt safe. Strange how that had changed.

Before splitting to find shelter, they discussed where to meet on the east coast. They'd agreed that New York was the best take-off point, but settled on meeting up first in Boston. Its proximity to Salem, they decided, might be helpful if their presence aroused interest. There was always enough weirdness associated with the crowd that went through there that their presence wouldn't be noticed. Indeed, it might even be welcomed. They agreed to meet in three days.

Yasmine and Dabir were given the task of setting up a safe house and establishing defensible perimeters. Because they could travel in daylight, they made great time and were set up in less than thirty-six hours. Yasmine contacted Mara who relayed their success to Terrill.

Mara and Terrill had decided to take the full travel time and send out feelers for both Victor and Angelica. They weren't able to learn anything new about Victor but did confirm that Angelica hadn't reentered the States. At least it was a start.

Mara hoped her dreams might provide more clues. After waking from a particularly vivid one she turned to see Terrill staring at her.

"I thought you were asleep."

He shrugged, "I've been in the habit lately of rising early. I wanted to see what happened in your dreams." His eyes bored into hers, demanding an honest answer. "Are you all right?"

She nodded shakily. "The other figures are starting to get clearer. I think that Celeste is the east point, but she's still unclear." She frowned. "It's going to take some time to get used to calling her Angelica. She's always been Celeste to me." She rubbed her temple in frustration.

He raised his hand to replace hers, and she felt a healing heat sooth the dull ache. "I know. But until you tell her about her past, it's probably best to get used to calling her by the only name she knows." She nodded. "Did your dream give you a location?" he asked.

She shook her head, disappointed in herself and the inability to find the answers she so desperately needed.

He raised himself over her and tenderly kissed the worried frown marring her lips. "Mara, it was worth a try, but it's not our only shot. Let's just rest. It isn't yet dusk and I'd feel better if you could get a little more sleep – real sleep."

"I don't know if I can."

"Try," he said as he lowered her down and wrapped her securely in his arms. It wasn't long before she wasn't thinking of anything at all.

CHAPTER TWENTY-FIVE

*W*e're all set outside Dabir's perimeter. We've made a few trips into town at random hours. Caleb hesitated. *Nothing out of the ordinary so far.*

Caleb, what aren't you telling me? Terrill asked gently, sensing something wasn't right.

It's nothing, man. Damn incessant buzzing, like a headache, has been driving me nuts for the last couple of days.

Is Morgan okay? he asked, knowing Mara would also ask.

Caleb smiled. *Yeah, she's fine. Whatever it is, it's not affecting her.*

Be careful, Terrill cautioned. *I don't want anything to happen to you.*

No worries, bro, talk with you later.

* * *

Mara jumped up. Something wasn't right.

Mara, we're under attack! Morgan cried.

Mara started to get jumbled bits and pieces of images through her communication path with Morgan. A log slamming into her . . . trying to hide . . . calling for Caleb.

Terrill, Morgan's under attack! Caleb isn't answering her!

Minutes seemed like hours before they got to the location of Morgan's broadcast for help. Mara felt the air thicken with power. An ominous creak of wood was her only warning as one of the massive branches making up the leafy canopy above Morgan took aim at her now-vulnerable position on the ground. Morgan rolled away and barely avoided a dead-on hit. The smaller limbs slashed through skin and clothes to rip angry gashes across her body as she scrambled out of its reach. By the looks of her, there had been more than a few successful hits already.

Where was the attack coming from? Mara spun to locate the source of the power. In the clearing yards away from her stood Caleb, tears sparkling in the moonlight as they streamed down his otherwise emotionless face. She saw him raise his arm toward Morgan.

Oh my god! HE was causing the attack! She stifled her scream and forced herself to breathe. She didn't take her eyes off him.

"Caleb, don't do this," Morgan whispered. "Don't let them control you. You're stronger than they are. I need you, baby, come back to me. Please."

Mara saw him hesitate and lower his arm. She breathed a huge sigh of relief, but it was short-lived. Seconds later he raised it again purposefully. The inner struggle once visible on his face was now wiped clean, replaced by the heartless mask of a stony-eyed and distant stranger.

Caleb's hand stretched out and he curled his fingers toward his palm, beckoning behind Morgan. Mara screamed but was too late in her warning. The tree branch cuffed Morgan in the back of the head before sailing by. Shaken and dazed, she was knocked to her knees.

Mara, something's wrong with Caleb. I don't have much time left. Help him.

One second Caleb faced Morgan, the next he was knocked off his feet by Terrill. Momentarily stunned, Caleb struggled to communicate. "I can't fight it, man. End it. Don't let me hurt her anymore."

Morgan heard his guilt-wracked voice and rose to go to him. Mara had to restrain her, not only to prevent her from causing herself more injury, but so she wouldn't incite Caleb to fight Terrill and finish the programming directive he'd received.

"It's all right, old friend, we won't surrender you so easily," Terrill told him as he kept him pinned to the ground. *We have only seconds before he tries again,* Terrill said, *I can feel it building in him, commanding him to continue. Merge with me.*

Mara did and felt their combined protective power form a shield of energy that whirled through the night in search of an invisible target. Guided by Terrill, it acquired one, and the blast it made upon contact left her drained and exhausted.

She felt Morgan collapse in her arms and she looked at Terrill.

He's safe. We forced out whoever was controlling him.

She sighed in relief. *Thank god.*

Morgan's ragged breathing recaptured her attention. Who could pit souls against one another? Her eyes turned glassy. No, she wasn't going to cry.

She needed to find out how badly Morgan was hurt. The biggest concern appeared to be the wound to her abdomen. They needed to get the wood out, but doing so would cause more pain and bleeding. She sent a nervous glance over her shoulder at Terrill as he helped Caleb up.

Caleb looked dazed and confused, like he was having trouble focusing. They saw him take in the damage caused to the tree and then shift his gaze to Morgan's chalky pallor and listlessness. He staggered and nearly fell when he saw the crimson stain soaking her clothes.

Slowly, he sank to his knees beside her. "Morgan, baby, I'm so sorry," his voice broke as tears streamed down his face. "I'm sorry."

Mara saw Morgan weakly squeeze his fingers. She didn't have much strength left. "It's not your fault, Caleb. It wasn't you. Remember that, no matter what. Promise me," she whispered.

Mara signaled to Terrill, and he placed his hand gently on Caleb's shoulder. Caleb clutched at his heart but released his grip on Morgan's hand. "I promise baby," he whispered.

Terrill helped him up. "Let us help her now, Caleb. Mara has healing powers. Morgan's going to be okay. We're not going to let her go."

"Don't let her die," Caleb begged. "Please don't let her die."

Terrill knelt opposite Mara and swallowed hard when he saw the nature of Morgan's wounds. He linked a hand with Mara.

Can you do this? he asked her.

I've done it on myself many times, but the wounds were never this severe. Determination shone in her eyes. *I can do this. She accepted me from the beginning. No way will I let her slip away. No way.*

He nodded and lowered his gaze back to Morgan. "Show me what you need me to do."

Mara gathered her energy and trusted the merge with Terrill to provide any additional strength she needed. She closed her eyes and moved her free hand slowly over Morgan's body. She concentrated on the most life-threatening wound to her stomach.

She opened her eyes and looked up at Terrill. *I'm going to need both hands for this. Can you keep the bond between us strong without physical contact?*

Absolutely. Do whatever you have to do. Nothing more will harm her.

Mara nodded and closed her eyes. She placed the hand Terrill had been holding over Morgan's head. The other remained centered over her heart. She built up the energy around her and used her control over the elements to raise the wooden shaft still embedded in Morgan's skin out of the wound. Mara worked fast to repair the damage as she removed it, but the pain was so much that Morgan whimpered and began to thrash. Afraid she would succeed in moving and undoing all the good she had accomplished so far, Mara ruthlessly held her friend still, slowing her heartbeat and breathing the best she could. She used Terrill's additional strength to try and dull the pain.

Her face grew gray and drawn from the effort, and she felt Terrill's concern. She removed the foreign contaminants and stimulated cellular bonding and growth with her mind. Inch by torturous inch she mentally sutured, stitched, and cajoled cell regeneration until the last of the wood was removed and she could direct all her efforts at replicating the epidermis and closing the last of the surface damage.

At Mara's cue, Terrill took hold of the offending wood and incinerated it. They couldn't afford to leave any trace of themselves there.

Mara rose on her knees, moving her hands over Morgan's entire body from toe to tip, seeking out other internal injuries or bruising. Each time she discovered another injury, she repaired the damage and increased circulation and oxygen release to that spot, helping speed healing by removing the swelling. Morgan's body had already begun to heal the minor scratches so she didn't worry about them.

Satisfied she'd done everything she could, Mara slumped back on her heels and lowered her hands to her sides, using them to brace herself upright. She nodded to Caleb, who immediately knelt at Morgan's side and reached for her hand. "She'll be fine," Mara said, "but she needs blood to regain her strength."

Tears of guilt and anger shimmered in Caleb's eyes. Terrill spoke to him gently. "We'll go as soon as you feed her. There's time enough to make it to the safe house Yasmine and Dabir found."

Terrill and Mara retreated to give their friends a little privacy but kept up a vigil for any signs of danger. The threat was still too close.

Caleb lowered his head to Morgan. "Can you ever forgive me?"

Morgan slowly opened her eyes and smiled weakly at him. "There's nothing to forgive. Not now, not ever."

"I don't deserve you. I never have."

"Caleb, I'm going to be fine."

"We can talk about it later," he said, his voice gruff with emotion. He pulled her into a tender embrace and gave her access to his neck as he leaned over her.

It was nearly dawn when they arrived at the safe house. The shock and concern on Yasmine's face at seeing Morgan in Caleb's arms was mirrored on Dabir's.

"What happened? Is Morgan all right?" she asked.

"You ran into trouble," Dabir stated.

"We think they were attacked by a Viajante. Caleb . . ." Mara hesitated.

"Caleb was attacked and under someone's control. He was forced to attack Morgan," Terrill said. "We were barely able to get there in time."

Yasmine gasped and looked at Mara in confusion. "You couldn't find any trace? How?"

Terrill shook his head in frustration. "I don't know."

"Interesting," Dabir said, "and disturbing."

Mara indicated for Yasmine to follow her. She wanted to check on Morgan and needed a second opinion. Morgan looked better. Her color was back and she appeared comfortable, but Mara was afraid she'd missed something.

"She's going to be fine, Mara. You have your mother's gift."

Mara felt a heavy weight lift. There truly was no finer praise she could have received.

I told you that you hadn't missed anything. Look, Caleb's pacing out here. If you two are finished, I think they'd appreciate some time alone. Otherwise, he's going to start climbing the walls.

Mara shook her head and tried not to laugh. As usual, he had a way of making her fears seem trivial.

We're done. By all means, send him in.

She rose to leave as Caleb entered the room. "She'll need rest," he said. "She hasn't gotten a lot of that lately."

Mara's interest piqued. She stopped Yasmine at the door. "What do you mean, she hasn't been sleeping?"

He nodded reluctantly. "Some sort of dream or nightmare has been keeping her up. I don't understand it. Seems I can't even protect her in her sleep."

Mara sent waves of reassurance. "You do a fine job protecting her, Caleb. She knows you'd give your life for hers. I know she would give hers for you."

"She nearly did!" he spat out bitterly.

"That wasn't your fault," Mara said softly. "You fought against it, giving us time to get there and help. That you could fight says a lot about your strength and dedication to each other. Most would have succumbed."

She watched him sink dejectedly into a chair beside Morgan's bed. "Caleb, just talk with her."

She left him holding Morgan's hand to his lips. She hoped the quietly murmured words she heard them exchanging were the start of a healing process for both of them.

She didn't get a chance to talk with Yasmine in private about the bombshell Caleb had inadvertently dropped, but they both had plans to look for Morgan in their dreams that night. Could she be the missing one? Mara thought about telling Terrill about it, but exhaustion won out and pushed her over the abyss into a healing sleep. She hoped the darkness would bring the answers she sought.

CHAPTER TWENTY-SIX

Mara awoke again abruptly, as she did now whenever she dreamt. The fourth figure was coming into focus, but she couldn't yet tell if it was Morgan. Maybe Yasmine had seen more. She silently left the bedchamber and headed outside to enjoy the late afternoon sun after making a detour by the kitchen for coffee. Confident she'd find Yasmine outside, she was surprised to see Dabir waiting for her instead.

"Yasmine needed some extra sleep. She told me you two often talked before the others awoke, so I thought I might keep you company if that's all right?"

Although he phrased it as a question, Mara got the impression it wasn't. She seated herself in one of the chairs. "What's wrong?"

He chuckled, "Now what makes you think something's wrong? I just said I wanted to talk."

Mara raised an eyebrow. "Oh, I don't know. Only maybe that every time you wanted to have a serious talk with me, it usually started something like this?"

"Fair enough," he said. "I'm concerned about your aunt and these dreams. What's going on?"

Mara's brow wrinkled in surprise. "Yasmine hasn't told you about them?" That didn't sound like her. When Yasmine had given her a hard time about talking to Terrill, she'd assumed she'd already told Dabir everything.

He waved his hand in dismissal. "No, she told me about the dreams and that you're in them, but I get the impression they have something to do with Morgan as well."

Mara did a double take. She didn't think anyone had caught their reaction when they'd left Morgan's bedchamber just a few hours ago. She doubted Yasmine would have said anything before talking with her. Dabir and Terrill hadn't been in the room, so how could he know about it? "What makes you say that?"

"She now wears that same weary look Yasmine does. And then there's the attack to consider. What are the odds she'd be the only Vampire for miles around singled out? Why her? And why now?"

They were good points. The attacker could easily have controlled Morgan and turned her against Caleb, instead of using Caleb to attack her. The chance that it had been an attack of opportunity seemed less and less likely.

"Yasmine and I didn't suspect anything until after the attack. How could our enemies have learned who Morgan is before we did?"

He frowned and cast a preoccupied glance off into the distance. "We may never know. Maybe someone said something that was overheard when we were in Viajante territory. It's hard to say." Mara sighed. True. "And now there are these dreams to contend with," he said. "They're like nothing I've ever heard of. I can't access them and I worry about Yasmine's safety. Both while she dreams and when awake."

Mara heard the frustration and concern in his voice. Terrill probably fought the same demons. "So far there's been nothing alarming or threatening about them," she said. "They seem to be a guidepost of some sort. We're still trying to figure them out."

Then her brain finally caught up with what he'd said. "Wait a minute. Are you saying you can normally access dreams? Just not these dreams?" If he could, that would make him one of the most powerful Viajante she'd ever heard of.

Her questions caught him by surprise and he shook his head in denial. "No, of course not, I can't influence dreams. No one can. I meant only that I wish I had insight into them, so I can better protect her. I don't like being this powerless to help – not after everything Yasmine's been through."

Mara relaxed. That made a lot more sense than what she thought she heard the first time. He usually said what he meant she must have misunderstood. Clearly, she needed more coffee before talking. "Of course," she said. "Terrill feels the same."

She felt him stiffen slightly at the mention of Terrill's name. Why would that still bother him? It didn't bother Yasmine. Before she could ask, she felt his attention shift to something behind her. She turned to see Yasmine pause in the threshold, surprise and confusion written across her beautiful face.

Dabir was at her side in an instant. "Yasmine, you're up. Please join us." He led her almost reluctantly to the chair he'd just occupied and left them alone to talk.

The instant he left, the weight of Mara's gaze focused on Yasmine. "What's going on?"

Yasmine looked back over her shoulder in the direction Dabir had taken and shrugged. "It's nothing."

Mara continued to stare at her. "Nothing?"

After casting another glance back at the house, Yasmine turned back to Mara and took a sip of her coffee. "When I woke this morning, Dabir was watching me. I swore I saw a cold look in his eyes I'd never seen before. Before I could blink, it was gone – like I'd imagined it. Am I losing my mind?"

"You're not crazy," Mara said as she lowered her cup. "We've all been under a lot of pressure lately. Are you sure you didn't just dream it?"

Yasmine shook her head. "I don't know . . . maybe. The next thing I knew I was overcome with exhaustion. I had to close my eyes. Then I woke again and found Dabir out here with you."

"He's concerned about you, Yasmine. It wasn't too long ago he thought he'd lost you. The attack last night must have brought it all back again. He said he's worried about the dreams, that he couldn't help you if he didn't understand what you were going through."

"He's upset I don't broadcast them to him."

"Why don't you?"

Yasmine stood and paced restlessly. "I don't know. Part of me wants to, knows it's the right thing to do. He's my soul, right? But another part of me warns me not to."

Mara nodded compassionately. "I know what you mean. I finally told Terrill about them after Sanctuary. He wasn't too happy, but I think we've worked it out." Yasmine usually had a great sense of intuition about these things. "You taught me to trust my instincts. If yours are telling you to hold back for now, there must be some reason."

They were interrupted by Terrill's appearance on the twilight-darkened porch. "Caleb and Morgan are up. We need to talk about what happened."

Mara's eyes were snared by his as she attempted to walk by. He motioned for Yasmine to enter and waited outside with Mara.

"Are you all right? I saw Dabir come in after Yasmine joined you. Did he say something that upset you?"

Mara shook her head. "No, nothing like that. We had a pretty good talk." She pushed aside the doubts trying to sneak into her head. She wouldn't be surprised to learn Terrill had somehow placed them there. "He's worried about Yasmine and now with the latest attack . . ."

I won't allow anything to happen to you.

And Caleb? Do you think he allowed something to happen to Morgan? How do you know you can resist what he couldn't?

He pulled her to him. *I would give my last breath in your defense. Caleb was caught unaware. I won't be. Nor will he again. I'm sure of it. Now that we know what to expect, it will be harder for our enemies to use it against us.*

How is he? she asked.

See for yourself. He kissed the top of her head and led her back inside.

CHAPTER TWENTY-SEVEN

Morgan sat on the couch with Caleb standing protectively behind her. His hand on her shoulder and the intense eye communication between them said volumes. Mara had been afraid their relationship might have suffered as her body had.

"Are you all right?" she asked Morgan as she took her hand.

Morgan smiled. "I'm fine and I've been ordered to take it easy. How exactly that translates to invalid status, incapable of doing anything for myself, is a complete mystery to me." The teasing twinkle in her eyes melted the heat of her words. She saw Caleb's look of displeasure so she swallowed her smile. "I see. Well, it seems wise to be cautious."

Caleb growled in light-hearted frustration. "All right already! I'm not a bloody ogre. Terrill, help me out here. Tell me you wouldn't do the same thing."

Terrill raised an eyebrow and maintained his typical aloof pose. "Perhaps, but I would have accomplished it with more tact."

Mara shoved him. "Tact, my ass. Like that's even a word you recognize." She sat down as they all laughed. "Morgan, Yasmine and I were curious how you two met." She glanced up at Caleb who was watching her with a puzzled expression. "I know it sounds strange, but we think it may be related."

"How the hell could it be related to the attack? It happened years ago." Sheer frustration and not a small shade of guilt colored his tone.

Mara hated to see him upset. She could tell he wanted to put the attack behind them, but there were still too many unanswered questions to safely do so yet.

He kissed Morgan's troubled mouth and sat down on the other side of her. He pulled her toward him and took possession of her hand. "All right, if you think it has some relevance, why not? Go ahead, baby, tell them."

"I was born mortal. I grew up in an orphanage in England. Once I turned fifteen, I was farmed out to foster homes." She grinned. "I wasn't too big a fan of the majority of people they placed me with. I ran away a lot. They labeled me a troublemaker, not that I cared what they thought mind you."

Mara smiled at the cheery lilt of her voice but heard the pain and loneliness beneath it. It was too easy to visualize just how hard her life had been.

"Just after I turned seventeen, I ran away again. Unfortunately, this time I got myself in a spot of trouble." Her hazel eyes darkened to a green-fringed mahogany. "I got involved with someone who wasn't all he appeared to be. He got drunk and left me in a bad part of town. I had no money and no idea how to get out of there. Words can't describe the impression of evil that swamped me without warning that night. I panicked and ran." She grimaced. "Ran right into a dead-end alley. How stupid can you get, right? Well, then it got worse."

Mara gripped Terrill's arm, unaware of how tight she was squeezing until he patiently pried her fingers apart. She made an apologetic gesture and placed her hands in her lap. He winked and reached into her lap and took back her hands.

"I was attacked by a Vampire and left for dead." Morgan shuddered at the memory. "The pain was so intense, I thought I was going out of my mind. I'd never experienced anything like it before."

Mara knew only too well how painful it could be. She turned sympathetic eyes to Morgan.

"Then this vision appeared and he promised to take away all the pain. I believed him. My soul believed it."

Caleb tenderly stroked her face. "I arrived too late to stop the attack, but I was able to convert her – to save her."

He saw the surprise his statement caused. "I'd been tracking her for weeks, only I hadn't been able to pinpoint who or where she was. My soul recognized her presence in the city, and I felt an urgency to find her. I guess part of me knew something would happen if I didn't. As it was, I barely got to her in time."

"He saved my life, and finding him changed mine. I became a Vampire and found the missing part of my soul. I can't even regret my life before that. It's what brought me to him."

"What does their story have to do with the attack?" Terrill asked. "I don't see the connection." Mara and Yasmine exchanged an electric glance. Terrill sat up in his chair and focused the full force of his gaze on Mara. "I think you'd better explain."

She shifted her gaze from him to the floor. "Yasmine, tell them what you told me about what happened to my mother before I was born." She waved off their confused looks. "Trust me, it's relevant."

In her slow and dramatic way, Yasmine retold the story of Mara's mother, how she was left behind in England, her rape and subsequent pregnancy, and finally her escape to Ireland.

Mara kept her eyes on Morgan's mesmerized expression as Yasmine recounted Nicolette's futile attempts to locate the daughter she'd left behind and the deep regret and feeling of failure that never left her, not even as she lay dying.

"You think Morgan is your half-sister?" Terrill asked. He looked at her for a heartbeat. He only said one word. *Trust.*

It cut her deeply that he thought she still didn't trust him. She had planned to tell him. She'd only just found out last night.

She fought to keep the impact of his disappointment out of her voice. "I only started to think about it last night after the attack. I think Morgan's father must have been mortal, thus she was born only partially Viajante. I think she would have converted later, but the Vampire conversion happened first. Maybe she'd already started to develop some skills, but didn't recognize them for what they were."

Morgan looked like she was considering it. "There were things I was able to figure out that others didn't, but it often backfired and I ended up making as many wrong guesses as right."

Mara looked into Morgan's tear-stained eyes and felt her mother's sorrow and shame for having lost her. "Morgan, I am so sorry you never got to know her."

Morgan raised incredulous eyes to Mara's and exhaled a shaky breath. "I have a family?" Mutely, Mara and Yasmine nodded.

Morgan opened her arms slightly but it was all the invitation Mara needed. She immediately rushed into them with Yasmine right behind her.

"Mara, how did you come to suspect Morgan was your missing sister?" Terrill asked. "What about the attack made you think it was related?"

She looked at Yasmine. It was time they told everyone. "It was the dreams."

"The dreams?" Caleb asked, "How did you know about them? We hadn't told anyone she was having trouble sleeping." He looked apologetically at Terrill. "I meant to talk with you once we got here, but events . . ."

"No need," Terrill said. "Mara?"

"Last night, Caleb let slip that Morgan was having trouble sleeping, and both Yasmine and I latched on to it." She took a deep breath. "We've both been having the same dreams and can communicate with each other in them. The dreams are related to the prophecy Shaba told us about."

The silence was so deep she swore even the crickets had paused their night symphony to listen.

"There are four pillars in the dream, like the four corners Shaba mentioned. Before you ask, Viajante don't dream like this and Terrill told me Vampires don't either. So . . . putting it all together, it seemed too much of a coincidence not to consider the possibility."

Morgan smiled as Caleb lifted her hand to his lips. "Since I first met Mara," she said and turned to her, "back when we were asked to keep an eye on you, I felt comfortable around you. I knew it was strange to have felt that way, but I never would have dreamed it would be because of this."

"And I with you." Mara smiled at the memory. "Here I was hunting Vampires, and I found myself breaking all the rules to develop a friendship with one. I guess I fooled myself into thinking I did it to help me succeed at my goals, but part of me always questioned that motive."

"That only explains some of the questions," Caleb said. "If Morgan is one of the four corners, how did the Society find out?"

Mara rose and started pacing. "That's been bothering me too. Morgan, when did the dreams start for you?"

"Right after we left your Sanctuary."

"Did you mention it to anyone while we were still in Viajante territory?"

Morgan looked at Caleb in confusion. "I told Caleb I was having trouble sleeping. I think we may have talked about the dreams at some point. But there was no one around to overhear. We never sensed anything."

Too late Mara realized they didn't understand the magic and control over the elements her people had. She should have warned them. She hadn't thought about it – she'd just assumed they knew. It was her fault Morgan had been attacked.

It wasn't your fault, Terrill said.

But I should have warned them. It didn't occur to me.

Mara, hindsight's 20/20. There are going to be mistakes – assumptions that will be made, both wrong and right. No one blames you.

Mara's eyes pleaded with Morgan to forgive her. "No one may have been there, but in Viajante territory, there could have been something that was overheard and it got back to the wrong ears. I didn't do a very good job of preparing you to deal with the powers over the elements that my people have."

"Mara, it's not your fault," Caleb sank back into the couch. "I'm more upset with myself that I didn't recognize it for what it was. To think I could have fallen for it to start with!" He punched the sofa in frustration. He sheepishly pulled his hand out of the arm cushion. "Damn," he muttered. "Forgot my own strength. Sorry about the furniture, Yasmine."

Yasmine's eyes sparkled with laughter. "It's nothing. Easily replaced. The Viajante who put that spell on Caleb must have been very strong. How many of our kind can cause the soul to turn on itself?" she asked Dabir. "Usually, if we have to employ a tactic like attacking the mind, it's defensive. Nothing so cold-blooded as this. We would normally direct it against the weak, weak of mind, resolution, or age. It's that lack of focus that lets us in. The ones prone to depravity are the easiest. The pure of heart are very resistant. That's why targeting soul against soul is so difficult."

Dabir nodded in affirmation. "Absolutely. Yasmine's right. Our people don't generally engage in this type of attack. It's used more to confuse the enemy so that we can prevail where outnumbered or to help us escape." He frowned. "It would have had to be a powerful ancient to do this, for all the issues Yasmine mentioned, even ignoring distance."

"And to remain undetected," Terrill cut in.

"Especially to remain undetected," Dabir echoed.

They were all silent.

"The discovery of the fourth will lead you to the third," Yasmine murmured.

Mara tapped her finger against her nose for a second, then turned and pointed it at Morgan. "Angelica was the third and you're the fourth. So where . . ."

Morgan shook her head sadly. "I don't know where she is."

"Maybe you just don't realize it yet."

Morgan looked at Mara, doubt swimming in her eyes. "The dreams."

"The dreams," Yasmine said. "We can't get a location, but there is a feeling of familiarity."

"And there's the sea coast," Mara interrupted.

"It's Ireland," Morgan said. "The dreams. It's Ireland. I'm certain. Caleb and I traveled there shortly after we met. I felt an irresistible tie to the land. Something pulled me there. If what you say was true, maybe I was subconsciously trying to find Nicolette."

Mara sat dazed at the implication and curious about why she – her own mother's daughter – had failed to pick up the connection.

"Perhaps we were too close to it," Yasmine guessed. "Morgan didn't have strong emotions for Nicolette masking clues and indicators like we did. Her thinking was clearer, and she was able to analyze without doubting the outside influences we might have."

"What about Celeste?" Dabir asked.

Did Morgan's translation of the dream location mean Celeste was there? Mara chewed on her lip nervously.

"If she's of your blood, she too should be having these dreams – or she will once we arrive," Terrill said. "I think she'll be drawn to us, but if not, we should be able to find her ourselves."

"Ireland, huh? It's been a while." Caleb looked at his soul with concern. "Morgan, are you sure you are up to it?"

She rolled her eyes dramatically. "I'm fine!"

Caleb looked like he wanted to disagree, but he nodded. "Ireland?"

"Ireland," Terrill said. "Get some rest. You're going to need it."

CHAPTER TWENTY-EIGHT

They descended the ladder onto the tarmac in Dublin. The air smelled salty and almost magical. Mara breathed it in joyously. Terrill herded them into the dark and cool interior of a Lincoln Town Car for the short ride to the private hangar. Terrill closed the hangar door and dismissed the driver after implanting the image of leaving them at a posh Dublin hotel.

Mara marveled at his seemingly effortless ability to control his environment and wondered again, just how powerful was he? It didn't take long for her to realize Dabir wasn't too comfortable with the continuous display of power either. She chuckled. Dabir never had been comfortable around those as, or god forbid, more powerful than he.

The surprisingly ordinary vehicles in the hangar didn't seem like Terrill's style. Her lips pursed. Was he seriously giving up his passion for fast cars?

He noticed the questioning gleam in her eye and winked.

Smart ass, she taunted him.

Takes one to know one, darling. May I?

By all means. Mara sent him the impression of an exaggerated bow, which he ignored.

Morgan coughed delicately and Caleb grinned like a loon as he waited for them to stop messing around.

"What's first, bro? Drive these things to our real vehicles?" Caleb asked hopefully.

Terrill smiled and shook his head. "We need to blend in. I don't expect we'll be staying in the city much. We'll need to keep a low profile as we go through some of the smaller villages around here. These should help."

Dabir nodded in approval. "We'll count on our powers to get us out of tight spots, using them only if necessary. Keep a small power footprint. Smart."

"But no cool cars?" Mara laughed at the disappointment in Caleb's voice.

Terrill laid out some of the basics of their plan. They'd discretely search the countryside for clues about the dream location or any Viajante or Vampire activity in the area. The primary focus would be to locate Celeste.

Before they left the hangar, Terrill touched base with Gabriella and Lauris.

"No word on Victor," he told the others unhappily. "He remains in Europe as far we know. The longer he remains hidden, the more time he has to plot and scheme and the less time we'll have to react."

They hid the vehicles with simple camouflage spells and settled into the cottage Terrill had rented on the outskirts of a sleepy village in County Cork.

That night the dream was even stronger. The mists cleared as Mara stepped out of the cave. Without hesitation, she traveled the footpath she now recognized would lead her to the stones and found the others waiting there. This time though, all four were visible.

"Join us," Mara said to Angelica.

Angelica looked confused. "Who are you? Why have I dreamed of this place for so long? You were never here before. Why are you here now?"

"It drew us as well."

Angelica turned her sapphire gaze back on Mara. "You've come for me – you more than the others."

"Yes. Though I knew you by another name."

Angelica nodded. "Very well. We'll meet soon. During waking hours," she said before she faded out of the dream.

The others cried out as the dream rippled and broke, waking them each in their respective resting places.

Angelica didn't seem frightened of them, Mara mused. It was almost as if she'd been expecting them. She was young but brave. She'd allowed the dreams to lead her where they would, despite the risk. And if what Angelica had said was correct, they'd find her soon.

Surprisingly, it took three days to locate her. She seemed to delight in jumping into and out of the dream at will, making it difficult to find her. More disturbing, Terrill discovered she traveled with a companion – a male companion. No one knew anything more.

"I don't like it," Caleb paced as he spoke. "What if it's Victor? We won't get her away from him without a fight." He flung his hand toward his companions. "Would you believe this motley assortment of characters over the man who raised you?"

Morgan looked at Mara with questions in her eyes. "He has a point. None of us were close to her before. Why should she believe us?"

Mara extricated herself from Terrill's iron grip on her hand and started to pace as well. "What we do know is that she seems to enjoy flouting the rules. This is the first time she didn't return to school after the holidays, but they have a long record of other indiscretions."

"She's sixteen, Mara," Yasmine said. "Flouting the rules isn't all that surprising, is it? In our family?"

Mara laughed, "Maybe, maybe not. But that was before the dreams. In the dream, she said she was expecting us. That may change things."

"She seemed as curious about us as we are about her," Morgan said.

Terrill came to his feet. "We won't know how she will react until she does," he said. "Caleb, you and I will have to be on high alert. If Victor's with her, he'll do whatever he can to stack the deck in his favor. He won't dare take us on directly. He'll send in reinforcements to do his dirty work." Caleb grinned and cracked his knuckles.

"You don't intend for Dabir and me to go, do you?" Yasmine asked.

"No," Terrill said.

"I hadn't even thought about that," Caleb said with a smile. "Shit, I'd begun to think of you two as part of the pack."

"Terrill, Yasmine should be there," said Mara. "Angelica is her family too." There really was no choice, but it still didn't seem right.

"I can't guarantee their safety, and we don't know how Angelica would react to Viajantes approaching," he said. "You know that. Once we know what we're facing we'll make other arrangements for them to meet."

Mara nodded reluctantly and looked at Yasmine, hoping she understood.

He's right. Yasmine said. *It would be too great a risk, especially if Victor's there.*

I'll send for you as soon as I can, Mara promised.

She watched as Yasmine and Dabir became smaller and smaller in the rearview until they finally disappeared. She sighed and turned to face forward. There was no going back now.

CHAPTER TWENTY-NINE

S he'd be face-to-face with her sister in minutes. A sudden dread seized her. What if she didn't believe them? Could she take losing Celeste a second time? She felt Terrill squeeze her hand without touching it. *You worry too much,* he said.

She drew invisible pictures on the armrest with her fingers. *I wish I could believe that.*

You should trust yourself and your destiny a little more. You just need to have a little faith.

She looked at him like he'd grown two heads. *Since when did you get so Pollyanna on me?*

He laughed silently. *I didn't. You're merely encroaching on my turf so I figured it would be fun to turn the tables. It's usually my job to be pessimistic and worried. One of us needs to be positive, so you better get with the program quick or we're going to end up confusing the hell out of ourselves.*

Mara rolled her eyes but swallowed her retort as they rolled into the parking lot of a small pub Angelica and her companion frequented. She let out a long breath.

She didn't want to think about the risks Angelica had been taking by using her powers daily to prevent mortals from questioning why someone so young was staying out late and drinking. She started to shake her head and then stopped herself. If she'd had the opportunity when she was her age, she probably would have done the same thing. Maybe they weren't so different after all. She smiled.

"So how do we do this?" Caleb asked. "What if she isn't there yet?"

"She is," Morgan said. Mara didn't question the certainty in her voice. "She doesn't know we're here yet," Morgan added and turned to look at Terrill and Mara. "That wouldn't have anything to do with your ability to mask yourselves and others would it?"

Terrill took point without commenting and they entered the bar, heading to the private corner where Angelica and her companion were already seated.

Angelica's eyes widened at their entrance, but she remained seated. Her companion made to rise, but she placed her hand on his arm and he stayed seated in reluctant compliance. "Four. And I had counted only two," she said. "Impressive."

It wasn't Victor. The dark eyes of a stranger stared at Mara with cryptic intensity. *Who is he?* she asked.

I've never seen him before, Terrill said, *but he's had training as a Warrior.*

How do you know?

I just do.

Mara returned the stare with a curious one of her own. His dark features and olive skin contrasted with Angelica's porcelain complexion and clear eyes. She couldn't determine his ethnicity. And the insight Terrill had just provided didn't make her feel any better about his presence. Who was he, and what were his intentions toward Angelica?

Terrill looked around the bar and scanned the patrons watching their interaction with avid interest. "Perhaps we ought to take this conversation to a more private location."

Angelica shook her head. "No. I like this location. I think I'll stay here. Feel free to go if you wish."

Mara found herself grudgingly impressed. Angelica looked like the delicate Barbie-doll type with blond hair and blue eyes, but obviously, the delicate part was just an illusion. Mara suspected a streak of stubbornness lay underneath. Either way, she was smart. A location change would mean a change in the balance of power and she obviously wasn't about to give up any advantage she had. Mara couldn't blame her. She hoped her sister wouldn't learn the hard lesson that the illusion of safety in public was just that – an illusion.

Mara matched stares with her sister. Only an oak table stood between them. "We need to talk."

Angelica's blue eyes locked onto Mara's darkening green ones as tension arced between them. Angelica's eyes sparked, and Mara knew the reds of her own hair were reacting, shifting and deepening in the dim light. She hoped none of the mortals around them picked up on the changes.

"I know you somehow, don't I?" Angelica asked

"Yes," Mara said. "May we join you?"

Angelica nodded as her companion stiffened in displeasure.

Caleb cocked an eyebrow and looked at Terrill. "Who's this cat?" he asked. Terrill shrugged.

After they took seats, Morgan took the initiative. "Perhaps you would introduce us to your friend?"

"You first," Angelica's companion demanded in a heavily accented voice.

Terrill crossed his arms and stared back. The man locked eyes with him and bit back a growl.

Angelica laughed and took a sip of the Guinness in front of her. Mara watched her companion slowly relax his highly vigilant posture to one less confrontational, but still hyperalert. He seemed protective of Angelica, but not in the same way Terrill was of her.

Angelica set the glass down and favored them with a bemused smile. "Very well, you all seem to know who I am, so it would be redundant to state the obvious, and I hate the obvious. So . . ." The man next to her looked at her in weary exasperation. She beamed at him and turned back to the group. "This is Filip."

Mara realized she didn't plan to say anything more and exchanged glances with Terrill. He made their introductions and kept returning his gaze over and over to Filip.

Mara nudged him with her toe. *What gives?*

He's not a young Vampire. I would guess he's at least a couple of hundred years old. What's his connection to Angelica?

I don't know. Why don't we ask?

Before he could caution her to be careful, she jumped in. "So Angelica, is Filip your soul or your protector? Did Victor send him to watch out over you?"

Angelica nearly spit out her beer. Well, at least it didn't look like she was harboring more than a mild school-girl crush on him. "No, Filip's not my soul, nor is he my protector. We simply enjoy each other's company."

Mara raised her eyebrow at her obvious lie, and Terrill looked disapproving. "I find it strange that a male of your age would spend your time with a child instead of with your soul. What are your intentions?"

Angelica's face turned bright red and Filip almost choked, actually inhaling the beverage he maintained the illusion of drinking. "A child?" she asked. Filip placed his hand over hers to silence her. She swatted his hand. Mara saw anger burning in her eyes.

"I would never dishonor her that way," he said.

"Then you were appointed her protector?" Terrill asked.

"No, not exactly."

"But you offer her your protection?"

Filip sat silent.

Mara saw a great sadness through his silence. "You gave up your soul to protect her."

He smiled bitterly. "No. It was I who was given up on many years ago by the one who gave me immortality. None of that has anything to do with Angelica."

Mara cringed at the self-mocking laughter in his voice.

Terrill looked at him in disbelief. "You were turned by one who was not your soul?"

I don't understand, Mara said.

Remember what I told you about how Vampires find their souls? It is almost unheard of to turn a mortal with whom you have no connection.

Now she understood the cause of Filip's bitterness clearly.

Filip shook his head. "I was in love and believed it reciprocated. Only much later was it betrayed. Now I remain alone except for the rare friendships I now fight to keep."

"So how did you come to be with Angelica?" Mara asked.

Mara now saw the truth behind the smile he sent Angelica. It was the type a father gave a daughter. "Angelica had already decided not to return to school when I ran into her and offered my protection. I helped facilitate her exploration into areas Victor, in his ignorance, would have insulated her from."

Angelica laughed. "Such a modest description. Don't let him fool you. I ran into a few of the truancy officers and Filip helped me elude them."

"It didn't seem fair, four against one, and not knowing the situation, I thought it best to intervene and ask questions later."

"Anyway, after that, we became fast friends," Angelica shrugged. "Filip didn't give a damn what people thought about him, and I didn't give a damn about doing what people wanted me to, so we decided to have a little fun."

"I take it you and Victor aren't close?" Morgan asked carefully.

"Me and Rob? Not hardly."

Morgan looked confused. "I'm sorry, what? You and who?"

Angelica laughed and shared a conspiratorial wink with Filip. "Sorry, inside joke. Rob's short for robber. He HATES when I call him that. Sometimes I do it just to provoke him."

"You call your father a thief?" Morgan asked.

"Well, he is, isn't he?"

Mara and Terrill looked at each other in mock horror.

And you thought I was bad? she asked Terrill.

I take it back.

Angelica saw their exchange and adopted a more defensive tack. "Let's face it. He's not exactly a saint. How do you think he got where he is today? Generosity? And then there's the taboo topic of my genealogy. What's he hiding anyway?"

Mara hid a smile at the imperious note in her voice. Obviously, she was used to getting her way. "Actually, that's part of what we want to talk with you about."

"Victor's misdeeds? Sorry, you've confused me with someone who cares. I've got enough of my own problems. I'm not interested in his."

"Oh, I think you'll be interested in this one," Mara said. "You were right to question your lineage. Victor didn't rescue you. He took you after he had your parents killed."

Angelica held up her hand, using it to shield herself from words she didn't know how to accept. "Say what? No. My parents were mortal. Victor found me and converted me to save my life."

It was really hard to watch the disbelief and pain building in her eyes. "No, honey," Mara said, "your parents were killed." She looked nervously at Terrill and then back at Angelica. "Your parents weren't mortal. They were Viajante."

Angelica stiffened and clenched her glass so tightly that Mara was afraid it would shatter. Filip clearly had the same thought as he hastily pried her fingers off it before something happened.

"How can you possibly know that?" Angelica asked. "How could they be Viajante if I am a Vampire? You're lying." She pushed back from the table and stood to leave.

Filip gripped her arm so tightly she cried out. Everyone stared at the angry expression on his face that transformed itself into a stone mask of determination. "Listen to what they have to say."

Angelica looked as shocked as they were at his behavior but relented. She sat back down and tucked the few strands of golden hair that had worked their way out of place back behind her ears.

"Fine. Tell me why I should believe you," she demanded.

Mara squared her shoulders. It was better to get it all out there. Piecemeal was just too damn painful for them both. "Because I was there. I saw him take you, Celeste."

Angelica's jaw quivered and she fought to maintain her composure. "What did you call me?" she asked breathlessly.

"Celeste," Mara said. "That was your given name when I saw you last."

Angelica looked shell-shocked. That's my fault, Mara thought to herself.

No, it's not. It's Victor's, Terrill argued.

Yes, but convenient for him, he's not available, isn't it?

She raised her eyes and was surprised to meet Filip's penetrating stare. He watched her, no doubt trying to determine if she told the truth, then he nodded.

Filip turned to Angelica and raised her head so that she looked into her eyes. "What is it that bothers you most?" he asked. "The truth that they tell you, or that he tried to make you forget and almost succeeded?"

"You remembered?" Mara gasped. "You were only two."

Angelica nodded. "He told me they were nightmares and sent me to see special doctors. They took blood and did all sorts of tests trying to find out why I couldn't remember what woke me screaming night after night. Finally, they just stopped. I never mentioned them again, and Victor never asked. He shipped me off to boarding school and we both pretended it had never happened."

Caleb shooed away a waitress approaching the table. "These doctors took your blood?"

"I was still pretty young, but I remember that the doctors were like us."

"Did they give you shots?" Terrill asked.

She shrugged. "Sometimes. I tried everything they offered. I just wanted to forget. I didn't know they were memories at the time."

Filip locked eyes with Terrill. "Why is that significant?"

"Mara, tell them about what Victor did to your family and what we've discovered about the Society," Terrill said.

"The what?" Angelica asked.

Mara scowled. She retold the story of what happened before she entered LA and what happened to her and Yasmine. The skeptical look on Angelica's face melted into a stunned one as she listened to what they had learned about the Society.

They had just covered what they knew of the prophecy and the dreams when Angelica stiffened. "Something's wrong. Some sort of danger's coming. You all need to go . . . like now." Filip was already clearing the way for her to escape out the back. "Hurry!" she warned them, "There isn't much time."

As they were about to exit the front door, Mara felt drawn to look back at her sister.

Come to the Morrigan's ruins tomorrow night at nine. Bring Morgan and Yasmine, but not the men. I believe you.

Mara almost smacked into the door, so great was her shock. She hadn't expected her sister to accept the truth so quickly. *Where?* she asked as they cleared the building.

Angelica gave her the directions and disappeared.

CHAPTER THIRTY

I told you so you wouldn't worry, not so you could dictate what I can and cannot do!"

"Why do you insist on doing these things when I'm not around? Don't you know how crazy that makes me?" Terrill shoved his hand through his hair and sat down beside her on the bed.

"It's not like I'll be there alone," she said. "Morgan and Yasmine will be there. It's only Angelica we're meeting."

"So you think," he said. "How do you know she's coming alone? Maybe she's working with Victor and it's a trap. Did you think of that?"

She jumped up from the bed and turned to confront him. "You don't believe that, do you? You saw her reaction last night to what we told her about Victor. Do you think she faked that?"

He sighed. "No, I didn't get the sense she was playing us. Though I have no doubt she's experienced at playing others, her reaction seemed genuine. What about Filip?"

"She said she would have him meet you at the bar."

"And you think he'll be willing to do that?"

She shrugged. "I guess I never thought about it. You don't think he will?"

"I don't know," Terrill said. "He's hiding something."

"Do you think Victor sent him?" she asked. He'd denied it before, but that didn't mean he'd told the truth.

"What about Dabir?" he asked

She shook her head. "We told Angelica we'd come alone. Can you take him with you? If he stays behind, Yasmine's afraid he won't let us go alone." She turned puppy-dog eyes at him and batted her eyelashes dramatically. "Besides, if you tell him you need his powers to help ferret out last night's threat, it might appeal to him more."

He gave her his are-you-kidding look. "You know how difficult he is to work with, right?" She waited. "Fine," he relented. "Caleb and I will take Dabir with us, but we want to know where Filip is before you leave the house."

"Deal."

It took some time to see the guys off. A lot of it due to Dabir's reluctance to accompany them and the arguments he made for staying with Yasmine. Mara saw the angry look he tried to mask. He was such a sore loser. She kept her promise and waited in their cottage until Terrill let her know they'd met up with Filip.

"You ready to meet your other niece?" she asked Yasmine.

Yasmine grinned. "You kidding? From what you two have told me though, she sounds like a handful."

"Where are the ruins she mentioned?" Morgan asked.

"According to the GPS, not far from here."

"What's their significance?" Yasmine asked. "There are lots of ruins in Ireland. Why this particular one?"

"I think it has something to do with the deity related to it. There's a lot of references about Morrigan in Celtic and Nordic cultures," Mara said. "One definition told of her status as a triple goddess who concentrated her powers for war, death, prophecy, and passionate love. She's also been associated with female energy and sought out as an advocate for those on a Warrior path."

Morgan snorted. "If I didn't know better, I'd have thought you made that last part up. I mean, seriously, can there be any more appropriate deity to symbolize the chaos we've embarked upon?"

Yasmine rose and opened the door. "Well, then, let's not keep fate waiting, shall we?"

"Indeed." Mara smiled and stepped out into the night with her family.

Mara led them to the path leading down to the ruins. The green of the familiar landscape shone brightly in the dark and the ruins themselves lay bathed in the gentle glow of the nearly full moon. Shadows sprinkled dark spots and partial images on the ground between the remaining pillars and their time-worn surfaces.

Angelica appeared from around one of the larger stones. She smiled and looked into Yasmine's eyes. "You're my aunt?"

Yasmine froze in midstep. "You look just like her," she said, "but your eyes are much darker, a deeper blue – perhaps your father's." She took a deep breath. "We believed you lost. I'm so glad we found you."

They clasped hands. Mara had millions of questions, but let Yasmine do most of the talking. After a while, she was shocked to realize the night was half gone, and they hadn't even discussed what brought them there to Ireland.

"How did you find this place?" Mara asked as she walked the circle and the stones placed at the corners. She swore she felt a surge of power as she drew closer to the southern one. "There's no doubt this is the place of our dreams, but we couldn't find it. It was only Morgan that realized it lay here in Ireland."

"Filip and I arrived here weeks ago. Like you, I was drawn to Ireland. I spent many nights wandering remote fields. We started farther north, but I was pulled toward this area. I snuck into the university library after dark and dug through books until I came across the legend of Morrigan. That's when I knew I'd found what I was looking for."

Yasmine nodded. "I can feel a power building around us – something I didn't feel when we first arrived."

Morgan rubbed her hands over her arms. "Goosebumps," she said. "Something is definitely here.

Mara walked back to the southern pillar. She wasn't crazy. It vibrated as she approached. What sort of power did it hold?

"What is it?" Yasmine asked as she stopped just to her right.

"I'm not sure. There's something here, but once I get to the pillar, it seems to fade." She squatted down to stare at the base of the pillar. The dust swirled softly around the base and then embedded itself into the pillar sediment. Before her eyes, a permanent image was burned into it.

"What do you see?" Angelica asked.

"A symbol of some kind, but I don't know what it means."

"I could tell you."

The sudden sound of an unfamiliar, childlike voice caused them all to whirl around.

Mara straightened and stared into the too-wise eyes of a small red-haired child. Too late now to question how she got there. "You know what the symbol means?"

The child smiled and nodded. "There are four symbols, just like there are four of you."

Last night seemed to indicate that Angelica had inherited their mother's gift of judgment and truth determination. Time to test that theory now. *What are you thinking?* Mara asked her.

Angelica cocked her head in appraisal. *She isn't what she appears to be. I sense immortal, but not Vampire and not Viajante. Something else.*

But do you sense a threat? Mara asked.

Angelica shook her head.

Yasmine?

I can't pick up anything different. Immortal, but not what we know as immortal.

Recommendations? Mara asked the group.

This feels like a test, Angelica said.

I agree. Morgan? Yasmine?

No one disagreed. Mara turned her gaze back to the child in front of her and prepared to address her.

The child smiled in approval. "You've made the right decision. Self-defense sacrificed for knowledge. Yes, you're the ones. Wait here and you will get the answers you seek." She blinked and disappeared into the mist.

* * *

They were frustrated. Terrill read it in their body language. He'd been surprised, but Filip seemed to have welcomed the chance to help search for the threat they'd discovered last night. He'd even been excited to meet Dabir. He said he'd never met a real Viajante before. Dabir, however, had been less than accommodating, and Filip had transferred his attention back to Terrill.

Caleb halted abruptly, and Terrill's wandering mind snapped back on task. "You found something?" he asked. He scanned the area and picked up the faint Vampire trail Caleb had just discovered by the bar entrance. There was something extremely familiar about it, but that wasn't possible. Was it? He sighed. It was. "I know that scent."

"Who is it?" Caleb asked.

"It's the same female presence I sensed outside Mara's home in LA. She never intended us to recognize her presence here." He patted Caleb on the arm. "I guess she never figured on your tracking skills, huh?"

Caleb straightened and took a mock bow and waved to his invisible fans.

"Then we have an advantage, no?" asked Filip. "If she thinks her presence undetected here, we have an advantage. Who did you suspect back in LA?"

Terrill thought about it. They hadn't been able to definitively identify the threat. There had been several possibilities, but one seemed more likely than the others.

"We never knew for sure," he said, "but there was a new addition to Victor's entourage we considered briefly. I don't know much about her, but they seemed close."

"Do you think this woman is Victor's soul?" Filip asked.

Terrill shook his head but didn't respond right away. "There's some sort of relationship there, but I couldn't figure it out. One thing is clear though. If it's her, she's here looking for Mara - or for information about her."

He kicked himself again mentally for letting Mara out of his sight. This would be the last risk he allowed her to take. Even as he touched her mind and reassured himself that she was okay, he knew with their bonding incomplete, she still had the power to project whatever image of events she wanted. It was time to take action and guarantee her safety, regardless of his promises or her wishes.

They split up to continue their search for additional clues about Victor's mystery minion or her future intentions. Terrill had a gut feeling she was long gone but hoped she might have stuck around. He had a few questions of his own he wanted answers to.

CHAPTER THIRTY-ONE

A sudden clap of thunder and blurring of the moon announced the arrival of the one promised to answer their questions. The mists cleared and they saw before them a slightly hunched figure, attired in some sort of flowing dress. She straightened slowly and supported herself with a uniquely carved staff topped with an oddly familiar amulet.

"Yes, child," the old woman cackled as she looked at Mara. Her faded green eyes glowed with mischief as she looked at her staff. "The symbol is what you think it to be."

Angelica noted faded red strands in the woman's long, intricately bound hair and her eyes widened in recognition of who stood in front of her. "You were the child that appeared before."

The old woman's eyes shone warm with approval. "Yes."

"Why the disguise?" Morgan asked. "Didn't you bring us here?"

"She needed to know our true intent," Yasmine said.

"If we had failed the test, the door would have remained closed," Mara continued, picking up and speaking aloud Yasmine's unfinished thoughts.

The old woman nodded again. "We have little time. What know you of your common history?"

Mara started to relate the story of her family, only to have the old woman stomp her staff into the ground angrily.

"No, no, no! You're thinking too small. Widen the scope. What you speak of is what drew you together, but it's not what I speak of."

Surprised at the irritation in her voice, Mara searched for something to say. She looked at the others in confusion and got only shrugs in response.

Angelica spoke softly and with respect. "Forgive us. It's obvious you possess knowledge deeper than ours – more ancient. Where within ourselves do we go to find the answers you seek?"

The old woman shook off any attempt at assistance and seated herself on the center rune stone. "I had hoped that the ancient teachings were not forgotten or lost, but I'm saddened to find it appears they were."

Mara seated herself at the woman's feet. Morgan, Yasmine, and Angelica followed suit. "Would you tell us? Help us understand. Our Shaman may retain much of this knowledge but the Council of Elders kept it close. The meaning may have been lost as our Shaman moved around."

The old woman rubbed her back in an unconscious gesture and nodded. "You need to know. Once there were but two species, mortal and immortal. Much changed for immortals over time, but mortals continued on, blissfully unaware of our existence, let alone our struggles."

Mara felt goose bumps crawl across her skin as she keyed in on the old woman's words. "One immortal species?"

The woman cracked a crooked smile. "Others like myself. Most died out, their hearts broken by the division. Others allowed time to transform them into emotionless objects, inuring themselves to the continual pain and sadness of awareness, transforming into something altogether different."

"Your magic and your spirit predate everything we know," Morgan said in an awed voice. "It's not Vampire or Viajante, is it?"

The old woman raised weary eyes. "Our people have been known as many things, in many times. Gods or Goddesses in more respectful times. Witch or Warlock in the more cynical ones."

"What happened?" Yasmine prompted gently.

"A few thousand years ago there came a period of great discontent. A movement formed among the warlocks. Some of them sought power and dominion over their surroundings, including mortals. They formed an alliance that drew on forbidden magic to attain their goals." Her eyes grew glassy with unshed tears. "The rituals and the oaths changed them. Turned them from what they were into something more powerful. But that power came at a great cost."

Morgan's sharply indrawn breath was loud against the night silence. "Costs like the inability to tolerate the sun and the need for blood to sustain their powers."

"Yes," the old woman said sadly. "To develop their powers, they had to embrace the darkness. As their power grew, the dark stain spread from their heart, until it sought to make itself a part of them, drawing them into the darkness it emerged from. They began to shun the light, seeing it as a source of power that robbed them of their new ones. Eventually, they could no longer tolerate it, even if they chose not to shun its brilliance."

"And the need for blood? Why did they seek it from mortals instead of other immortals? With the breaking of so many other rules, why didn't they seek the power immortal blood held?" Yasmine asked.

"Their numbers were far fewer then, but they certainly had the strength to have done so. I believe they thought that turning their backs on the old ways was redeemable, but feeding on their own kind never could be. That oath became the foundation of the strong division between both your species. To commit violence against each other was inexcusable, just as it remains today."

Well, at least to some of them, Mara thought bitterly to herself.

"We didn't know at first that the need for blood would result in the death of their victims. But they justified killing mortals to sustain themselves. At first, they stuck to the sick and depraved, but one bite left no room for error, no second chances. Eventually, I think some of them stopped caring."

She rubbed her neck, as if weary from retelling the tale. "Some of the witches joined their side, but more remained with the growing counter-movement dedicated to balancing the actions and power of the Vampire, as they called themselves. Perhaps the smaller original gene pool is part of the reason why their procreation has been so difficult, often taking hundreds of years before a child would be born to a joined couple."

She sighed. "No one knew what consequences to predict back then. It's only now, after so many thousands of years, that we begin to see."

"What happened to those who started the counter-movement? How did they become Viajante?" Mara's eyes swam with unanswered questions and implored her to continue.

"It's a time in our history of which I am not proud." The old woman closed her eyes.

"Please," Angelica begged her. "The truth has been hidden too long."

"Things were done, spells cast. The most powerful of our people mated with mortals. These matings caused gene mutations in mortals, mutations that would activate if the Vampire population grew too strong. It wasn't long before true Viajante as you know them were born without our interference.

"Remorseful of having robbed mortals of the choice to live as they'd been destined, the new Viajante were gathered into safe havens, and we sought to impart our knowledge to them, warning them of the Vampire and giving them the tools to defend both themselves and mortals should the need arise. They also passed on the story of the prophecy, divined by a powerful witch upon the eve of the split between our peoples."

"Sanctuary," Mara whispered. "And our Shaman?"

"Descendants of our original immortal elders. It was hoped they would retain the secrets of their creation, but much was lost during the long years awaiting fulfillment of the prophecy."

"How did this happen?" Yasmine asked.

"You have to understand, it was a time of great distrust. We barely prevented a war among ourselves. We were afraid of what would happen if word of the prophecy got out, and what steps some would take to destroy its existence. Very few of the original elders were even told. Many like myself chose to remain apart from both worlds, waiting until signs of the prophecy revealed themselves."

"So our family holds the key to the prophecy." Mara frowned in concentration and looked over at the stone that captured her attention earlier. "Shaba said the secret was in the blood, but familial blood flows through each of us in different amounts. It's not the same—"

"Balance," Yasmine interrupted and looked eagerly at the old woman. "That's what we need to attain."

The old woman nodded solemnly. "Yes," she said. "I can only guide you. You must find the way yourselves." Slowly she raised herself up, once again brushing off attempts to aid her.

"What of the prophecy?" Mara asked.

The others waited anxiously.

The old woman shook her head. "It calls for a joining. This is the location and you are the corners, but I am not permitted to tell you how to proceed."

Mara screamed silently in frustration. Well, wasn't that about perfect? She took a deep breathe. "Okay, so what happens after the joining?"

The old woman's eyes twinkled. "Ah, that is where my knowledge ends. We believe it heralds a new beginning – a new hope for all immortals. But it also strengthens the determination of some seeking to keep the species apart."

"So more Vampires and Viajante chasing us," Angelica said. "Big surprise." Mara grimaced at her flippancy and exchanged looks of consternation with Yasmine. The old woman smiled patiently.

"Will we see you again?" Mara asked.

"You no longer have need. I pass the legacy into your hands." She looked so sad when she said it. "I will promise you this, if you are ever in trouble and return to this place of power, you can call on me."

"How shall we do that?" Morgan asked.

"I have been known by many names. The one of my greatest folly is probably most appropriate to be known as now. You may call on me as Cassiopeia."

"We are honored to have met you," Mara said and inclined her head. "We will try to live up to the prophecy we've been charged to fulfill."

Cassiopeia cackled softly to herself. "It won't be easy. Many will seek your failure, but you already know that. I wish you success."

The girls were suddenly engulfed in darkness and smoke. Seconds later it cleared and they found themselves alone.

"Well," Angelica's eyes twinkled as she rose and planted her hands on her hips in her typical dramatic fashion. "Can't wait to see what we do to top this tomorrow."

Morgan laughed out loud, and Mara found herself unable to smother a smile. Even her usually reserved aunt fought to prevent a giggle from escaping.

"Well, if she's right, we've got our work cut out for us." Mara ran her hands through her hair.

"We need to figure out what we hope to achieve before we commit to following a course blindly," Yasmine said.

Mara wrinkled her brow but reluctantly nodded her head. While she agreed in principle, the odds weren't good they would really find out anything before jumping in any deeper. And she knew she planned to jump at least waist-deep before learning anything else. "Angelica, do you see anything about the joining or the prophecy?"

Angelica closed her eyes. "The bloodline brings change. Once joined, we will be stronger together as well as individually." She opened her eyes and turned indigo irises to Mara in regret. "I'm sorry. I can't see anything past that."

"It's like you thought, Mara. Some answers will remain clouded until after our joining," Yasmine said.

Mara found herself drawn back to the stone from earlier. "We need to figure out how to conduct this joining."

Yasmine watched Mara warily. "It's related to the pillars and the symbols Cassiopeia mentioned."

"And the center," interrupted Morgan.

"We've been assuming the center to be Ireland and these ruins," Mara thought out loud. "What if we overlooked something even more obvious?"

Angelica moved toward the center of the ruins where the old woman had been. "The center is both the beginning and the end."

"Angelica, be careful," Morgan said as Angelica reached the center then gasped as Angelica's body went rigid and her head rolled back.

CHAPTER THIRTY-TWO

Wait," Mara said as Morgan moved to interfere.

Angelica's head slumped then slowly rose. Black eyes devoid of any white stared unblinkingly into the distance.

Mara felt a chill when Angelica spoke. The voice that came from her mouth was no longer her own. "Earth, Water, Air, and Fire. Four elements become one."

She faced Yasmine. "North. Of the earth. At peace with one's surroundings, grounded and focused. These are your strengths."

Next, she turned sightless eyes toward Morgan. "Water. Forever changing, emotions in movement. Forger of friendships. Creative in ends and means to attain. Strength in blue, of the water or sky. Your place is west."

She locked eyes with Mara. "South. You and fire as one. Fire brings energy and your ability to heal, to overcome. It is the truth.

"I am the east. Air. Seeking knowledge and enlightenment. I face east."

Morgan leapt forward and caught her as she sank to one knee, obviously spent by her psychic exertion. They crowded around her.

Mara took Angelica's clammy hand in her own. She'd never seen anyone but a Shaman do that sort of channeling, and Angelica was only a child. "Has that ever happened before?"

She nodded. "It's not usually so intense, but it's one of the things that developed after the nightmares ended." Mara helped her up and Angelica rose unsteadily to her feet. "Should have kept my mouth shut about that encore, huh?"

Mara rolled her eyes and managed a stern look for all of about three seconds before she gave in and shook her head. Was she really that bad when she was her age? Yasmine just grinned.

Mara smiled. "Well, if that wasn't a cue, I don't know what is. Angelica, are you good with this?" She gave the thumbs-up sign. "Let's take our places then," Mara said.

She watched the members of her family fondly as they approached their respective stones, each intent on discovering its secrets.

Mara ran her hand over hers and the symbol appeared to glow faintly as her hand skimmed the surface. She pressed down on it unconsciously and jumped as her skin caught and ripped on the jagged surface. The jolt she felt when her blood touched the symbol shocked her. Her eyes lit in excitement and a grin covered her face. That had to be it!

It's in the blood, she said. *Mix your blood with the stone. The stone holds your power source and blood releases it. You must become one with it to draw upon it.*

She watched excitement replace confusion as they moved to do as she'd instructed. Morgan and Angelica used a lengthened nail to cleanly cut their palms. Yasmine pulled out her dagger and accomplished the same.

Mara felt something open as soon as her blood splattered on the ancient stones. By the whispers of surprise from around her, she could tell she wasn't alone in her observations.

It's done, Angelica intoned.

Simultaneously they turned to face each other then they approached the center. Once in place, Mara grew a little nervous under the attention as they waited for her to speak. She didn't know how she knew the words to say, but what came to her felt right. "Feel the source of your power flow through your veins. Bind it to you. Make it part of your every cell. You must become one with it before we go further."

They closed their eyes and did what she asked, letting the spirit of their element seep into them. It seemed like hours passed but was in truth only seconds. They opened their eyes and felt a new mental path between them open.

"The prophecy is about the blood that binds us together as a family. Now we seek to strengthen those bonds as sisters of a new world. We have embraced once more the world elements, now we must find balance. The blood that flows through the veins of one must flow through the veins of all. Do we stand so committed?"

"Yes," Angelica said.

Morgan nodded, her eyes alight with conviction. "Yes."

Yasmine slightly inclined her head and met her niece's eyes. "We stand so committed."

Mara raised her palms up to her sides and held them at shoulder height. As she did, an invisible force gnashed deep cuts across the already-healed surfaces. Morgan mirrored her actions, then Yasmine, and finally Angelica. They reached toward each other and grasped hands, completing the circle and sparking the change.

At first, each heard only their own heartbeat, then it grew until they heard two, then three, and finally all four. They merged and blended until there was only one strong heartbeat between them.

Hands still joined, they opened their eyes and saw each in a way only four of the same center could. They brought their joined arms to point at the center of the circle. A white light appeared around them, bathing them in its warmth as the center stone was consumed by an unearthly violet flame. The flame and the light surrounding them gradually faded and they dropped their arms. Mara looked at her newly healed hands in amazement.

"I can feel it," Angelica said in wonder.

"It's like a humming rushing through my veins," Morgan said.

Yasmine was quiet and Mara shot her a concerned look. "Are you all right?"

"The bond between us is so strong. I didn't think there would be anything stronger than that of making whole one's soul. The intensity should be different, shouldn't it?" she asked uneasily.

Mara and Morgan exchanged looks. It was possible the Viajante bond was different than the Vampire one, but . . .

"Do you think it's made us different?" Angelica asked as she twirled and flashed around the corners of the ruins. "Will I be able to walk in the sun? Or," she winked wickedly, "is Yasmine gonna start craving blood?" She made an irreverent boogeyman face at her aunt.

Yasmine made a sound of disgust and shook her head. "Mara," she asked, "how has this changed us?"

"I don't know. But if this magic is as ancient as the prophecy, it may reveal itself with the full moon."

"I don't think we should tell anyone about this yet," Angelica said

"Why not?" Morgan asked. "The guys know we came up here. Secrets don't exactly sit well with Caleb or Terrill." She gave Mara a meaningful look.

"No, I don't mean to never tell them," Angelica said. "I just sense a need to delay revealing everything until tomorrow night." She looked at Mara pleadingly. "Not doing so averts some sort of danger."

Mara didn't sense what Angelica had picked up on, but she'd already shown she had power to sense what the others could not. It would be wise to trust her now.

Mara nodded. "We can keep the details of the joining secret until tomorrow. We tell them about Cassiopeia and bring them out here tomorrow night to tell them the rest." Mara looked at the others for their assent, which they gave immediately.

Mara sensed Terrill's growing impatience at their prolonged absence and frowned uncomfortably. "It's almost dawn and they're expecting us. We should head back."

Even Mara was surprised by the anger in Terrill's voice.

"Damn it, Mara! You let some super-powerful being into your circle, and put yourself and your own family at risk. Do you have no concept of self-preservation whatsoever?"

Mara's hair turned vibrant colors of red and green flames flashed in her eyes. Before she could say or do anything, Morgan jumped up and headed toward Terrill. Caleb barely managed to grab her before she reached him.

She glared at both of them. "So you're saying that none of us have any ability to take care of ourselves? Is that it? Terrill? Caleb?" She paced around the room, working herself up until she trembled with rage. "You think because we're women that we're somehow without defenses, or even the ability to sense and respond to danger? That we're stupid?"

Both Terrill and Caleb looked shocked at Morgan's outburst. "That's not what I meant," Terrill said. "And I was talking to Mara." He fixed Morgan with a look so fierce she finally backed down.

He turned his granite glare to Mara. "I don't understand why you insist on doing everything the hard way. You take far too many risks. For once I wish you would stop and think about the consequences. Not just to you, but to others around you. You didn't just endanger yourself, you endangered your family. One of which isn't even of age yet. If that old woman had attacked you or them, would you have been quick enough to stop her?"

Mara tried to reply but he threw his hands up. There was no getting through to him when he was this angry. Nothing she could say would make a difference.

"Our plan is to go back tomorrow night, for the joining," Angelica said, breaking the silence.

Filip looked at Angelica in surprise. "Why tomorrow night?" he asked.

She laughed and grinned impishly. "Duh! The full moon of course. All the crazies will be out. Who'd want to miss that?"

Dabir shook his head in disgust and rose to his feet. He reached for Yasmine's hand. "We're calling it a night." Yasmine reluctantly gave him her hand and he helped her up. "It's been a busy day," he said.

Angelica nodded and she and Filip also rose to go. "We won't be far."

Call me if you have a need, she told Mara.

Mara was relieved that the drama of the night was finally over. Terrill ignored her and left the room as she said goodnight to Morgan and Caleb. She sighed and made the solitary walk to their sleeping chamber.

Still no sign of him. She sat on the end of the bed and let the day's events drain her of her remaining energy.

Her skin tingled and she felt Terrill's eyes on her as he appeared at the door. He latched it closed in a deliberate motion and stared at her intently, his arms folded in resolve. She didn't like the look of sheer determination chiseled across his rugged features.

No Mara, the night isn't over yet. Not by a long shot.

She swallowed convulsively, frozen in place as he crossed the room. He moved like an animal stalking its prey. A very angry animal she corrected herself. She shrank back on the bed and watched him warily as he approached.

Now, Mara, we WILL have truth between us.

CHAPTER THIRTY-THREE

Mara sucked in a deep breath and ran her tongue over suddenly dry lips. "I don't know what you mean. How have I been untruthful?"

"Don't! Don't act as if you have no idea what I'm talking about. You insult us both."

The bite of his words caused her eyes to sting and she wiped at them involuntarily, angry he could cause a reaction with just a few words. And worse he'd seen it. She rose and went for the door. She found herself thrown back on the bed, pinned in place by his strong body and the anger burning in his eyes.

"Where did you think you were going? We haven't even gotten to the interesting part yet." Although he spoke with velvet tones, Mara noted that he didn't bother wasting energy to conceal his fury at her defiance.

Too late she realized she'd pushed him too far this time. Mara tried frantically to come up with an argument to calm him down and change his mind from the course she saw carved on his face. He'd promised her he wouldn't. Her well-planned argument melted the second his lips made contact with hers. He tasted like anger and a dangerous desire. Mara felt herself falling under his spell and she struggled against it. She needed to maintain her wits tonight – especially tonight.

He strengthened his assault on her senses. "You will surrender to me tonight, Mara," he vowed. "Forever in my keeping. Under my protection. No longer will I tolerate your defiance. You will not hide your intentions – not from me. Everything. Tonight you will give me everything. No more half measures, Mara – not between us."

Mara gasped at his words and the deadly intent behind them. He wasn't giving her a chance to think. She felt him thrust into her mind, broadcasting his desires and how he expected her to fulfill them.

"I can't breathe, Terrill. You have to stop."

"You don't want me to," he said, his voice deep with masculine confidence as he scraped his teeth seductively over the pulse hammering at her neck. She shivered, unable to deny her reaction or the truth of his words. "Later," he promised. He lifted his head from her neck and recaptured her mouth.

Clothes were quickly becoming an impediment. The second she thought it, he acted, rending them with teeth and nails. She squirmed and hitched in her breath as he ran his fingers gently over her sensitive skin. "So smooth," he murmured.

Mara thought she was going to lose her mind when he shifted position and replaced his fingers with his mouth. He drove her again and again to the edge, but stopped just short, denying her release.

"Terrill, please," she gasped. Her body quivered with each deliberately accidental stroke of his fingers. And his tongue . . . oh god, his tongue.

"Say it, Mara. Say you recognize me as your soul, your other half. Take me into your soul. Surrender to me."

She shook her head in negation as she looked into his eyes. What he did to her affected him as well. He wouldn't be able to deny himself much longer. She shivered at the dark hunger in his eyes.

He held her gaze. "I would not place my faith on that hollow assumption. You have no idea the levels of my self-control or my determination that you obey me in this." She paled. "I will not be denied, Mara. You will surrender tonight, even if it takes an eternity."

She nearly screamed as he lowered his mouth again. He flicked his tongue once more, a promise of release only he could deliver.

"Mara," he said as he raised his eyes to stare into her passion-glazed ones, "would you deny us both?"

Tears of frustration and desire welled up, making her eyes sparkle like glittering emeralds. "No," she whispered. "I cannot. You are my soul. Together. Unable to exist without each other."

He trembled above her. "Give me your surrender, Mara." Ruthlessly he allowed his hand to accidentally touch her again.

She moaned. It wasn't fair. "I surrend . . ."

The words were torn from her as he gave her what she – what they – needed. He captured her scream in his mouth.

"Forever mine, Mara," he whispered as he lowered his head to her neck, flicking his tongue once, twice against the pulse beating frantically. He pierced the skin. The sensations of their joining rocked through them and sent them over the precipice again, erasing her gasp as if it had never occurred.

He closed the marks on her neck with an erotic sweep of his tongue and shifted position to lie down next to her. He cupped her face between his hands and kissed her tenderly. "The ritual is now complete. You are finally mine, just as I am yours."

"It feels even stronger now."

He nodded. "It is."

"You took my blood," she said, upset he had removed her choice in the matter. "You said you wouldn't until I was ready."

"I could no longer protect you with the ritual incomplete. You left me no choice."

Sparks flashed from her eyes. "This is the partnership of which you speak? You decide what's best for both of us?"

"You kept things from me – things that put you in danger."

"You took away my free will," she accused.

"No, I opened your mind so that I can sense danger to you from any distance. All you lost was the ability to hide things from me."

He dragged her close. "Mara," he whispered against her ear, "I would not seek knowledge you are unwilling to give, but I will not allow harm to come to you because your mind is shut to mine."

She glared up at him. A mocking smile curled his lips and Mara saw him swallow his pride. She looked up at him, surprised by the vulnerable light now reflected in his eyes.

He sighed. "I'd be lost without you, Mara. I know I promised you I wouldn't force it, but I had no choice. I had to. I couldn't keep you safe. I can't lose you."

Damn it. It was impossible to ignore his emotions lying naked before her. She wasn't willing to let his arrogance drive them apart.

"I don't want to lose you either," she admitted.

She saw the relief and joy in his eyes as he read her thoughts. He dragged her under him. "You won't."

He lowered his head and kissed her. She lost herself in the sensations the completion of their bonding had released.

CHAPTER THIRTY-FOUR

Mara woke early. She sat up and stretched. The peaceful expression on Terrill's sleeping face, conspicuously absent during waking hours, made him look almost innocent. She resisted the urge to wake him. They had the rest of their lives together. The thought filled her with wonder. She might still disapprove of his methods, but she had to admit, he'd only forced her to go where she would have eventually. Now she understood what Morgan meant about the intensity of a soul joining.

She brewed a pot of coffee and let the gentle percolating sounds soothe the slight sense of unease tugging at her. She again considered waking Terrill to tell him about it, but it was still early afternoon. It was probably just nerves anyway.

She walked outside the cottage, and the innocence and beauty of the Irish countryside enveloped her in a fragrant embrace. She sipped from the steaming cup in her hands as she enjoyed the early afternoon light. The gentle breeze carried a potpourri of floral scents and the occasional delicate petal or two. She sighed. Despite everything, tranquility eluded her. The chord of uneasiness from earlier still plucked at her, persistent but undefined. She was about to go inside when Dabir contacted her.

Yasmine went back to the ruins and the witch attacked her. Mara, I don't know if I can save her. Hurry, please!

Her coffee cup shattered on the stone walkway. She stared uncomprehendingly at the pieces. Fear for her aunt choked her. She didn't hesitate, but ran, using every power at her disposal to cross the distance to the ruins. The horror in Dabir's voice meant she couldn't afford to waste another second. God, let her be all right!

She crested the hill leading to the ruins. She blocked out everything around her, focusing with laser precision on Yasmine lying broken on the center rune stone like some discarded pagan sacrifice. Blood seeped down her face from a gash over her eye and grotesquely stained the sacred rock, forming an ominous crimson bracelet around her at its base. Mara dimly registered a strangely silent and detached Dabir moving to stand at her side.

"Dabir, how long has she been like this?" she asked as she tried and failed to reach her aunt on their old and new communication pathways.

Shadows began to flicker around the pillars in the gathering twilight. Her eyes grazed across their dancing movements, but she didn't spare them a second thought and focused her attention on Yasmine as she tried to staunch the flow of blood from her numerous wounds.

It took her a few minutes to realize that Dabir hadn't answered her. "Dabir?"

She turned to see what had prevented his response. A sudden sense of menace assailed her. Cold steel plunged into her before she could react. She gasped as the blade struck deep. It stung bitterly as it slid in. She raised pain-filled eyes to Dabir in shock. *Terrill!*

"Why?" she asked as unshed tears of betrayal threatened to blind her.

Dabir's lips twisted into an icy grin and he reached his free hand around her neck and pulled her toward him in a cruel embrace. She cringed at the death in his eyes. His chest rumbled in a satisfied laugh as he brutally ripped the knife from her body and shoved her away. He contemptuously wiped the blood from its blade on his pants. She fell to her knees and clutched her stomach in an attempt to control the bleeding.

"Is this because of Terrill and me?"

"Terrill?" he sneered the question.

"Why hurt Yasmine? She's your soul."

He barked in derision. "The hell she is! She's what I convinced her she was."

"And what is that exactly?"

He kicked Yasmine's inert body and Mara cried out. She tried to move toward her aunt, but he was too fast. He scissor-kicked her chest and she went down. She sucked in air, trying to recover her breath. His laughter chilled her like nothing ever had.

"Yasmine was a means to an end, and thank god that end is finally here. If I had to put up with her weakness and dependency another day more, I'd go mad."

Shock robbed her of speech. How had he fabricated the bond between them so expertly and for so long? He'd pretended to be her soul for years! They'd all bought it. How was that even possible?

He laughed at the transparent questions in her eyes. "You two never gave me enough credit. Always assuming I was ordinary, of average powers. You tried to keep your little secrets from me, but you never succeeded as much as you thought you did. I always knew this day would come, and the thought of how satisfying it would be sustained me."

"It really grated on you that we dared keep secrets from you, didn't it?" Mara rose shakily to her feet as his tirade and stomping around had at least temporarily increased the distance between them. She continued to goad him, hoping his need to justify his actions would make him reveal things he might not otherwise. And, more to the point, hoped to stall him long enough to reach Terrill. Why couldn't she? "That we didn't acknowledge you as the powerful being you are must have made you angry. Is that why you joined the Society?"

"I was a member long before I made it my mission to find you."

Mara's eyes widened. Oh, shit. That meant he was much, much better than she'd originally thought. That wasn't good – not good at all. "You used Yasmine to get to me."

"Bingo," he said as he pointed the tip of the knife at her in mock congratulation.

She tried again to contact Terrill, but her mind screamed in pain at the attempt.

She swore the smug expression on his face grew at her discomfort. He tilted the blade from side to side in mock concentration then raised his eyes to meet hers. "A truly beautiful weapon, don't you think?"

Her eyes were drawn involuntarily to the intricate handle as he toyed with it. It was Terrill's knife! The one she'd lost during her capture.

"Yes, I thought you might recognize it," he said. "I took the liberty of adding a little something extra from my personal collection to the surface of the blade. I believe you've sampled it before."

"The shot they gave me," she said dully. He was responsible for creating that too?

He nodded. "Useful stuff as it turns out. Wouldn't you know, with just a slight modification, it's just as effective on mortals? It prevents them from accessing too much information and impairs their abilities to pass anything but what we wish."

Mara started to inch away from him.

Terrill, can you hear me? A little help here would be nice. She felt the faint stirrings of a response. Encouraged, she tried again.

She needed to keep Dabir occupied. If he suspected she was having any success, he'd finish her off before—

He squatted down and grabbed her ankle, halting her movement. It shocked her into breaking off her attempt to contact Terrill.

"Uh-uh," he tsked. "I don't think we're done here yet."

"So what did the Society want with me? And why would you risk that to destroy me now?"

"What risk? We knew about the prophecy and that you were the key years ago, but until the other pieces fell into place there was little we could do about it. Until we had enough information to prevent the prophecy, you were nothing more than an aberration, a curiosity, to be studied and experimented on." He flashed an evil grin as he flipped the knife blade. "Not to worry. We managed to keep busy ourselves with other scientific research while we waited."

Bile rose to her throat as she remembered the experiment results she'd come across. How could he have been part of something so vile? He'd conducted experiments on his own people?

He laughed, reminding her that her emotions ran too close to the surface. She'd have to do a better job of masking them if she wanted to survive.

"We learned of Victor's daughter years ago when he brought her to us. It wasn't hard to figure out she was really Celeste." Mara couldn't prevent her gasp. He smiled. "In his defense, he never meant to bring her to us, but Vampires like him are so easily led. A whisper here or there about the dangers of a ward with such, ah, issues and tales of magic cures was really all it took."

"The idea of a Society of Vampires and mortals working together for supremacy over Viajante appealed to him, just as the idea of a mortal-Viajante alliance seeking supremacy over Vampires appeals to our Viajante recruits."

She turned her head away in disgust.

"And when we found that Victor's interest in you coincided with our own . . . well, we had all kinds of new directions to explore."

"You were the one leading the way into this new future? To what end? Mad scientist to some genetic mutation? Destruction of your own species? Great goal, Einstein."

He slammed his fist into her face, smashing her head against the rock and dirt floor.

Well, maybe that wasn't the smartest thing she could have said, she thought to herself as she wiped the blood from her mouth and forced herself upright. If she wasn't careful, her smart mouth was going to get her killed even faster.

Terrill, I could really use a little assistance here.

His response was weak, but there. He was slowly waking. Finally!

She maintained an outward impression of anger and hopelessness that she prayed would cover her elation at having finally made contact.

Terrill read her thoughts and caught up on what he'd missed while sleeping. She felt him cursing under his breath and knew she'd get another lecture about leaping before looking. If she survived that long, she reminded herself.

She was forced back to the present when Dabir dragged her to her feet by her hair. He glared at her. "I can't stand to even touch you. You let that filth violate you." He wrinkled his nose in disgust and sniffed contemptuously. He reared back and spit in her face. "I smell his stench all over you. You're nothing but his stinking whore." He grabbed hold of her and lifted her feet off the ground. He heaved and tossed her effortlessly into the far pillars.

She heard the crack as she hit, shattering what remained of the pillar. She tried to focus, her vision muddied with bloody forms multiplying and weaving throughout her field of view. Her left arm dangled uselessly at her side. She couldn't control the shaking of her fingers as she tried to position it to grasp her aching head or contain the continuing flow of blood from her knife wound.

Mara? The voice was slight, but she hadn't imagined it. She invoked her iron discipline not to look in that direction. Yasmine was still alive! If Mara even glanced that way, she wouldn't be much longer.

He's coming to finish you off. I have little strength left, but if we combine it, we might be able to hold him until the others arrive.

He grasped her ankle with both hands and she heard him chuckle as he prepared to whirl her into a full-body spin. She clenched her eyes shut and tried to brace herself.

Now! Yasmine yelled.

They focused their powers on unlocking his mind. Mara followed Yasmine's lead and pushed hard. He dropped her to the ground and grabbed his temples in an attempt to squeeze them out.

The depravity and desire for violence she found shocked her. She lost focus and Dabir got enough control back to retaliate by landing several vicious kicks to her ribs. She could barely draw in a ragged breath by the time he stopped. He turned away from her and stalked toward Yasmine.

Focus! A new voice in her head yelled.

She almost wept in relief. Angelica. Both she and Morgan had joined through their new link and lent their powers. She focused again on Dabir. She had to save Yasmine. This time she held on until she had enough control to freeze him in place. Dabir growled and screamed in rage as he struggled against their invasion. He was so strong. She was afraid that in their weakened states, even with the extra help they wouldn't be able to hold him for long.

Hurry, she whispered silently to Terrill.

Dabir broke through her control and clucked his tongue at her. He started back toward her. She tried to get to her feet, knowing she wouldn't be much of a challenge to him. But at least the longer she kept him busy, the longer Yasmine would remain safe. Just as he reached her, Terrill, with Caleb and Filip close behind, exploded onto the scene.

Released from Dabir's grip, she fell back to the ground and stared up at the suddenly dark and forbidding sky in confusion. The next thing she remembered was Terrill's presence, warm inside her, healing her as she'd healed Morgan.

Where'd you learn to do that? she asked him as the pain that had her biting her lip slowly lessened.

He smiled tenderly at her. *A stubborn woman taught me.*

The soul thing, right?

His warm laugh ran through her. He nodded and Mara saw his attention turn from her eyes to her lips. *You have to stop distracting me, Mara,* he whispered seductively as he lowered his mouth to capture the trickle of blood her bitten lip had caused.

She felt her pulse quicken and groaned in frustration. *Stop! Talk about a one-track mind.* Even her body refused to listen to her.

I've healed the worst of your wounds. Besides, there's nothing wrong with your body . . . or how it responds.

She ignored his efforts to keep her prone and made him help her up.

Everything came flooding back. "Yasmine, is she all right? And Dabir? Did he escape?" The questions poured out one on top of another.

She scanned the area. They were still at the ruins. A small fire burned just off the north pillar. "Dabir?" she asked sadly.

He nodded. "I'm sorry. I know it was a horrible betrayal, but we couldn't allow him to recover."

He held her quietly as she cried. Tears finally spent, she pushed him away and wiped her eyes. "The worst betrayal is to Yasmine. He controlled and manipulated her for years. I think somehow deep down, we both struggled with doubts, but we didn't trust our instincts."

"I know you don't blame Yasmine, so Mara, you can't blame yourself either. He fooled a lot of people, including your Shaman, for a very long time."

She shook her head in sudden remembrance. "Sinjon must have known something was wrong. Somehow Dabir got the jump on him and eliminated him before he could raise the alarm. Could that have been the reason Sanctuary was attacked — to cover up the murder of one man? What makes someone so evil? And how did he learn to hide that much evil so well?"

She shuddered, still feeling the after-effects of having been in his mind and in the company of the sickest and most twisted part of him. He must have been extremely powerful to have hidden his real self from her, she'd always been able to pick up on violence — at least she used to be. Thank god Terrill had gotten there in time.

"You heard me when I reached out to you," she said. "Dabir said he used the same potion they shot me up with on the knife to prevent our communication. How did you hear me through that? Last time it was a while before it wore off enough to break through."

He shrugged. "Apparently Dabir never tried that potion on someone soul-bonded before. He assumed we'd already bonded the first time he used it, so he expected the same results."

"Did you know the ritual would make us stronger than what had been used against us before?

"I'd hoped it would make the bond between us strong enough for anything. Even without it, we were stronger together than most. It seemed reasonable."

Mara looked over at Morgan and Caleb, deep in conversation with Yasmine.

"Dabir was behind the attack on Morgan?"

"It looks that way."

Caleb turned his head toward Terrill as they communicated. He nodded and returned his attention back to Morgan.

"It looks like Dabir overheard their discussion about Morgan's dreams and decided to act on them," Terrill said.

"And you know why Dabir chose now to attack Yasmine?" she asked nervously.

He looked less than pleased, but not as angry as she'd expected. He nodded. "I saw the completion of the joining through our link as I healed you." He held up his hand before she could speak. "I saw that Angelica sought to prevent something, possibly this attack, so I understand why you didn't say anything. I didn't exactly encourage more confessions last night either." Her lips twitched in an involuntary smile. "The others have already talked about this too. Everyone's aware of what happened."

He helped her to her feet, and she exchanged embraces with Morgan before they moved out of the circle to where Yasmine rested with Angelica and Filip in attendance.

Mara dropped to her knees beside her aunt. "Are you all right?" The words struck her as stupid and rhetorical. Of course she wasn't all right. How the hell could she be?

Yasmine nodded and Mara was surprised to see the suppressed fury in her eyes. She'd expected defeat or sadness. She wasn't sure if this was better or worse.

"It's kind of ironic," Yasmine said. "I had conflicted feelings about so many things for so long, I'd started to doubt my own sanity. If only I had trusted myself!"

"Dabir was extremely powerful. He fooled everyone, even the Shaman. There's no way you could have known," Mara reminded her gently as Angelica and Morgan echoed her sentiments.

Yasmine smiled wryly. "He was my so-called soul. I should have."

"Yes, I see what you mean," Mara said, striking a pose of great reflection. "You with all your experience in finding your soul — not that anyone finds more than one soul within their lifetime. You should have been able to intuitively know he wasn't really your soul and seen past his façade to the layer of evil that even the elders didn't see."

Yasmine glared at her. Mara adopted a look of innocent confusion. "No? Or maybe," she said, "you're being just a little too hard on yourself."

"Fine," Yasmine snapped. "You made your point."

"Good," Angelica said. "So now what are we going to do about it?"

"I don't understand," Morgan interrupted. "Dabir's no longer a threat, right?"

"Dabir was involved deeply in Society business, in its leadership. His treachery is still in play and lives remain at stake." Yasmine looked up at the family and friends surrounding her. "There was a lot Dabir revealed against his will, before . . ."

Mara placed her hand on her aunt's shoulder. She didn't need to go on.

Terrill ignored Mara's look of warning and dropped to her level. "Go on."

"There's a Society stronghold close by. I couldn't get every twisted detail from Dabir's mind, but I'm certain they're involved in the capture and torture of innocent mortals and immortals for their sick purposes. I'm not leaving until it's destroyed."

Terrill shook his head. "We won't deny you your justice, but you won't avenge these innocents alone. We will help you." The others nodded.

"Is this one location more significant than others?" Caleb asked.

Yasmine nodded. "I think this one is very significant. Dabir held it in high esteem because it wasn't contaminated with Vampire collusion." She smiled ruefully. "Sorry, his words, not mine."

Angelica rose abruptly and scanned the area. Filip immediately went to her side. "What is it?" he asked. "What do you sense?"

"There's been a lot of power generated here, in this spot. The joining and now this attack. Attention has turned to our location, and we'll be sought out soon to explain." She turned back to look at Yasmine. "We won't have much time before they arrive."

"How much time?" Terrill demanded.

She shrugged. "Tomorrow evening. Maybe the next night. I'm not sure. I suspect we won't leave the island without a confrontation of some kind."

"I think it best we retire and regroup early tomorrow," Terrill said. "Yasmine, will the attack on the Society keep until tomorrow? We have plans to make and I want us all at full strength before taking them on." He looked at Angelica. "And anything else that might come up."

Yasmine nodded reluctantly.

Mara, said Terrill, *make her promise you not to do anything until we go as a group.*

I can't make her do that! She has the right to vengeance.

Mara, please, I know you don't want to lose another family member.

That's not fair.

Ask her.

She smothered her anger and turned pleading eyes to Yasmine. *Yasmine, promise me we go as a group tomorrow. No heroics. Promise me.*

Yasmine's eyes blazed, but weariness overtook anger and she nodded her head slightly.

As a sister, now so joined by the prophecy, you promise not to act alone. Mara deliberately widened the communication to include her sisters.

Yasmine exhaled and glared at her. *Fine. I wait to go as part of a group. But know this, I will not be held back in safety while an attack is conducted. I WILL be allowed to punish the transgressors.*

Agreed, Mara assured her. *No one will interfere.* She turned to Terrill. "Let's get out of here."

He nodded. As they left, Mara felt compelled to turn and face the ruins. It wasn't over, whatever it was. No, she thought to herself as she shook off the shiver of apprehension that cloaked her, it wasn't over by a long shot.

CHAPTER THIRTY-FIVE

While the others hunted, Yasmine reluctantly allowed Mara to hook up an IV for a blood transfusion. "I don't like this."

Mara sighed. "I know, but I won't risk your health. You and I are still weaker than the others because of the attack. Terrill won't allow me to go into trouble without taking his blood, and unless you've changed your mind . . ."

She waited for Yasmine's inevitable look of distaste at the thought before she continued. "Then it's a blood transfusion for you."

"How do you know it will help?"

"Well, I don't, not for sure." Yasmine arched a brow at her niece so Mara hurried on. "But since we've mixed blood, it should help amplify your powers like it used to mine."

"I thought our new bond alone was supposed to make us stronger. Why are we doing this?" She waved her hand at the transfusion equipment and curled her lip in disgust.

Mara sighed. She really couldn't blame her aunt for questioning. It probably was unnecessary, but she wasn't willing to take that risk. "Until we can test the theory in a little less, ah, high-stress environment, this is the compromise you're going to have to make. I know you'll heal and replace the blood loss over time, but time's a luxury we don't have." She softened her voice and looked her aunt in the eye. "Yasmine, I won't give you up. You're just going to have to deal with it."

Yasmine tossed her hair and scrunched up her face in irritation. "When did you get so bossy?" Mara arched a brow. Yasmine laughed and shook her head. "I know you worry, sobrina mia, but I'll be all right. I need to be able to do something, anything, to undo what Dabir did." She lay back in the chair. "Fourteen years of lies is a lot, but I will not let my desire for vengeance put anyone in danger."

Mara smiled. "I know, but I worry you won't forgive yourself. It's the danger you'll put yourself in that concerns me."

"I should have known about Dabir. When I look back now, I see when our bond started to break, but I didn't recognize it at the time."

Mara squeezed her arm. "Dabir fooled all of us. You know every one of us trusts you with our lives. We just need you to trust yourself, okay?"

Yasmine nodded and Mara watched her struggle with her emotions. She was going to be all right.

Mara sensed the others' impending return. They unhooked the transfusion apparatus and put it away. They didn't have long to wait.

Preparations for the assault started within minutes of the last arrival. Mara watched Angelica's enthusiasm with a cautious eye. She didn't want her sister involved, but Filip was needed. With the ambiguous threat hanging over their heads, it wasn't safe to leave her behind either.

Terrill stood at the head of the table, the unquestioned leader. "Yasmine, tell us again about the safe house and the people inside. I don't want any surprises."

She nodded. "Nor do I, but I didn't see everything. Dabir had many secrets. So, know there may be missing parts or, god forbid, parts he was able to keep hidden from us."

Terrill grinned grimly and indicated for her to continue.

She described the building and as she did, Mara projected it graphically on the wall. "I know there are a few Viajante involved as well as mortals that act as decoys for the curious or misguided that might show up. I only dragged three faces from his memories." Her voice cracked and she momentarily lowered her head before raising it bravely.

She wasn't going to let herself get upset over him. Good for her. Mara saw her intent and combined with Angelica and Morgan to feed her strength.

Terrill pretended not to notice the lapse, and Mara blew him a kiss across their private path. "So at least three," he said, "but probably more. If we're lucky, the odds will remain even."

"Actually, there will be four of us going in," Angelica broke in.

"Excuse me?" Terrill asked.

She didn't let him intimidate her and rose to stare him down. Mara hid a smile.

Remind you of anyone? Mara asked him.

Not funny, he said.

No, it's not.

"I can see things that will help with the initial attack," Angelica said. "I'm going."

I don't like it either, but she does have a point, Mara said.

I'm only agreeing because we don't have a hell of a lot of choices, he said. *It's up to you girls to keep her safe.*

Mara smiled and gave Angelica a thumbs-up sign. *We have it covered.* I hope.

Terrill scowled at Angelica's enthusiastic response. He moved to tower above her like an overprotective brother. "You will listen to everything they tell you. Follow their instructions to the letter. No deviation. None."

Mara was impressed by his intensity. Terrill could be downright scary when he wanted to be. Angelica didn't exactly cower, but he'd managed to wipe the look of excitement off her face and replace it with one of serious concentration and determination to impress them.

Mara stole a glance at Filip. The expression on his face indicated his approval. Angelica wouldn't be a mission liability.

It was decided that the girls would approach in mortal guise. Mara would mask their true identity and Terrill would help through their bond if needed. He'd use his powers to mask his, Caleb's, and Filip's presence as the girls got into the facility.

Mara was sure the new connection between them would tip things in their favor if it started to get dicey, but Terrill wasn't as convinced.

Be careful, Terrill admonished Mara.

She knew he hated the idea of her being in danger, but she was looking forward to proving herself once and for all. She started to blow him a kiss, but he dragged her to him and, to the amusement of all, engaged in a kiss that succeeded in raising both of their breathing to an uneven and somewhat jagged hitch before finally releasing her.

Just a little something to think about while you're gone, he said with a wicked grin. *Come back safe to me, Mara.*

She nodded stupidly as the girls pulled her into the car.

The girls took a circuitous route through town to throw off suspicion before going to the stronghold. After they left, Terrill signaled to Filip and Caleb and they took off. They arrived before the girls, undetected by mortal or immortal, and faded silently into position outside their target.

A lorry roared into the drive and slammed on the brakes. It spun out on the gravel drive, stopping just shy of the building. The girls got out of the car and staggered drunkenly toward the building.

Beer bottle in hand, Yasmine banged on the door. "Hey, in there! Are we late?"

They collapsed into giggles.

"Aidan's gonna to be so mad at you," Morgan said as she wiggled a less-than-steady finger in front of Yasmine's face. "You told him we'd be here hours ago."

Yasmine adopted an air of annoyance and put her hands on her hips. She tilted her head in Angelica's direction. "Like I had any idea it would take Princess Anna here hours to prep!"

"Very funny. It's not easy to look this good. You might do better if you only put in a little effort. I mean, really, just look at that outfit."

"What's wrong with this outfit?"

Mara stepped between them to stop the mock fight as the door finally opened. She breathed a sigh of relief. Just what they were hoping for, mortal guards. She wasn't sure their plan for access would have held up against Viajantes of Dabir's skill.

Within seconds the girls talked their way into the building. It was almost too easy. They knocked the guards out. Mara knew Terrill would come behind and make sure they never rose again. She didn't like it, but she understood it. They'd agreed before they left to spare Angelica what violence they could. Mara and Yasmine took off while Morgan and Angelica stayed behind to let the guys in.

"Not much in the way of defenses, huh?" Caleb whispered to Morgan as he brushed his lips against hers.

Her brow wrinkled. "I know. Either they're supremely confident they're above detection, or else there's something we've missed."

Even as the words left her mouth, they felt a power release. Terrill took off after Mara while the others closed in on Yasmine's position after taking care of the guards outside Angelica's sight.

Mara planted her feet as her opponent chose a frontal attack. He thought he could use his size as an advantage. She felt the bulk of his two-hundred-pound frame whisper against hers and crouched down just as he was about to hit. She shifted her center of gravity giving her the force needed to catch him off balance. She struck at waist height. To his surprise, she used his forward momentum and tucked her shoulder so that it acted as a lift, tossing him over her head. He grunted as he hit the ground. Mara knew he wouldn't be down long, so she used the distraction to open the distance between them.

"So, you're the chosen one," he said as he stood and dusted himself off.

She didn't trust the calm way he said it. He had to know she wasn't alone, yet his movements remained unhurried — like he was unconcerned she might renew her attack. Or if she did, that he could handle it. "I could say the same about you," she said, "although we might disagree on what you were chosen for."

His lips curled in a feral smile. "If only you put as much effort into learning to fight as you do quick-witted comments, you might have made a worthy opponent. Dabir was right about that."

Mara's eyes narrowed.

Hard on his words, he flew at her. This time he veered at the last minute and sent a blow directed at the base of her neck. He was done messing around and wanted her out of commission. She used her Vampire speed and inherited masking power to give the impression of being in two places at once and repositioned in front of him. She slammed her fist squarely into his jaw. The impact stopped his advance and snapped his neck back hard. He hit the floor with a muffled thud.

She sensed Terrill's arrival and, flush with the thought of her impending victory, relaxed her posture only the tiniest bit. It was enough for her opponent, who had silently gathered himself on the floor, to lunge at her. The blow would have been fatal had it not been deflected by a powerful blast from Terrill. Not content to let the battle drag on further, he delivered the death blow.

Mara slowly straightened and turned to look at him. He was pissed. She could feel the anger radiating from him, even at a distance.

He placed a finger over her lips, preventing her from speaking. *Never lose your concentration. The enemy will use any advantage they can. You gave him that opportunity. You know better.*

Pissed at herself for making such an amateur mistake, she had to agree. When would she learn?

They raced off in the direction of the others, but the battle had already ended by the time they got there. Filip was tending to a cut on Angelica's face. Mara whipped around to look at Morgan and Caleb in accusation.

"What happened?" she asked.

Yasmine wiped the blood off her hands and adjusted her clothing. "Angelica stepped into something headed for me. We've taken care of the problem," she said as she pointed to the body at her feet, "and you could say, training has been conducted."

Mara wanted to stay mad, but the look on Angelica's face showed she'd learned how costly mistakes could be and had been properly yelled at, so she let it drop.

"Did you recognize either of them?" Caleb asked.

Mara and Yasmine both shook their heads.

"Mine was Viajante, but no one I recognized," Mara said.

"Mine too, same thing. Dabir never brought me to Ireland before so I didn't know him either. The last time I was here was before I found Mara."

Caleb nodded and turned to Angelica as she and Filip approached them. "What do you sense?" he asked.

"Someone else is here. Not the source of the violence," Angelica's eyes widened, "but the cause."

Yasmine tore out of the room. The heavy steel doors of various chambers being flung open echoed through the complex. Mara borrowed one of Terrill's favorite curses and bolted after her aunt. Something extremely violent had happened, and Yasmine was about to find it. Mara didn't want her to be alone when she did.

Too late, she thought to herself as she skidded to a stop just inside a larger antechamber. A tattered and horribly wounded man hung from chains attached to the far wall. Yasmine was already by his side opening the shackles. Tears streamed down her face. "We're too late. He died because of me — because I didn't get here in time."

"Yasmine, stop!" Terrill yelled as he entered the chamber.

CHAPTER THIRTY-SIX

At Terrill's voice, the seemingly motionless corpse snarled and came to life. He grabbed Yasmine and blanketed himself with her body, an effective shield that halted their approach. He'd fashioned a crude sort of metal weapon and apparently kept it hidden from his captors. He pressed it now against Yasmine's neck and caused a small trickle of blood to flow. As her blood touched his fingers they both jumped as if electrified by some invisible current.

What is it? Mara asked her.

I don't know — an elemental recognition of some kind, she said, *but I swear I don't know him! We've never met before.*

Mara watched his grip on her tighten and confusion flash across his face. He switched the knife to his hand at her waist and wrapped his other arm around Yasmine's neck in a choking embrace.

Yasmine signaled the others to hold.

Mara started to take a step forward, but Terrill snatched her back as Yasmine's captor tightened his hold. *Don't provoke him!* he scolded.

Yasmine, what do you want us to do? Morgan asked as she and Caleb moved to the right and cleared a path in front of Angelica and Filip, allowing them to position to the left for attack if needed. Their actions agitated the stranger and Mara saw his muscles twitch.

Give him some space, Yasmine said.

No one wanted to give up their position, but they slowly moved backward a little, infinitesimally increasing the distance between them and Yasmine. Mara wanted the man to see they were willing to think before acting. God only knew what Dabir and his cronies had driven him to. Yasmine's eyes shone with encouragement.

"We don't want to harm you," Mara said. "We just want our friend back safe."

He opened his mouth to speak, but nothing came out. He cleared his throat painfully, and Yasmine winced. When he spoke, his Irish brogue was muted by the crunchy gravel sound of his voice. The starvation and torture had obviously taken their toll.

He locked eyes with Mara. "What are you? Not Vampire like those," he pointed at the others beside her, "and not Viajante like we." His step backward with Yasmine made clear who he meant by 'we'.

Curious. He threatened Yasmine, yet he moved away from the Vampire in their group like he wanted to protect her. She shared her thoughts with Terrill.

Mara started to move forward, and the man jerked Yasmine tightly against him in response. The knife rose and replaced his arm at her neck. Yasmine gasped as the blade punctured the skin. His eyes darkened.

"I see I have your attention. Know this, I have no problem killing her, but if you want her back alive, you better start explaining. I've had about as much bullshit as I care to take."

Mara nodded. "We understand. You're right. I am neither Viajante nor Vampire, but a mix."

He barked in derision. "No more lies!"

Mara raised her hand in acquiescence. "I am not lying. Why would I claim something so unbelievable if it weren't true? You asked for the truth and I gave it."

Mara, Yasmine said, *I don't understand how I know, but - he wants to believe you.*

He hesitated and Mara pressed her advantage. "Will you please lower the knife? Give our friend the opportunity to speak?"

His grip tightened and the trickle became a steady stream.

"Please," Mara said.

He looked at his hand in shock, as if surprised by his actions. He immediately lowered the knife and used his hand to staunch the flow. He didn't, however, release her.

Mara exhaled in relief. *It's a start*, she said to Terrill, who watched the exchange cautiously.

"Thank you," she said. "No one here wishes further bloodshed."

He snorted. "You expect me to believe that rubbish with the stench of violence so strong on the lot of you that it stings my nostrils? How stupid do you think me?"

"Not stupid at all," Angelica said as he looked at her. "Our violence was directed at the destruction of the Society — the ones who held you here. We merely wish the chance to be heard. Surely that's not an unreasonable request, is it?" Mara heard the push behind the words and congratulated her sister for recognizing that in his weakened condition, he would be susceptible.

Mara was truly shocked by the venomous look he shot Angelica. "Do NOT play games with my head. I'm much stronger than you could ever imagine, and I won't hesitate to protect myself."

"Interesting," Caleb mouthed to Morgan.

Mara nodded. "That won't happen again. But if I were you, I wouldn't make assumptions about how much power you think you hold over us."

He narrowed his eyes and braced himself for some sort of assault. He stared at Yasmine in shock as she switched projections from Viajante to Vampire. Mara saw him shudder as if a cold chill ripped through him. He turned accusing eyes back to Mara and watched in disbelief as the girls morphed to mortal, to Viajante, and back to Vampire. Mara maintained her mixed projection.

"What the hell?" he asked as he pushed the words past his cracked lips.

Part of the prophecy, intent on destroying the Society and anyone who supports it, Yasmine whispered inside his mind and to their girls through their new link.

Terrill moved forward as the stranger tightened his arm around Yasmine's neck, nearly cutting off her airflow.

"Wait," Mara said, grabbing his arm. *Yasmine, what's going on?*

Trying to reach him. Give me a minute.

Mara communicated Yasmine's intent to the others. They opened a link that would allow her to communicate with them all while talking with him as well.

Be ready, Mara cautioned them, *in case this doesn't work.*

You . . . are . . . making this . . . hard . . . to . . . to explain. Yasmine choked out the words.

What the hell? he asked. *No one's ever broken into my mind before. How did you?* He released the pressure against her neck and she sucked in hungry gulps of air.

If I gave you access to my thoughts — total access — would that prove our intentions to you?

His eyes widened in surprise, then narrowed suspiciously. *You'd risk offering me your mind?*

Yes, she said and dropped the barriers.

Through their shared viewing link, they all watched him access her memories, her ties to her family, their souls, the prophecy, her determination to stop the Society, and ultimately her betrayal by Dabir and the lingering vulnerability she couldn't hide. Angelica stifled a gasp as she witnessed the torture, his stubbornness in spite of his helplessness, and his fierce determination to destroy those who had betrayed him and his kind.

Yasmine, Mara said gently, *you shouldn't be able to see his thoughts like this.*

I know.

Then you realize what this means?

Yes.

Mara nodded and closed the link between the girls so Yasmine could communicate privately if she chose.

The stranger looked at Yasmine and noticed her tears. His hand rose slowly and gentle fingers dried the errant tear that had gotten away. He swallowed hard. "You saw into my mind?" he rasped.

She stared at him, seemingly mesmerized by the sparks of a fragile bond forming in his gun-powder irises. She nodded.

He didn't break eye contact with her as he slowly lowered his arms and freed her from his embrace. He looked at the group before him, knowing they could hear his every word. "Then you know why I cannot harm you. Go back to your friends."

"What will you do?" she asked.

"Probably get myself in trouble."

"Most likely. Join us anyway."

"Would that include the chance to take out the Society?" he asked.

"Oh yeah," she said smiling. "Among other things."

He returned her smile with a heated one of his own. "Done." He released his grip on her and stepped back slowly, dropping the knife.

Why did he let her go and why isn't she out of harm's way? Terrill asked.

He won't harm her, Mara said.

Did you miss the blood on her neck and his multiple attempts to strangle her just a few minutes ago?

No, but unless I miss my guess, he's Yasmine's true soul.

Her what? Terrill did a double take when he saw she was serious.

"So, what should we call you?" Mara asked the man.

"My name's Connor," he said.

"What can you tell us about the Viajante we fought here? Were there others? Or other Vampires?" Terrill asked.

"You killed the only blighters I had the pleasure of knowing. Turned against their own kind. Thought I'd never see the day that happened."

He straightened his back with a grimace. "No Vampires until now. I saw a few mortals time and again, but mainly those two. I remember another one showed up and seemed to be in charge, but I never saw him. Could that be your Dabir fellow? I heard him speak with the others once about someone named Victor."

He noticed their reaction. "Ah, so I see you have an interest in him as well. I thought it a bit strange they never let that one come by."

"Did they say anything specific about Victor and his relation to the Society?" Terrill asked.

Connor shook his head. "Dabir gave instructions to the others to limit what they shared with Victor. They weren't to tell him about the experiments they were conducting."

"What kind of experiments?" Mara asked with trepidation.

"None that warrant repeating in front of ladies, I'm sure," he said. "They sought a few donations from me during my visit. Not that any were given willingly to be sure." He clenched his jaw tightly. Mara saw remembrances of violence darken his eyes. Further questions could wait.

"So Victor was interested in what they were doing here," Caleb said, "but Dabir wasn't sharing."

"It fits our earlier theory that Vampires were being duped by the Society and allowed to believe they retained control," Terrill said. "But in truth, the control remained not mortals but with Dabir and his supremacy-seeking cronies."

Yasmine nodded sadly at Terrill's assessment. "Unfortunately, that sounds a lot like the sort of game Dabir would have loved playing." She shook her head in disgust. "He would have especially enjoyed stringing along a powerful, well-connected Vampire such as Victor."

Angelica turned to face the building entrance. "Ah . . . guys," she said nervously. "That threat I warned you about? Well, it's kinda here now."

Connor looked confused for a second. "What's going on?" he whispered to Yasmine.

"Can you stand?" she asked. "We need whoever's here to think you and I are Vampire. If you limit your movement, we can mask you."

"You can do that?"

"Yes," she said, "but we have to hurry."

He nodded and Yasmine immediately moved into action. She placed his hand on her waist and joined forces with the girls to project the image of Connor as a Vampire instead of his true weakened Viajante state. They faced the doorway as two Vampires appeared in a swirling mist.

"Is all this drama necessary?" Terrill asked drolly, his tone sharply in contrast with his vigilant pose.

The taller of the two bristled at the disrespectful tone and spoke with a hiss of displeasure. "Would you be so rude to emissaries of King Cedric and Queen Evangeline?"

"We hold no allegiance to them," Terrill said tersely, "but also, mean no disrespect."

The Vampire glared suspiciously at him and surveyed the area, taking into account their appearance and their surroundings. "There's a Viajante stench here," he said in a monotone voice.

"Yes," Terrill said. "How astute of you to notice what we had not."

He's pissed and not doing a very good job hiding it, Mara said to Angelica, who stifled a giggle. She saw Terrill's lips quirk in amusement.

The messenger shifted his eyes between them, almost as if aware of their private communication. "You're to accompany us to the High Court of King Cedric and Queen Evangeline. They would have an explanation of your recent actions."

Terrill raised his brow at the thinly concealed demand. "I see. I would ask that you send our regrets. We have not been to their realm to create disturbance recently and find ourselves, regrettably, indisposed. Perhaps some other time."

The shorter of the two emissaries came forward. Mara immediately recognized him as the more powerful of the two.

"You misunderstand," he said. "That wasn't a request."

CHAPTER THIRTY-SEVEN

Terrill's eyes narrowed and flashed tombstone gray before his features smoothed back out. "As I have no memory of pledging allegiance to your lord, how could it be other than a request?"

The shorter Vampire's face twisted in anger and he raised his hands slightly.

Mara felt power building but before she could react, Angelica stepped forward.

What are you doing? Mara hissed.

Let me handle this.

Terrill moved to put himself in front of Angelica, but Mara's hand on his arm stayed him. *Let her try.*

"Perhaps we can come to some arrangement that meets the intent of your sovereign's wishes while taking into consideration our special circumstances?" she offered.

Angelica's voice wove a strong magic, her ability to push extremely well developed, and by their visitors' reactions, stronger than their own. Yasmine, Morgan, and Mara added their powers to Angelica's. A sly wink from Angelica was the only acknowledgment they received before she continued.

"We have no wish to offend, but we've been under duress and must tend to our wounded. We would meet your liege in full health and able to answer all his questions. Surely that would be his desire as well, would it not?"

The taller of the two nodded and raised eager eyes toward her, anxious to please. His companion was slower to agree. His ramrod stiff posture evidenced his fight against the compulsion being planted. Angelica re-doubled her efforts.

Why don't you use your Viajante powers to control him? Terrill asked Mara. *As Dabir did on Caleb. They were extremely effective.*

It's a much more invasive form of attack. While the compulsion is being planted, he could fight, and here in this confined space . . . well it's not a risk I want to take. Besides, we don't want our interference discovered.

But most victims of that sort of attack are not aware they were victims. How much more secure can you get?

Mara shook her head. *There are some immortals who can detect interference like that. How else have the rumors of what we can do gotten out?*

Terrill appeared to consider it. *So how is what Angelica doing less undetectable?*

It takes significantly more power to convince someone to do something they don't want to than to convince them to do what they want to do. And if the influence is part of their own makeup . . .

Vampire vice Viajante.

Mara nodded.

And if they want to deliver their message and have us accept . . .

Exactly. She smiled. *We're just tweaking the delivery a little to buy us time to prepare. They leave here happy, and we get what we want.*

Terrill studied her face and Mara squirmed under the intensity. *I misspoke before when I said you weren't prepared to fight. You may still lack certain physical skills, but not strategic ones.*

Mara grinned. He'd never given her that much credit before. Clearly, he should have. She turned her attention back to the messengers. They wouldn't be leaving with what they sought tonight. But neither would blood be shed over it. Not if she could help it.

"Tell us where to meet you three days hence and we'll be there," Mara said.

Terrill made a sound of impatience. *I'd promise them no such thing.*

If we don't, they continue to hunt us. Better to set the stage for our confrontation at a time of our choosing rather than one of theirs, no?

He glared at her.

"We can speak. Angelica's controlling what they hear."

"I don't like promising anything," Terrill said. "Three days isn't enough time to find out what we need to."

"Three days isn't much, bro," Caleb said, "but more would be a harder sell. At least it gives us some time, and right now that's better than the alternative." He looked over his shoulder at the messengers held under Angelica's thrall. "I'm for finishing the discussion and getting the hell out of Dodge."

"All right," Terrill conceded. "Set the plan and let's get out of here."

Angelica finished implanting the suggestion that an escort was both unnecessary and insulting and that they would meet them outside Cedric's Court in three days, ready to answer whatever questions their liege might have.

After the two emissaries left Yasmine sank into the nearest chair. Mara looked at her in concern until she realized it was just the strain of masking Connor's presence and the events of the past few days that had finally caught up to her. Mara had turned back to Terrill when she heard Yasmine's cry. Connor had collapsed. Yasmine managed to cradle the worst of his fall. The pain rolling off him caused her to gasp, and Mara felt it through their link.

Terrill knelt by his head with a grim shock of amazement stamped on his face. "He stood there in this much pain without even a whimper? Mara, can you help him?"

She was already by his side. "Yes, but I'd rather we get out of here first."

"Agreed."

"Yasmine," Mara said, "we need to go. Caleb and Filip will cover our tracks."

"Give him to me, Yasmine," Terrill said. "I'll keep him safe. Go with Angelica and Morgan. They'll help you prepare everything. We'll meet you there."

"Don't let anything happen to him," Yasmine begged as they dragged her out of the room.

Mara watched Terrill gently pick Connor up. *Ready?*

She nodded and they took flight. Filip and Caleb would follow later. They had to take care of the Viajante bodies and erase all traces of their presence or anything else that might give away clues to their future plans.

* * *

"Who are these people?" Yasmine asked in horror as she saw the extent of the damage done to Connor's savaged body.

Mara shook her head. The torture had been deliberate and methodical, designed to prolong pain without causing enough damage to kill him before they were done. She couldn't imagine the kind of individual it took to do such horrible things over and over.

"When I began this journey, I was convinced only Vampires could be this depraved and have so little regard for life," Mara sighed. "But now, I just don't know anymore."

Mara shook off her gloomy ruminations and embraced Yasmine. "We've had a long night, you most of all. Connor will heal. If he rises or you have need of us, just call."

One by one they said their good nights and faded off into the darkness leaving Yasmine at Connor's side.

CHAPTER THIRTY-EIGHT

Terrill stood and the chair he'd been sitting on flew across the room and slammed into the wall before finally landing in pieces on the floor. "We can't take the risk and that's final!"

Eyes blazing defiance, Connor stood, his slow ascent a mocking indicator of his fury. "See how far you'll be getting without a shadow then."

Terrill moved toward him only to run into Mara parked obstinately in his path. *Enough!* she said. *You can't convince him, and you won't be able to stop him from doing what he feels best.*

Watch me.

Really? Just how easy do you think it would be to stop me or for me to stop you once your mind's set? Does anything about his Irish temper and desire for justice give you some hidden indication he'll magically bend to your will?

Terrill exhaled slowly and indicated for Connor to sit. He walked back to the table with Mara and stood behind her chair. *It's his desire to find action that worries me the most.*

Then tell him that.

"You realize the risk you run?" Terrill asked him. "We have to maintain the illusion you're one of us, but if things go wrong, you'll be uncovered quickly and we may not be able to help."

Connor nodded with a cocky grin. "Well, that's what makes it interesting now, doesn't it?" He twisted to look at the chair Terrill had destroyed and moved his fingers slightly. Before their eyes, it righted and reconstructed itself next to Terrill.

Caleb laughed. "I think Connor's going to fit in just fine." Terrill rewarded him with a hostile glare, and Mara bit her lip to swallow her smile.

Other than a brief comment acknowledging Connor's powers and how they might be useful, nothing further was said about excluding him. They spent the next few hours bringing him up to speed on Victor and the reasons behind their alliance. No one knew much about Cedric and Evangeline, but they all agreed that controlling what they revealed about the prophecy would be critical. God only knew how strong an alliance this court held with Victor. They needed to be cautious.

Angelica and Filip were the last to arrive at the agreed-upon spot. The group communicated silently to prevent detection and prepared to enter the huge, palace-like estate.

Terrill didn't shift his focus from the building in front of him but took Mara's hand. *Are you ready?*

She squeezed his hand. *We were brought here for a purpose, and I don't believe that purpose was to die. And if I'm wrong, well, we'll just have to take a few of them with us, right?*

Let's hope it doesn't come to that, he said grimly.

I was hoping for a little more confidence than that.

He gave her one of his unfathomable stares.

They were met at the massive wrought iron gates by two shadowy figures. Terrill merely raised an eyebrow at their attempt to intimidate.

Don't provoke them, Mara scolded. *We need to gather information, and like you always say, confrontation isn't the best way to get it.*

Since when did you start listening to me?

Terrill . . .

He chuckled silently. *All right, I'll try. But if it's a game of who has the most power they want to play, they're in for a rude surprise if they think they can beat me.*

The iron gates opened before them and they entered through a second set of wooden doors into some sort of gatehouse. As the doors closed behind them with a resounding thud, Mara couldn't help but feel a sense of dread creep over her.

It's what they want you to think, Terrill said. *What better way to win the advantage than to take away one's self-confidence before the fight even begins? Don't let it affect you.*

They quickly passed the warning among themselves and shook off the lingering despair the impression had left. The air cooled as they followed their guide down the stairs and exited into an underground garden walkway. The air was fragrant with the scent of night-blooming jasmine and a cornucopia of other exotic smells and colors.

Mara started to inhale deeply, letting the relaxing scents invade her consciousness when she realized a dangerous truth. *Don't!* she warned the others. *The smells are a trap. It's not only the aroma that gets inside you. It acts as a catalyst, designed to loosen barriers protecting our thoughts, giving its designer access.*

How do you know? Terrill asked.

Sinjon told me about this type of trap when I was a little girl. He was going to teach me about making them someday.

Their guide ignored their discomfort and led them into a candle-lit antechamber where he bade them wait as he announced their presence to the court. They watched him step between the guards in ceremonial garb and disappear through a hidden door.

Mara nodded as Terrill pointed out other subtly disguised doors that probably led to reinforcements or tunnels crisscrossing throughout the estate. The size of the labyrinth provided protection against outsider attempts to penetrate its inner sanctum should anyone breach the exterior.

The guards snapped to attention, the doors leading to the court opened slowly, and their escort reappeared.

Prepare yourselves, Terrill said.

For once, even Caleb didn't have a comment. They were passing into a realm more dangerous than any they'd yet encountered.

Mara heard the sound of bells in the background. Or was it chimes? Another trap?

No, not a trap, Angelica said as she read her sister's mind. *A preference.*

Terrill had told her that typically only those of royal blood entered the inner sanctum of such a High Court. The only exception to that rule would be for someone of great interest to the court, and usually, that didn't bode so well for the subject of that interest.

Terrill and his family had bloodlines that supported the preferred admission criteria. They were strong enough that they could lay claim to a crown and power such as this. Only he had witnessed such a scene before.

Is it what you expected? she asked.

It's about as petty and lavish as I remember them being, he said, *but the power they project here is fairly impressive.*

He made only the slightest attempt at obeisance, just enough to indicate his respect for the position while reserving judgment on their power. Mara saw that same acknowledgment in Cedric's eyes.

Anger radiated off Cedric as he looked down on the group. He focused his displeasure on Terrill. The calm, detached tone of his voice served as their only warning. "I wondered what reason you'd found to decline my invitation. I was especially surprised to discover that you opted to enter our territory without escort or protection." The handsome lines of his ebony-colored face blended with the darkness barely illuminated by the dim lights surrounding him.

Terrill pivoted and addressed the queen. "We were honored with the invitation, but found the escort unnecessary, so we released them back to your tasking."

"You released them?" Cedric challenged.

Evangeline placed her hand on Cedric's arm, amusement warming her face. "How very considerate of you."

Mara listened to the musical tones of her voice and looked at Yasmine in surprise. She had the same sub-Saharan accent as Shaba. And yet she was here, part of this royal court. What were the odds of that?

Mara concentrated on Evangeline. The power she projected was not her own. In fact, what power she had was masked by Cedric's, and definitely weaker than his. If Mara was any judge of age, he was hundreds of years old while Evangeline was barely seventeen or eighteen. A queen at her age?

If their messengers had not called her queen, I would have thought her a consort, Terrill said. *She's young to have such a position with as little power as she has. Too young.*

Consort?

Sometimes royalty chooses a companion as they search for their soul.

Why? she asked. *I mean . . .*

The bloodlines must be maintained.

Do you mean . . .?

Yes. It gets complicated once the soul has been found if an heir has already been created.

What?

Mara, can we discuss it later?

Mara looked up at Cedric, disturbed by the focused look he gave her. His expression shifted to a mildly puzzled one. Maybe he'd expected to access their thoughts. Thank goodness they'd figured out his traps before they were completely sprung.

"It seems there's much about you we do not yet know," he said. "Perhaps you might enlighten us on a few things."

"Perhaps if you would illuminate us on the reasons you requested our presence here, we might better be able to do so," Terrill countered just as politely.

Cedric winked at Evangeline and flashed a white-toothed grin. "Your activities in the region generated, shall we say, not a small amount of power." He shrugged at Terrill's arched brow. "I have people who keep their eye on such things and have generally found it wise to investigate such spikes."

Terrill nodded and crossed his arms in front of his chest. "And I assume these watchers of yours have kept you informed of the activities of a certain Society dedicated to the advancement of a master race?"

Cedric quickly extinguished the flicker of surprise that flared in his eyes, but not before Mara and Terrill saw it.

Cedric waved his hand. "Yes. I've been made aware of this mortal Society and its activities. They're harmless. They seek answers they'll never find." He rested his hand on his chin before meeting their eyes again. "The only troublesome thing is the barrier that protects their minds from us. We've been unable to penetrate it without detection. Quite strange actually."

As he spoke Mara noted the annoyance in his tone. Obviously, he'd expended some effort in attempting to crack this code. At least he seemed suspicious about the Society. Hopefully, that meant he hadn't bought into it. But still, it wasn't any guarantee. Mara signaled Terrill to tread carefully.

Terrill reached up casually and stroked his chin in contemplation. He paused mid-motion and snapped his fingers as if something had just occurred to him. "You didn't know this Society was created and controlled by Viajante?"

Why wasn't she surprised Terrill choose not take the subtle route? Seriously?

Almost instantly, pandemonium swept through the room. Mara and the others moved closer together.

Cedric launched himself up from his throne. "Silence!" Immediately the outcries quieted. Cedric lowered himself back onto his throne and patted his queen's hand before turning back to face Terrill, returning to the model of dignity and grace he obviously prided himself on. "Surely you're mistaken. I've had this Society researched and found no indication of any such thing."

"Perhaps your researchers missed something."

"Perhaps, but it's unlikely. Luckily for both of us, my most prominent researcher is here among us and can provide the detail you seem to lack." He motioned to the guards and they exited.

If it wasn't for the slight tapping of his fingers on the arm of his chair, Mara would have assumed he believed implicitly what he'd told them.

The doors opened and the guards ushered a lone figure to the dais. He climbed the stairs and stood at Cedric's left. He turned to face the group and removed his hood. Victor.

CHAPTER THIRTY-NINE

Victor saw their group and hesitated. The crack in his confidence was so slight it went unnoticed by the majority of the court. Mara cast a hooded glance at Cedric. By the look he exchanged with Evangeline, Mara knew he'd caught it too.

Victor's only real option was to dismiss Terrill's suggestion that the Society was controlled by Viajantes as ridiculous. She wasn't disappointed.

"I've seen the Society target mortals and Viajante alike," he said as he straightened his tie and pulled smooth the folds of his immaculate jacket for the third time. "They were seeking some sort of gene enhancement." He shrugged. "I thought involvement in the process would ensure their success was monitored and results limited to advancing Vampire defense."

Victor in front of an audience was like pouring kerosene over his already flame-engulfed ego. He ramped up the charm and turned on the magnetic personality Mara imagined had gotten him so far politically.

"Imagine being able to harness Viajante abilities like walking in daylight and more powerful mind control," he said. "Our limitations make us vulnerable. These mortals hope to tap into powers our enemies possess. All I did was seek a way to use that access for the advancement of our own kind. Encouraging their research can only benefit us. Of course, a strict eye is being kept on them to ensure no, uh, misunderstandings."

The audience discussed the possibilities excitedly. Victor was a good salesman — too good — not that it seemed hard to sell Vampires on violence against Viajante to start with. Mara frowned. He did seem to have the crowd. Not good.

He smiled an oily smile at Mara, daring her to comment. Her eyes narrowed defiantly.

"So while you were keeping an eye on them, you didn't happen to notice the multiple attempts, one successful, to capture Mara?" Terrill asked him in a dangerously calm voice.

Victor feigned a look of surprise. He looked at Mara as if recognizing her for the first time. "Your friend from the holiday party, right? I had no idea you were still together. Nor that you'd turned her." He faced Cedric and Evangeline. "I had no idea she'd been targeted."

"Then you admit you had no idea what the Society was up to in your own territory. No real control, as you claim?" Terrill asked.

Victor bristled and took a few seconds to compose himself. When he spoke his voice sounded almost defensive. "You misunderstood. I focused on the results, not the feeble attempts at success. There were simply too many insignificant plans involving mortals to track them all. I only followed the ones that led to something of interest."

"Then tell me, Father," Angelica said as she stepped forward, "what did you judge to be of interest?" She asked the question innocently enough, but Victor's reaction to the stubborn set of her shoulders indicated his familiarity and annoyance with the course she planned to take.

"Angelica, my dear, you should be in school. Remind me to speak to the headmaster about your truancy and the failure of the school to notify me of your absence . . . again." He straightened his tie. "In answer to your question, I haven't yet found much value. I do remain hopeful though."

Angelica placed her hands on her hips and cocked her head. "Ever the curious scientist, aren't you? Did you share your own hugely successful experiment with the Society?"

Victor froze, a murderous expression on his face. She ignored him and hit her hand on her head. "Of course not. Why would you? You deemed them unworthy of such knowledge no doubt. Or was it that they needed to prove themselves? No, that's not it either. Surely you shared your amazing skills and success with the court here, right?" She waved her hand to encompass the royal couple in front of her as well as the courtiers surrounding them.

"What's she talking about?" Cedric asked.

Victor shook his head at the murmur of interest around him and smiled a smile one uses to indulge a small child. "Angelica, you do not understand. I'm afraid I kept you too isolated as a child. Once again, you've gotten in with the wrong crowd and been lied to." He beckoned to her. "Come. We have much to discuss, away from this crowd."

"No."

Mara saw shock and anger on his face. She'd bet no one had ever defied his will so publicly before.

"Ah, youth. So young, so impetuous." Cedric sat back on his throne and spoke casually, but from his demeanor, it was obvious he expected an explanation, and a good one.

"Forgive her, my lord. She forgets her place." He all but growled the last words as he directed them at Angelica.

"My place. How interesting you would call it that. Where exactly is my place, Father? Would that be with my parents? The ones you had killed?" She turned to the stunned crowd around her. "Oh not to worry. Victor would never dare kill his own kind. My parents were not Vampire. But they weren't mortal either, were they, dear Father?"

Mara felt rage and fury roll off him in venomous waves. Evangeline's eyes widened in surprise. Cedric motioned for her to control her emotions.

"No answer?" Angelica continued. "You're right, maybe I should explain. After my Viajante family was killed, Victor showed up. He decided to conduct a little experiment of his own. He converted me into Vampire and his witch doctors worked hard to erase my memories of the event. For the most part, they succeeded. Until recently when my memories finally returned."

The shock and protests rose to such a crescendo that Cedric came to his feet again. "Enough!"

"You sign your own death warrant, child," Victor ground out between clenched teeth.

"But it's forbidden to convert Viajante, Father, not to be one converted."

Angelica, be careful! Mara warned.

Angelica smiled. "Now the question I had to ask myself was why my father would risk breaking such a rule? I struggled with that one for months, and then I met Mara and learned the real reason."

"What was it?" Evangeline demanded.

"What indeed your highness?" Angelica mused. She nodded to Mara.

"There is a prophecy to which Victor subscribes," Mara said. "It spoke of a chosen one whose actions would affect both species. The Society and many ancients feared it. Victor thought to gain power by controlling the outcome and the chosen one."

"This is utter and complete garbage," Victor spat out. "I may have bent the rules, but never for personal gain — only for the good of our species. If I sought control of this so-called prophecy, it was only for the greater good, not my own."

Mara didn't give him a chance to use his considerable powers of persuasion to convince the court of his so-called sincerity or virtue. "What he didn't know was that he risked everything for naught. In his quest to play god, he missed the simple fact that the child who would fulfill the prophecy had already been born."

"And died," Victor said smugly. "That power would continue through the bloodline."

Mara smiled thinly. "So he thought. Angelica had a sister, already several years her senior, who Victor thought was dead. Once he left with Angelica, she was saved by one of their Seekers."

"You lie."

"Try me."

"You?" The dignified veneer peeled off Victor's face. Mara saw him realize that those grand dreams of power he'd held on to were slipping out of his grasp. Unfortunately, he now had someone to direct that loss and hatred at.

Cedric motioned to the guards to close in. "You are Viajante?" he asked her.

"Partially."

He narrowed his eyes at Evangeline's puzzled look. "Explain."

"During the attack on my family, I was bitten by one of your kind. My mother and I appear to have some rather unique healing abilities. We changed my cellular structure to allow for the cells of your species to coexist with my own, preventing my death."

"You are able to be both Viajante and Vampire? At the same time?" Evangeline brought her finger to her nose and tapped it in contemplation. "Extraordinary."

Terrill and Mara exchanged glances. Clearly, their value and the risk of their existence were being assessed privately by the King and Queen. The Queen smiled and waved her fingers graciously at Mara to continue.

"I have the ability to pass as whichever species I need to." She changed her projection from Vampire to mortal to Viajante and finally back to Vampire.

"A parlor trick, nothing more," Victor snarled.

"Perhaps," Cedric said pensively. "But one very few can maintain so successfully and in front of so many witnesses."

He scanned the group in front of him. Mara felt him probing for answers and easily blocked his access to her mind. He no longer seemed surprised not to have succeeded. "I would have more explanations, but first I'll have your allegiance and a promise you do not conspire against this court and our people."

"You would trust these . . . these . . . imposters?" Victor sputtered.

Get ready, Terrill warned them. "I am sorry, but allegiance we cannot offer."

The guards moved in. Before they made contact, the girls arranged themselves to take the outer points of a diamond. The air pulsed between them, vibrating to create a power wave that effortlessly repulsed the would-be attackers and sent them sprawling.

Mara saw the calculating look on Cedric's face and held her position as they waited for his response. She hoped he realized they had the ability to cause serious damage to his guard — maybe even death — but had instead chosen to give a warning.

He signaled for the guards to stand down. "We seem to be at a standstill," he said. "You will not provide allegiance and I cannot trust you unless you do."

"Instead of allegiance, would you settle for assurance of our peaceful intentions toward this court?" Terrill asked.

Cedric raised a brow in inquiry. "Is that what your intentions are? Peaceful?"

Terrill nodded. "As long as our safety remains unthreatened, we will seek no violence here against you or your people." He maintained his gaze fully on Cedric.

Cedric smiled. "Well, then, I'm willing to give you a chance." His eyes slid to Victor and back to Terrill. "Let's see if you really can play nice."

He stood and addressed the court. "These travelers will not be molested within our territory as long as they keep their word to me." He fixed a hard gaze on his courtiers. "Is that understood?"

Without a backward glance at the astonished court, he led the way out of the chamber and indicated the visitors should follow. He paused at the exit. "Victor, you too should join us."

Victor bowed in acknowledgment and allowed Mara and the others to precede him.

In the privacy of a smaller chamber, Cedric locked eyes with Terrill. "I don't know what you're hiding, but I cannot allow your departure from my realm until this mystery is solved and this power explained to the court. Victor has been a trusted member of this court, and you made serious allegations that I cannot ignore."

"I agree. Victor should be investigated. But speaking of Victor, where is he? Since he neglected to accompany us here, I can only wonder at his intentions, both toward us and in response to these allegations, as you put them."

Cedric's lips stretched into a tolerant smile, but Mara wasn't fooled. He wasn't happy with Victor, but he wasn't about to admit it. "Victor need not concern you. I've declared it to be my pleasure alone to determine what actions be brought against you."

"If any," Terrill reminded him.

"And if Victor was disinclined to follow your orders . . ." drawled Caleb.

"That too would be my choice to resolve." Cedric made an annoyed motion with his hand and their shadowy guide reappeared. "It would be wise to focus on yourselves and the answers you owe me. We will continue this discussion tomorrow night."

Terrill nodded and they followed their guide out into the hallway.

Must you provoke him? Mara asked.

Was I? He appeared to seriously consider the possibility and fixed innocent eyes on Mara.

She shook her head in exasperation. *It's the authority thing, right? Do you have an issue with that?* He winked and turned his attention back to their guide.

The guide led them out a different way. Terrill fixed him with a steely stare when he closed a smaller gate behind them, locking them out of the palace grounds.

"You'll find your cars that way," The guard huffed and indicated a vague direction with his arm before catching the menace in Terrill's eyes and darting away in a hasty escape.

Connor chuckled. "Well, are all you blood suckers so much about the pomp and frill as all that?"

Terrill just shook his head.

They made plans to meet up the next night and split up to seek shelter. Mara said good night, and it wasn't long before she was asleep.

She woke with a start, like from one of her dreams. But there hadn't been any dreams since the joining. This wasn't a dream. She felt noxious smoke seep into her lungs and threaten to choke off her air. The flames she heard crackle angrily around her would reach them soon. There was no way out.

CHAPTER FORTY

Terrill awoke to the identical realization. His expression was grim, but Mara saw his determination to thwart the intentions of whoever sought their demise firmly stamped across his face.

If Terrill felt the tiniest sliver of fear, he certainly didn't show it. He pushed her hair back from her cheek and wiped off the soot that was already mixing with sweat from the heat of the fire to form dirty streaks across her face. He cupped her face and kissed her.

"Mara, this isn't over. We're going to get out of this. Do you trust me?"

She nodded and a dangerous smile broke across his face. His silver eyes gleamed in the sooty darkness and shadows of the flame-illuminated structure.

"I haven't tried this in years. No one knows I can do it. No one knows anyone can." Mara's gaze wavered between his face and the flames licking ever closer. "Mara!" She returned her eyes to him. He wouldn't let the flames get her back. She knew that, but still, turning her back on them didn't seem natural either.

"Remember when we first met, and I told you about the special skills I developed as a child?" She nodded. Where was he going with this?

An impish smile lit his face, but something over her shoulder erased the grin in a flash. He held out his hand in front of her and to her astonishment, the tip of his finger burst into flame. The glow of the flame twisted and bent until it slowly consumed his entire hand.

Mara stared at him in horror. What the . . .? Fire destroyed both of their species, without exception. There was no coming back if their body burned.

"Mara, look at my hand. Look at it."

She blinked. It wasn't burning at all! Through the flame, she saw it whole and untouched. "How did you do that?" she asked as she reached for the flame.

He used his untouched hand to quickly capture hers before she touched it. He blinked and the flame was extinguished just as quickly. "The flame I create is as real as those around us," he said. "You would have been burned if you'd touched it."

She smiled as he shared a memory of returning home with singed hair and clothes and Gabriella's reaction. He must have driven his parents mad with worry. Her levity died instantly in the scorching blast of flame that entered their room.

"Terrill, I don't know if I can do this."

"Your element is fire. You must have the ability."

"It's true I know of no other Viajante with the element of fire, but I've never attempted what you're asking me to."

"You are my soul. If for no other reason than that, this should work." He grasped her by the shoulders and stared into her eyes. "I won't let anything happen to you."

She saw the conviction in his eyes and nodded. Ability or not, she trusted him with her life. "All right."

Terrill lifted her in his arms and cradled her to him. She watched, mesmerized, as the flames started at his feet, building to engulf them both. The fire Terrill created around them acted as a barrier, a shield against the flames threatening their lives from outside. No longer could those flames destroy them.

Terrill dodged falling beams and leaped over burning furniture as he raced through the blazing structure and hurtled them out into the night. Once outside, he extinguished the flames surrounding them. He laid her carefully on the grass, steam coming off both of their bodies in the cool, early-morning air.

She realized they'd only been asleep a few hours.

"Mara," he whispered, "are you all right?"

She slowly opened her eyes and took a deep cleansing breath. The cool, clean air tasted sweet, and she savored the drastic change from the harsh black smoke she'd been forced to inhale. "I'm okay."

She sat up. She wasn't burned anywhere. A few singe marks on her sleeves where stray embers had caught hold remained the only evidence of their close call. When she woke up, she hadn't expected to get off so lightly.

She smiled wickedly at him. "My turn." She rose and walked toward the blaze consuming what remained of the structure. She closed her eyes and gathered the water particles in the clouds, then released them in a sudden rain burst directed over the fire. The torrent of water hit it hard. It hissed in defiance and struggled to maintain its former strength, but Mara persisted until it was forced into submission. Certain it had been extinguished, she slowed the rain to a light drizzle. It was Terrill's turn to stare at her in amazement.

"I never knew I could control the flame, so I focused on learning to control other elements. I can't control one within another though." She grinned. "Trust me I would have preferred to put out the flames, but while we were inside the element . . . well, I haven't quite learned that trick yet."

He shook his head and chuckled. "They'd lock both of us up if they knew what we were capable of."

"Terrill, watch out!"

He cursed under his breath and ducked just in time to miss the charred beam thrown at him. Silver eyes darkened and he turned to face this newest threat.

Before he could identify who stood in front of him, a gale-like blast of wind slammed his foe back against the fence. The force of the wind shattered the fence and threw their attacker down so hard the ground cracked beneath him.

Terrill turned back to Mara, who stood with her arms still outstretched. She started forward, ready to do battle. He gestured for her to stay put. "No, I've got this."

She started forward again, but the expression in his eyes stopped her.

"Hello, Victor," he said cordially as he approached their foe. The involuntary twitch in his jaw muscles was the only visible indication of his intense anger. "How nice of you to join us."

Terrill's powers held Victor to the ground, but they didn't prevent him from placing as many obstacles on the path as he could while he struggled to get to his feet.

Enough of this crap Mara thought to herself. The instant he got his feet under him, she hammered him back into the huge trees behind him.

Victor raised his head and locked eyes with her. She watched his lips move, but his words remained inaudible.

Shock poured over her like a bucket of cold water. *Terrill, I can't move!* She tried to lift her feet, but they stuck as if rooted to the ground.

Terrill whipped his head around.

Mara saw the tree limb missile heading for her chest, and Terrill's horrified expression flashed before her eyes. He couldn't get to her in time. This wasn't going to be pretty.

She crouched and felt the spear adjust its trajectory. A blast of power ripped her from the ground and threw her backward. The tree exploded in thousands of shards just inches from where she'd been standing. She rolled and shielded her eyes as the debris rained down around her.

Hard on the heels of the push that destroyed the spear, Angelica and Filip strode into the clearing. Guess that explained where the surprising burst of power had come from. She wanted to thank them but needed to deal with Victor first. She turned to face him and was shocked to see Filip materialize at his side.

"Filip?" Angelica's voice wavered as he helped Victor to his feet. Victor cast a disdainful look in their direction. Filip shrugged.

Connor and Yasmine appeared on the opposite side of the clearing at almost the same time Caleb and Morgan arrived just behind Terrill. Filip shook his head in warning.

Terrill indicated with his hand for Caleb to hold. Yasmine and Connor continued to approach the pair. Before Victor could react, Filip stretched out an arm and immobilized them as Victor had Mara.

"Why?" Mara asked him.

He sighed and Mara saw a weary sadness cover his features before it was replaced with a look of resigned determination. "I need answers, and only Victor has them."

Victor's look of gloating satisfaction faded to one slightly less certain, less confident. "You couldn't harm me," he said and raised his hand to Filip's face in a lover's caress. "You know how I feel about you."

"It's been so long." Filip shuddered at the contact

"I know, my love. I've felt it too."

"Have you?" Filip asked. "Tell me you had nothing to do with our separation, Victor. Tell me you had no choice. Make me understand why. Why you never sought me out. I need to know."

"Filip, you know I had no choice. I am, as I have always been, her servant." Victor placed his hand on Filip's arm and ran his fingers up and down its length.

Mara saw Filip hitch in his breath convulsively at the contact and the long-buried sensations it appeared to invoke. She didn't know what was going on, but she sensed he was about to make a decision that would affect them all.

"Tell me you still love me," he demanded.

Victor smiled the nervous smile of someone who hopes he hasn't been overhead. "You know how I feel."

"Yes," Filip said and embraced Victor before shifting quickly to snap his neck. "I do. And I'm done believing in you." He lovingly lowered the body to the ground at his feet. He silently closed Victor's eyes and wiped his own before rising to face the group.

CHAPTER FORTY-ONE

A ngelica ignored Terrill's warning and moved to Filip's side, her eyes full of tears. He didn't prevent her from taking his hand in hers. "He was the one who created you, wasn't he." He lifted his head to look at her.

Terrill hugged Mara to him. Now free of the temporary immobility, the others closed the distance to stand by Filip.

"Filip," Mara said, "Victor didn't deserve you. He let ambition blind him to that which matters most. You made a hard choice — one I am not sure even the strongest of us could have made."

Terrill nodded. "While we might not understand all the reasons behind what you did, it was the right thing to do. Victor was a risk to us all and to our species. But I think you already know that."

Filip looked at Mara, a myriad of emotions running through his eyes. "I'm sorry I cheated you of the answers you sought." Mara struggled to find the right words. "It wasn't Victor that masterminded the plot to kill your family," he said.

What? Mara swallowed the lump in her throat. But she had seen him there. Who'd ordered it then?

As if sensing her question, Filip shook his head. "No, he directed the attack and gave the order to his henchmen, but he too was following orders."

Mara looked at him in confusion. "Whose orders does Victor follow?"

"The orders of the same person who deemed my relationship with Victor an abomination. The one who forbade Victor to ever see me again."

Caleb raised his hand to his chin. "It would have to be someone close to Victor — someone very powerful. Victor rarely took the advice of others, let alone orders."

Terrill nodded. "We know little of Victor's family. It was a topic he didn't discuss."

Filip's mouth twitched in an involuntary half-smile. "I can't say I'm surprised. Victor's mother was — is — extremely strong. She enjoyed pulling strings and making those around her dance to a beat she chose." He shook his head. "I only met her once, when she discovered our relationship, but it was enough to know I didn't ever want to run into her again."

"Victor never spoke of family, yet his lineage was never questioned," Terrill said. "I always wondered why. Just how powerful is his mother?"

Filip shrugged. "There was a lot about his childhood Victor never talked about. The little he shared with me did nothing to prepare me for meeting her in person. I got the impression that they were somewhat estranged. Victor only talked about it once. You should know that something happened to his father, who disappeared under questionable circumstances."

"So what if his father disappeared?" Caleb asked him. "So Victor had secrets. Again, not surprising, as ambitious as he was. I don't see how that helps us with the current situation any."

Filip shook his head. "So impatient."

Caleb started to protest, but Morgan stopped him by placing her hand on his arm. She nodded to Filip to continue.

"There's more to it than that. Victor's mother took up as consort with a powerful Vampire after his father's disappearance. Victor was concerned that this Vampire knew of him and would seek some sort of vengeance or use him to get to his mother."

"And you know who she played consort with?" Terrill asked.

"I believe you met him last night."

"Well, I guess that settles the question of whether we should return to court now, doesn't it?" Caleb quipped as Morgan moaned melodramatically.

"Did Victor know?" Angelica asked.

Filip shrugged. "I think he suspected."

"Cedric and Victor's mother," Mara said, her eyes widening at the implication. "What if Cedric was part of this conspiracy from the start and played us?"

Terrill clenched his jaw. "It's certainly possible."

Connor stepped closer to Yasmine. "If that's the case, I'd recommend getting as far from here as we can, and quickly too."

"I know these weren't the answers you sought, Mara," Terrill said. "It's your call."

Mara looked into the eyes of those who had suffered so much because of her and shook her head. "No, we should go. Our focus needs to be on the Society. The battle with my parents' killers cannot take precedence over that. They'd understand."

"Mara," Terrill said, "we aren't giving up on the truth behind their death."

She raised her eyes up to his pleading ones and smiled as she squeezed his hand. "I know."

"All right, then," he said. "Connor's right. Things are too hot for us to stay here now."

"And what of King Cedric?" Filip asked.

Terrill grinned wickedly. "He's not going anywhere. At least we'll know where to find him when we're ready."

"You're not worried about the audience he demanded tonight?" Angelica asked.

Terrill shrugged. "I find myself suddenly disinclined to honor his request."

Caleb chuckled. "You know that's not going to go over well, don't you?"

Terrill smiled widely. "Ask me if I care."

"What happens next for you?" Mara asked Filip, somehow knowing he wouldn't be continuing with them. "You are welcome to stay with us."

He shook his head. "No, my path now lies along a different route. I have made right the wrongs I could." He turned and embraced Angelica fondly. "I leave you now in good hands. You will be safe with your true family."

"Will we see you again?" Angelica asked him.

His smile didn't quite reach his eyes. "Someday."

"Before you go, would you be willing to teach us that little trick you did?" Caleb asked. "Planting immortals like trees."

Filip sobered. "I think a skill as dangerous as that is best kept unlearned. Victor and I worked together to develop it and swore not to share its secrets with others. I believe that, if nothing else, he kept his promise. As long as I believe that to be true, I will not widen the circle."

Mara stepped forward to embrace him. After they said their goodbyes, Angelica's saddest of all, he turned and walked away. They watched him until his figure blended into the night.

Angelica sighed. "I feel his loss so strongly. I fear his heart will never heal."

Mara and Yasmine shared a sad smile.

At Morgan's nod, Caleb approached Terrill. "We've talked about it, and if it's all right with you and Mara, we'd like to take Angelica back with us."

"She needs to be in school," Morgan said cutting off Angelica's protest, "and we know one close to us that we can visit often."

"School?" Angelica snorted. "After all this you want me to go back to school?"

"Yes," they all answered in unison.

Mara laughed at her sister's shocked expression.

"Fine," Angelica said. "I'll go back to school under one condition."

Mara and Terrill exchanged wary looks. "What?" Mara asked her.

She smiled. "You enroll me under the name Celeste Martinovic."

Mara's hand flew to her heart and tears stung her eyes. "I think we can do that."

"Caleb?" Terrill asked.

He grinned. "Yup, got it. Celeste."

Celeste beamed. "What of you and Connor?" she asked Yasmine.

Yasmine smiled as Connor took her hand.

"We have some work to do here in Ireland," he said, "to repair the damage the Society has done within our community. I fear it's still a strong threat here, and I'm not willing to let it take root here ever again."

"But," Yasmine said as she saw Celeste's look of disappointment, "we plan to return to the States soon. We were thinking of visiting Shaba, and once you're done with school this spring, we hoped you might join us."

Celeste leaped into Yasmine's arms.

Mara laughed. "I guess that's a yes?"

Celeste giggled and embraced Mara and Morgan in turn.

Terrill's eyes hid a smile only Mara saw.

Caleb embraced Terrill in the way of Warriors. "Once we get Ang . . . Celeste settled, we're off to see Lauris and Gabriella."

"Is there anything we can tell them about your return?" Morgan asked.

"Tell them we look forward to seeing them soon," Terrill said, "but we have business to attend to first."

They exchanged warm farewells. Everyone was tired from the sleepless night but anxious to get out of Cedric's reach before daybreak. Soon all that remained was the charred structure, Victor's broken body, and Terrill and Mara's need to be together.

Mara walked across the field until she could no longer smell the fire smoldering. She turned her back as Terrill placed Victor's body in the ruins and closed her eyes as the flames roared in fiery delight at the offering. Terrill would make sure Victor's remains were completely destroyed.

"Is it done?" she asked sadly as he appeared at her side.

He wiped the silent tears from her face. "We'll find the ones responsible for what happened to your family."

"I know we will," she said. "It's just . . ."

"What?"

"We've come so far, and for what? More senseless destruction of lives, our friends and family hurt, threatened. Why did I ever start this?"

He hugged her to him and kissed her forehead. "Mara, you didn't start any of this. It started before you were born. And," he raised her chin with two fingers so that her eyes were level with his, "Your journey brought you to me. That's something I will never regret."

She blinked back tears. "Why do you risk so much for me?"

"Mara," he said, "how many times do I have to remind you that you are my soul — that there is no risk to me but your unhappiness?"

She wiped her eyes furtively. "So now what?"

"I have a few contacts in Spain. I thought we might spend some time there while we wait for things to settle down. Maybe we can learn more about the Society or about Victor's mother. The attack happened there, and if what Dabir told you about waiting for you is true, there may have been Society involvement there we can investigate."

When she'd started this, everything had been so simple — so black and white. She thought of the loss she'd seen, the betrayal. It was time to stop looking back. Time to stop wishing for what could have been. Her family and her soul were not just part of her present, but also her future.

She pulled his face down to hers and kissed him. "Let's go."

He held her tight and took off into the night.

ABOUT THE AUTHOR

An eternal scholar, Heather Beal best prefers delving into the worlds of fantasy and the supernatural. The "what if" is what fascinates her most. Since retiring from the Navy, she has settled in Seabeck, Washington where power outages in winter are a guarantee. She splits her time between nonprofit work, writing, spending her time with her husband, raising two children and taking care of two black cats who think themselves dogs. Still searching for her own super powers, she delights in the imaginary friends that whisper their stories into her ear, hoping their words will one day be read by others. Find out more at www.heatherbeal.com.

NOTE FROM HEATHER BEAL

Word-of-mouth is crucial for any author to succeed. If you enjoyed *Extinguishing Shadows*, please leave a review online—anywhere you are able. Even if it's just a sentence or two. It would make all the difference and would be very much appreciated.

Thanks!
Heather Beal

We hope you enjoyed reading this title from:

Subscribe to our mailing list – *The Rosevine* – and receive **FREE** books, daily deals, and stay current with news about upcoming releases and our hottest authors.
Scan the QR code below to sign up.

Already a subscriber? Please accept a sincere thank you for being a fan of Black Rose Writing authors.

www.ingramcontent.com/pod-product-compliance
Lightning Source LLC
Chambersburg PA
CBHW050138120726
47903CB00002B/408